For Ieuan

L. C. TYLER

Death of a Shipbuilder

CONSTABLE

CONSTABLE

First published in Great Britain in 2020 by Constable
This paperback edition published in 2021 by Constable

A CIP catalogue record for this book
is available from the British Library.

ISBN: 978-1-47212-853-9

Typeset in Caslon Pro by SX Composing DTP, Rayleigh, Essex
Printed and bound in Great Britain by Clays Ltd, Elcograf S.p.A.

Papers used by Constable are from well-managed forests
and other responsible sources.

Constable
An imprint of
Little, Brown Book Group
Carmelite House
50 Victoria Embankment
London EC4Y 0DZ

An Hachette UK Company
www.hachette.co.uk

www.littlebrown.co.uk

Dramatis Personae

John Grey – me, a former servant of Lord Protector Oliver Cromwell but, after His Majesty's glorious and long-looked-for Restoration, as good a Royalist as I need to be; for many years a lawyer, now a knight, magistrate and Lord of the Manor and fortunate to be husband (at the second attempt) to

Aminta, Lady Grey – noted playwright and also my childhood friend, born Aminta Clifford into a family that is (she tells me) much older, more distinguished and in every way superior to my own, hence her being admitted from time to time to the highest circles of the Court which include

My Lady Castlemaine – mistress of **His Gracious Majesty, King Charles II of England, Ireland, Scotland and France, Defender of the Faith** (other mistresses are available) and

The Earl of Dartford – a notorious rakehell, author of obscene verse and drinking companion of the aforementioned King, who has allied himself closely with

The Duke of Buckingham – the King's childhood friend, a distant kinsman of my wife (precisely how distant never satisfactorily explained, in spite of my asking) and the second most powerful man in England, though with many enemies, especially

Henry Bennet, Lord Arlington – the King's Secretary of State and spymaster, who, in the latter and grubbier capacity, was once my employer, though I have promised Aminta faithfully that I shall never work for him again, since he is a vain and untrustworthy scoundrel, unlike his deputy

Mr Joseph Williamson – a fine and honest servant of the Crown, whose only fault is to believe that the further north you were born the more worthy you are, though he has a high regard for the administrative abilities of

Mr Samuel Pepys – Clerk of the Acts to the Navy Board, who has rarely strayed out of London, other than to visit the estates of his patron **Lord Sandwich**, because there are in London more actresses, pliant maidservants and other men's wives, with whom he may spend a pleasant hour or two before returning home to his own wife (and her maidservants), and who is far richer than you might expect for a mere clerk, having profited from naval contracts with men such as

Abel Symonds – acting head of the royal dockyard at Deptford and

Thomas Cade – shipbuilder and owner of a small private shipyard hard by the Tower of London, who is married to

Mistress Cade – originally from Bromley in the charming county of Kent, where her brutish brother **Mr Cooper** is the worst blacksmith in that town, and who is very friendly indeed with Mr Pepys, much to the annoyance of

Harry Truscott – Cade's deputy at the yard, long-time admirer of Mistress Cade and the loyal servant of Thomas Cade just as

Will Atkins – is my own loyal servant, fetching, carrying, doing my accounts, nagging me incessantly and watching my back, though

Mr Sparks – my new partner in the Law practice, believes him capable of very much more and wishes to make him a lawyer like

Me – John Grey, though I would wish that dreary profession on nobody and am trying to give up the Law, as you will find out if you choose to read very much further in this story.

But that is your decision entirely.

Prologue

May 1669

Samuel Pepys reflected yet again on the great personal inconvenience he was put to when seducing other men's wives.

It was true that, on this occasion, the husband was safely out of the way. Pepys had himself sent Thomas Cade to Rotherhithe to examine a massy parcel of timber, newly arrived from the Baltic, that might be purchased for the King, on terms that were advantageous to almost everyone except the King, for possible use in constructing a warship. And yet, even as he thought about the doubly happy expedition that he had sent this husband and shipbuilder on, Pepys became fretful, as he so often did once his immediate objective had been gained. Had Cade not accepted the commission with too great alacrity? Had he not shown too little interest in the likely size and configuration of this purely imaginary ship? And, critically, hadn't Cade failed to question him in any way whatsoever as to the likely division of any profits from the enterprise? Moreover, Pepys was worried that Mistress Cade had been just a little too eager to see him. Perhaps just a little too willing to do his bidding in all respects. Some show of reluctance, some passing reference to virtue and modesty, was more conventional. In his experience anyway.

Suddenly he suspected a trap. It was not at all unknown for honest gentlemen such as himself, men utterly faithful to their wives for days at a time, to be lured into compromising positions by scheming couples, one of whom would do the luring and the other of whom would burst through the door with much show of well-wrought morality at the most awkward moment. Well, let them try. He had a wife who would not credit any such slanders on her husband's name or, if she did, could be bought off with a rope of pearls or a new gold-laced petticoat or private dancing lessons with a handsome young instructor. Say two out of three of those. Only a poor man needed to fear his wife's anger.

'I hope that was all to your satisfaction, Mr Pepys?' asked Mistress Cade, still seated on the bed. She held a hairbrush in her hand, perhaps not being able to afford a maid to brush her hair, or perhaps not caring to face her maid's enquiries as to why her mistress's hair needed brushing again before dinner time. Just for a moment Pepys imagined Mistress Cade brushing his own hair, the bristles gently caressing his head, her hand on his shoulder, her breath on his ear, her warm little body enticingly close. But he would not take the risk of requesting that service now. That was for another day, because Cade might return at any moment and for any reason: even if he set out honestly and trustingly, a thousand possible accidents on the road to Rotherhithe might force him to retrace his steps to his front door, then, failing to locate his wife in the proper place, up the stairs to his bedchamber, where she had no business to go if there was work to be done in the kitchen. The sooner Pepys was on his way the better. What was without question, however, was that there would most certainly *be* another day and on that day there would be another place to send Cade on another plausible errand that would again engage him for a whole morning or afternoon. Though one part of Pepys swore that he would never return here, never give way to temptation again, another part of him was calculating exactly how soon it might be done.

'It was all very much to my satisfaction,' Pepys replied, with a slight bow. 'Thank you, Mistress Cade.'

He looked again in the cracked mirror that hung on the walls of the Cades' bedchamber. The fracture in the glass ran down the middle of his face, making the left half slightly higher than the right. It gave him a villainous air that did not wholly displease him. There was nothing wrong with being a bit of a rogue. A bit of a rakehell. The King had set that particular fashion. It was very much in the spirit of the times. Pepys took up his periwig from the dressing table and placed it squarely on his head, hiding the real hair that he would so much have enjoyed having combed, if only he dared.

'I'm always saying to Cade that he should buy himself a periwig,' said Mistress Cade, head on one side. 'But he says that he doesn't want to give himself airs and graces. False hair and false promises are for the gentry, so he claims.'

Pepys waited for her to exclude him from the accusation of falsity, but she fell silent and stared out of the small leaded window, which gave on to a narrow street. The corners of her mouth dropped, as they so often did when something was not completely to her liking. It happened a great deal when she spoke to Pepys of her husband. But this time it seemed that it was the view that did not please her overmuch. The house they were in was large and comfortable, and must once have stood in open fields, but London had crept up on it, new house by new house, new street by new street, and overwhelmed it. Chimneys now smoked on all four sides and the leaves of the ancient apple trees in the garden were covered with a thin layer of soot the year round. There were more fashionable places to live, far to the west, where the merry King and his hard-drinking Court resided, but this place was cheap, practical and close to the river. Nobody here thought the worse of you for wearing your own hair. Thomas Cade would not have considered being anywhere else, however much his better half would.

'Everyone will wear periwigs ere long,' said Pepys. 'First it was the French Court, then the English one ... now every squalid little tradesman looks to buy one second hand, usually at his wife's instigation, and struts around in it as if he were a duke.'

Mistress Cade looked at Pepys as if expecting him to rule out any such accusation against her husband and herself, but it was likely that he was thinking specifically of them.

'Well ...' she said.

She placed the horn-backed hairbrush on the bed, stood and went over to the great iron-bound chest by the fireplace. She smoothed down the front of her skirt, preparatory to whatever it was she planned to do next, then opened the lid and took something from the very top of the pile. She turned suddenly.

Pepys, watching her curiously from the far side of the room, was for a moment alarmed. Could she be about to level a pistol at him? It again struck him that he was in a dangerous position, alone with a married woman, in a bedchamber, in a street that was neither where he worked nor where he lived. And he had not brought his sword with him. But what she held out was a roll of paper.

'Here you are, Mr Pepys,' she said.

'And what is that exactly?'

'The contract, dear Mr Pepys,' she said. 'Our contract.'

'Ah,' said Pepys.

'You said that the Navy Board would approve the contract for the construction of a new frigate. My husband needs the commission to keep his men employed. The ship they are working on is almost done. The matter is therefore now pressing. We have discussed it all before. As you know.'

'The board unfortunately awaits a number of decisions from the King as to how many new ships are to be built and of what rating. The King, sadly, pays no more attention to business than he has to. His dogs and his mistresses take up much of his time. Sailing, fishing, wine and horse racing take up the rest. Oh, and sometimes he sleeps. He's a busy man.'

'As you are perfectly well aware, the matter is already approved in principle. The drafts are drawn up. The King has nodded appreciatively while perusing them. His spaniel has pissed on them in passing. The King has made a few suggestions, sketched on the back of some dispatch or other. My husband has pulled a face, having strong views on how his ships should look, taken the sketch and lost it, perhaps having accidentally wiped his arse on it in the privy. In short, all is as it should be. It now merely requires the confirmation from the Navy Board, of which you are Secretary.'

Pepys laughed briefly and modestly. 'I am but one member of the board and, as Clerk of the Acts, the most junior one. And the poorest.'

'But you said that the board has discussed the matter and is of a mind to place the order?'

'I have of course persuaded them of the merits of your husband's proposal,' said Pepys. 'As I promised I would, when we last ... spoke. It is a question of the final approval of the very document you have in your hand. Therein lies the let and hindrance to reaching a happy conclusion.'

'In which case, approve it and sign yourself. Thus all is concluded. You know that the other members of the board will not question it. Or, if they do, you know how to buy their support.'

'That may not be cheap.'

'If you sign, you will not find us ungenerous, Mr Pepys. My husband would pay you what he paid before.'

'I hope you are not suggesting that the Clerk of the Acts to the Navy Board would accept bribes when allocating naval contracts?' Pepys laughed, to give her a clue as to what the correct answer should be.

'Of course not, Mr Pepys. Your devotion to the King's interests is well known. I am just saying that, once the contract is signed, entirely on the merits of our offer, Cade would be indebted to you in all sorts of ways. He would wish to show his appreciation. As he has done before. And, by pure coincidence, at an identical number of pence in the Pound.'

'I shall think on the matter—'

'Then there is the question of your wife. We should consider what it is right to do there.'

Pepys looked at her. She didn't have the face of a blackmailer, but only the most unfortunate of blackmailers actually did. The threat was clear enough anyway.

'Tell my wife about this morning if you wish. She won't believe a word of what you say. She trusts me utterly.'

Now it was Mistress Cade who laughed. The false tinkling note was almost as painful to Pepys as the threat of exposure. 'Indeed you misunderstand me,' she said. 'I mean that my husband would feel indebted both to you and to Mistress Pepys. We do of course understand that a present to you, given freely and openly, might make it appear that your decision to award us the contract was not impartial. But presents to ladies are innocent enough and leave no muddy footprints on a polished floor. Some lace. And a pair of gloves, perhaps with something more substantial tucked inside. Something metallic.'

Mistress Cade gave Pepys a wholly unnecessary wink. He knew which metal she had in mind. At least, he hoped he did.

'Whatever he wishes to do – not that I am requesting anything, mind – it may be given to me.'

'Entirely as you wish. But if he wanted to give your wife a small gift in addition? It would be no more than a courtesy. A monkey, if she would like one, or some fine Brussels lace or a set of china cups.'

'There is no need to reward my wife in any way whatsoever. She has done nothing for you. She is not aware of your existence.'

'Then let us by all means keep it that way, if you would prefer. I am agreeable that a happy ignorance should be part of our bargain.' She winked at him again. 'I have a pen and ink in the drawer over there.'

Perhaps it was the revived hint of blackmail, perhaps it was the second wink of complicity, implying an easy understanding of his baser nature, but it was enough to make Pepys cautiously honest, if only for a moment.

'Let me read over this agreement again,' he said. 'My duty is to His Majesty the King and I believe that the price demanded may be too high – even for this particular king. I shall study this and compare it with other similar contracts. Precedents are everything. Then I shall visit your husband as soon as I can and discuss the matter with him.'

'This was the price we agreed, Mr Pepys.' All trace of flirtatiousness had left her voice. The words were stonily polite.

'It was the price you proposed. That is not the same thing,' he said.

'Well, I did what *you* proposed and you made no distinction then between proposal and agreement. You assumed my consent to everything very easily.'

'That is another matter entirely.'

'Was it? Was it really? My virtue and yours are clearly beasts of a very different colour. Look, you've had your fun, Mr Pepys. Now it's time to pay for it. Like the gentleman we both wish you were.' She knew that she could have phrased that better, that she had not advanced her cause by attacking Pepys's origins and status in society, but she still held out the paper hopefully towards him. Business was business, after all. Surely he could see that?

But Pepys had decided he would have to comb his own hair in future.

'I'll talk to your husband,' he repeated. 'This is not the time or place to discuss official matters.'

'It's how the King proceeds,' she said. 'Most of his decisions are made in his bedchamber.'

Pepys picked up his hat. 'Precisely,' he said.

'You'll regret this,' she said suddenly and without wholly realising she was saying it. She bit her lip.

'There are other shipyards,' he said.

'Oh, that's it, is it? Well, if you've had a better offer from Pett, you only had to say—'

'Good morning, madam,' Pepys said. 'I can find my own way out.'

She watched him go.

A door opened behind her and, somewhat improbably, her husband appeared. He did not seem to be in Rotherhithe.

'What are you doing here?' she asked.

'That's my business. Back early. Where's Pepys?'

'Gone. Didn't you see him?'

'Came up the back stairs.'

'Why?'

'Just thought I would. They're my stairs. I can do as I like.'

'Were you listening at that door?'

Cade looked uncertain, as if he couldn't quite recall what he'd been doing a few moments before.

'Can't hear a thing through that door,' he said eventually.

'So you *were* listening then?'

'I said, I couldn't.'

'Makes no difference to me,' she replied. 'Some men trust their wives.'

'So, did he sign?' he demanded. 'Yes or no? Do we have a contract?'

'No,' she said. 'He didn't sign.'

'But you tried everything?'

She looked at him. Had he really not heard anything that had been said? Or that had been done? Of course he could be lying. Most people did lie all the time, in her experience. Especially men.

'I did everything an honest woman might do,' she replied,

ignoring the things she had also done that an honest woman possibly wouldn't. 'He still said no. He's no gentleman, that one. Jumped up little nobody with a rich cousin to buy him a place on the Navy Board.'

'That's that then,' said Cade. 'No contract. No new work. The yard is finished. That's the end of us. Unless I can get Pepys to make me commissioner at Deptford. That's a snug little nest. What do you think?'

'I've told you I'm not going to Deptford, miles from anywhere.'

Cade sighed. His wife normally complained about every aspect of living by the Tower. Deptford, a few green miles downriver, should have been an improvement for her in most ways. A better house. A garden with roses and quince trees. But it clearly wasn't what she wanted either.

'Anyway, we've still got a trick or two up our sleeves before we abandon the yard here,' she added.

'Really?' he said. 'What trick's that then, my girl? You're going to get the whole Navy Board in here, are you?'

She considered this possibility for a moment, then shook her head. They didn't have that much time. 'Pepys is scared half to death that we'll go to his wife and tell her he tried to lead me astray. It won't be difficult to convince her. She's caught him at it before. In the act. With her own maid. That always concentrates a wife's mind.'

'You know that for sure?' he said.

'Oh yes. Our maid knows the Pepys's maid well, the dirty little slut.'

She looked at Cade with an enquiring eyebrow but, unexpectedly, he shook his head. 'This is wrong,' he said. 'I've done all I can to keep this yard running. And I've done it honestly – sometimes anyway. But at every step we sink deeper and deeper into the slime. I don't mind blackmail, but we'll get nowhere with trumped-up accusations ... They *are* trumped-up, I hope?'

'Trumped-up? Course they are, my pet. You know me.'

'Still, we know a lot about how Pepys conducts his business,' said Cade. 'That could be the way to go.'

It was Mistress Cade's turn to sigh. Was the man a complete fool? 'I grant you he's done a lot that's wrong, but so have we. We could go down with him, unless we're careful. Actually we'll go down alone, because, unlike him, we can't afford to bribe the jury.'

'Men like Pepys – they shouldn't be allowed to get away with the things they do. We should go to the authorities—'

'Don't start on that again,' she said. 'Denouncing him to the King is as dangerous as blackmailing him – and there's nothing in it for us.'

'Maybe it's not that dangerous. We could get a pardon, if we give evidence for the Crown.'

'We'll get hanged more like. Blackmail's one thing, but this is certainly no time to decide to become an honest informer – don't even think about that.'

'We might as well be hanged than die of starvation. The yard's finished. Look, why don't I see how much I need to pay Pepys to give me the commissioner's job?'

'I've told you – I'm not going to Deptford.'

'Why? You're always saying how you hate it here.'

'Well, now I'm saying I'm not going.'

'So, what do we do? We can't say Pepys tried to seduce you if he didn't.'

'That's true.'

'And we can't risk accusing him of taking bribes without admitting we gave them to him.'

'That's also true.'

'But don't forget we know about the Ruby.'

Mistress Cade pulled a face. 'The Ruby?' she said. 'We don't want to be digging that up. You tried that once and it didn't go well. Forget hanging after a fair trial – the Ruby will get us knifed as soon as we step out of the house.'

Cade shook his head. 'Then let's give bribery another go. Even if Pepys thinks he's too good for us, his wife may be more sensible. She won't look a gift horse in the mouth. And Pepys knows she'll make a fuss all over London if he tries to get her to return whatever we give her – he won't want to risk that. So, once she's taken our little present, and Pepys knows she has, maybe he'll feel he has no choice but to give us a hand.'

'Pepys is no fool. If we're to save the yard, we need divine inspiration.'

'A parrot,' he said suddenly. 'We'll give his wife a parrot.'

Mistress Cade looked out of the window in case that idea had come accompanied by a sudden shaft of sunlight from Heaven.

But it hadn't.

Chapter 1

Lincoln's Inn, June 1669

'I t's good to have you back with us, Sir John,' says Will. 'Here in London. Just like old times. You and me working together. Happy days they were, sir. And it will be happy days again.'

My clerk rubs his hands together, as if this will make what he says true.

'I'm only here for a week, Will,' I say. 'Long enough to hand over the remainder of my work to my new partner, and no more than that. Then I'm returning to Essex for good. I'm not going to alter my decision.'

Will draws a deep breath of disapproval. I should be here, drafting contracts, advising on bequests, writing codicils, earning streams of golden sovereigns for us both.

'Lady Grey is well, I trust?' he asks. 'And young Master Charles?'

'Both wife and son are well,' I say, 'and Aminta sends her best wishes to you. She holds you in genuine affection, Will.'

He nods. He holds Aminta in genuine affection, in most ways. But not all.

'It isn't my wife who is making me do this,' I say. 'I have responsibilities in Essex that mean that I no longer have time to practise as a lawyer here in London. And I certainly don't have time to take on work for Lord Arlington. It's entirely my own decision. It's what I want to do. You need blame nobody but me.'

Will looks at me silently. I too am suspicious of any witness who protests their innocence overmuch. I resolve not to say anything further that can only make things worse than they are. Anyway, I'm done with the Law, except for serving as a magistrate in Essex. I'm Lord of the Manor of Clavershall West. I can't be that and a London lawyer, even to keep my clerk happy. Nor can I be the creature of Lord Arlington. Arlington will have to find other creatures. And maybe pay them better than he paid me, if he wants to keep them.

'How is Sir Felix?' asks Will.

'My wife's father is well,' I say. 'Some aches and pains last winter, but less now the warm weather is with us.'

It's a hot summer and even hotter here in London than in Essex. The air in the chamber drips and sticks to my skin. Will has, unusually for him, discarded his coat and waistcoat and stands before me in shirtsleeves.

'Sir Felix isn't bored in the country?' asks Will.

'Why should anyone be bored in the country, Will?'

'No reason at all, sir,' says Will. 'Lots to do in the country, as you say. You'll be out hunting a great deal, of course.'

'I don't hunt,' I say.

'And shooting.'

'I don't shoot.'

'And fishing.'

'You've made your point, Will,' I say. 'There are other things to do in the country.'

'Such as?'

'Such as lots of things,' I say.

'So, you're not taking on any more clients?'

'No,' I said.

'Not ever?'

He can ask for as much clarification as he likes. It won't change things at all.

'No,' I say. I take out a kerchief and mop my brow. Will's a Londoner born and bred. He can survive here. He doesn't mind the heat rising up from the cobblestones at midday and the evening stink from the soupy river. But it's an art I've lost myself. The sooner I'm out of London the better.

'It's just that there's somebody who's been trying to see you,' says Will insistently. 'He comes here every evening.'

'What's his name?' I ask.

'Thomas Cade. He's a shipbuilder.'

'I've never heard of him. He can see my partner, surely?'

'Only you will do, it seems. Says he wants to talk to an honest lawyer. Says you're the only one he knows of.'

'That's flattering—'

'Don't worry. I told him you were no more honest than was strictly necessary. But I also told him, honest or not, you're the best in London. The very best.'

'That's an exaggeration. And I'm not a lawyer any more.'

'He says it's a matter of great importance. Says you'll want to help him when he tells you what it is.'

'Well I can't see him. There would be no point. This time next week I'll be in the country again. He'll have to find an honest lawyer elsewhere. If he can't find one here, at Lincoln's

Inn, he could try the Middle Temple. There was rumoured to be one there, when I last heard.'

'I told him to come back tonight, sir, between half past nine and ten o'clock. Your letter didn't say exactly when you'd arrive, but I thought it would be before dark.'

'And did you tell him I'd see him then?'

'Yes, sir. I said you'd be pleased to counsel him.'

'Ten minutes,' I say. 'No more.'

'I'll advise him to be brief,' he says.

Thomas Cade holds his battered leather hat respectfully in his hands. He wears a rough woollen coat and breeches – good sturdy cloth, cut in the new fashion – and a plain linen cravat twisted round his neck. He shaved yesterday or perhaps the day before. Like me, he has not yet affected a periwig. His black hair is clean and tied back neatly.

'My clerk says that you wish to see me,' I say, 'but I must warn you that I am in London for a short time only. If I can advise you, then I shall, but I may not accept any case that cannot be resolved in a single interview.'

'I don't rightly know who else to take this to . . .' he says uncertainly. 'I asked around and was told that you were the best. And this is a matter that is far from being easy. More to the point, you have a friend at Court. Lord Arlington.'

Well at least, unlike Aminta, he does not appear to be about to chide me for my foolishness in having anything to do with the King's Secretary of State. He seems to think it may prove advantageous.

'I've worked for Arlington in the past,' I say cautiously. 'I don't know if he regards me as a friend. But, as with my legal practice, that is work I no longer have time for.'

Cade nods. 'You were a spy,' he says bluntly. 'For Lord Arlington.'

'Arlington is head of intelligence, amongst other things. I carried out some tasks for him. My exact role was rarely given a name. I was a spy, if you wish to call it that.'

'Is that how you got the scar on your face?'

'Yes,' I say.

'And is that why you have that limp?'

'It is only inconvenient in damp weather. Or, like today, when I have been long in the saddle, journeying here from Essex.'

An almost-cool evening wind is finally blowing in through the casement. Outside, in Lincoln's Inn Fields, I hear the dry rustle of the leaves on the plane trees.

'Like as not, he owes you a favour or two, in that case?' says Cade.

'I doubt that Arlington sees it that way.'

He nods again. Perhaps he knows Arlington. If he does, he'll also know that Arlington never acknowledges debts of any sort to anyone. He doesn't need to.

'Are you acquainted with a Mr Samuel Pepys, sir?' Cade asks.

'He's Clerk of the Acts at the Navy Office. He is a kinsman of Lord Sandwich and has the ear of the Duke of York. And of the King. When London was burning – I mean during the Great Fire – it was Pepys who persuaded the King to blow up houses to create a firebreak. At the moment of greatest danger for the City he asked to see the King and the King saw him straight away. And the King did what he said. That's the influence he has. He's a clever man. And hard-working.'

'You don't say honest?'

'No, I don't say that.'

'And not a friend of yours?'

'No,' I say. 'I admire his abilities, of course . . .'

'But you disapprove of some aspects of his conduct?'

'I'm no Puritan,' I say firmly.

'I didn't say you were, Sir John.'

Good. Perhaps I look less of a Puritan than I once did. I mean less than I did before I married Aminta. This deep red velvet coat, for example, which Aminta chose for me. The lace on my cravat, to which Aminta urged me. The new gold watch in my waistcoat pocket, which Aminta gave me. Still, I don't approve of Pepys for all that. I wouldn't leave him alone with a daughter if I had one. I wouldn't leave him with my wife either, but for his safety rather than hers. I've watched Aminta skin a rabbit and wring a chicken's neck with one simple, economical twist and pull.

'His morality is no concern of mine,' I say.

'Provided he stays within the Law,' says Cade.

'As a magistrate I can hear cases only within my own county. So long as Pepys keeps his nose clean in Essex he has nothing to fear from me in the City of London or in Middlesex.'

'I'm not asking you to try him for breaking the Sabbath,' says Cade.

'What are you asking me to do then?'

Cade pauses for a long time. When he finally speaks, he says: 'Do you know anything about shipbuilding, sir?'

'Not much.'

'Well, it's what I do, as my father did before me. I own a yard by the Tower. We built the Dunbar for Oliver Cromwell. Finest ship in the fleet until the Dutch captured it two years ago when they attacked us in the Medway. They've renamed it now, something Dutch I expect, and it patrols the Channel for them.' He shakes his head. We both know it was the most shameful defeat the English Navy has ever suffered. Our best ships gone and we didn't even put up a fight. 'I build merchantmen for private customers, when I can get the work, but they're all going to the bigger yards downriver these days. So we need the Navy contracts. We build mainly the third and fourth raters for them – the smaller ships – and usually only when the royal dockyards have more work than they can handle. And we repair them, of course. Actually, it's mainly repair work now, to tell you the truth.'

'But you must be busy with the constant threat from the Dutch?'

'We've kept the men fully employed up to now, thank the Lord.'

'That must be a great comfort to them,' I say.

'Yes. When we manage to pay them, sir. Pay is several months in arrears at the moment, because payment from the King is slow to arrive. It's not as bad with us as in the royal dockyards, but it's bad enough.'

'Parliament has failed to vote enough money?'

'No sir, the money is there, but it's a pot everyone dips their hand into. The King can't buy goods at the same price as other men. Everyone takes their allotted pence – or Shillings – in the King's Pound, as it passes through their hands.'

'Including Pepys?'

'Yes, sir. Especially Pepys.'

I look him in the eye. In my work for Arlington I've been asked to believe a great many things by all manner of people. Information that might hang a man is rarely provided out of the goodness of somebody's heart. Does Cade have a grudge against Pepys? His face suggests he is an honest man or a practised liar. Definitely one or the other.

'And does nothing ever come your way?' I ask.

'A little,' he says. 'That's how it is.'

I shrug. 'Everyone regards a tithe of the King's money as their own.'

'You're right, sir. But it hasn't always been so. Oliver would never have countenanced it. There was discipline in his Navy and decency amongst those who ran it. More godliness. Less lace.'

'That is certainly how I recall things myself. But everyone wears lace now if they can afford it. We must forget Oliver Cromwell. The Republic is dead.'

'And have you changed with the times?' he asks.

'Enough, and no more,' I say.

'I wish I could say the same, sir. I told myself that was what I had to do if I wanted to continue to build ships. I've winked at wrongdoing, both my own and other people's. But I've thought a lot about it, sir. I'd rather the yard went under than allow things to continue as they are.'

'Then take your concerns to the King. He is not unapproachable. He'll see almost anyone, if he has a mind to. He does not fear assassination the way Oliver did. He thinks the people love him. As for my help – I know nothing at all about ships. You don't need me.'

'The King will never listen to me, sir. You know that. Even if I could get an audience with him, he wouldn't believe me rather than Pepys.'

'That's not true,' I say. 'He might well believe you. He's nobody's fool. It's just that he'd then take the easiest path and do nothing.'

'It would be different if you told him.'

'Not so very different. He might hesitate for a minute or so. He might consult his dogs as to their opinion. But in the end it would be the same.'

'Please try, sir. Between us, I think we can do it. I'm offering to give up my livelihood, if I have to. I want to put things right. I'm just asking you to arrange one meeting.'

'So, you want me to go to the King—'

'Or to Lord Arlington.'

'But we'll have no proof.'

'I have the proof, sir. All the proof you'll need. Contracts. Letters.'

'Evidence against Pepys?'

'Not just Pepys. And not just shipbuilding contracts. There are other ways of making your fortune at the country's expense.'

'Can I see these documents now?'

'It wasn't safe to bring them, sir. I couldn't be sure that I wouldn't be followed here. In fact, I'm still not sure I wasn't followed. Better the information lies where it is – where it can speak, whether I live or die.'

'But why are you doing this, Master Cade? What concern is it of yours?'

'Because we're constantly fighting the Dutch and the French, sir. Yet we never have enough money to build the ships we need and supply them and pay the sailors. If we can't keep the fleet at sea, then however well I build the ships, we're lost. It's as I said: when the Dutch raided the Medway two years ago, our fleet just sat there waiting to be sunk, burned or captured. There weren't enough men aboard The Royal Charles to load a cannon. The rigging and ropes were all rotten. The ship's in Amsterdam now. It was one of the vessels towed away without a shot being fired. This canker at the heart of the administration is shaming us all.'

'Have you considered the consequences for yourself?'

'I've been plain with you about my own wrongdoing. If I give evidence, maybe you can get me a pardon or maybe I'll have to take the consequences. But, if we all sit on our hands, this will continue for ever and a day. You've been a spy, sir. You know that nothing happens unless somebody turns informer. I'm offering to come over to the King's side. Together we can stop this.'

I wonder if he has been as plain as he might be. Still, the rest of what he has said is true enough. A double agent is a most valuable piece in the game. Unfortunately, even the best double agent is of no weight unless he is properly used. And I doubt that Arlington will want to acquire this one, unless he's already decided to move against Pepys or his master, the Duke of York. That's unlikely. The main thing a double agent needs is somebody to protect him. A completely friendless double agent cannot expect to see the sun rise on another day. I have no wish to lead Mr Cade on to a path that presents only danger for him.

'My advice to you, Mr Cade, is to go home and forget what you've told me. Perhaps I could get you a pardon. But Pepys is both well protected and unforgiving. And, as you say, far too many benefit from practices of this sort. Lord Arlington will see little advantage in stopping courtiers making easy money. He has enemies enough at Court without that. Anyway, take Pepys away from the Navy Office, and all that will happen is that another, less efficient and more grasping, will be set in his place. England grows richer by the day. The country has money to spare. We have more ships and more shipyards than they do. We'll defeat the Dutch next time, even with Mr Pepys clipping the King's coin on its way through his hands.'

'I'm sorry to hear you say that, sir. You wouldn't have done once.'

'Wouldn't I? Who told you that?'

'Your clerk, sir. Mr Atkins.'

I pause. Is Will right? Have I really changed that much? Am I, as Lord of the Manor of Clavershall West, prepared to overlook things that I, as a young lawyer, would have fought against tooth and nail? Would I, in happier times, have gone to Lord Arlington's predecessor, Mr Secretary Thurloe, or to Cromwell himself? Things were different then. I am no longer in the habit of drinking myself into a stupor every evening, either.

'Very well,' I say. 'Forget the personal danger. Think of the men you employ. Have you considered that, if you upset Pepys, you will never get another naval contract again?'

'Then so be it,' he says. 'But, for me, there is no going back. I've already told others – others too cowardly to come with me – that I intend to act. The die is already cast. Pepys and the others will hear of it whatever I do. The danger lies in not following my purpose through to the end. I need your help, Sir John. I'm a dead man without it. If you're not already convinced, let me tell you about the Ruby—'

I hold up my hand. I do not need to know about this, and the less he says, the less danger he will be in. At the moment, whatever incautious words he may have let fall, the danger is still quite small. But he can make it as great as he believes it could be. 'Go home,' I repeat. 'I know Pepys. He's hardly the sort of person to lie in wait for you with a pair of pistols just because you spoke against him.'

'I beg you, Sir John—'

I hold up my hand again. '*I know Pepys*. You have my assurance that you are safe so long as you say nothing more. Trust me, Mr Cade. I'm right.'

'I'm sorry, Sir John . . .' he says. But whether he is sorry to have troubled me or sorry that I am not more use to him is left unsaid. Both perhaps. I'm sorry too.

He turns, claps his hat on his head, and walks away, out of my chamber, clattering down the bare wooden stairs and into the night. I hear the outer door close and his footsteps receding. They pause – perhaps Cade has momentarily lost his way in the dark – then I hear them again briefly. Then there is silence.

Will enters the room. He raises an eyebrow.

'My apologies, Will, but there was nothing to be done for him,' I say. 'It would have been irresponsible for me to have encouraged his belief that he could take on Pepys.'

'*You* could have done it, sir,' says Will.

'To what end?' I ask.

Will looks at me. Of course, I know the answer to my question.

'None at all, sir,' says Will. 'You're quite right. These things can't be remedied. It's the times, sir. They make honest men dishonest without their knowing. Can I bring you a tankard of ale?'

I wonder whether to send Will after Cade. If he ran fast, and I know that Will would run fast, I could get Cade back here. Perhaps if I questioned him further I could find some way to do as he suggested. A younger John Grey would not have let it rest there. A younger John Grey would have considered how justice could best be served. I look out of my chamber window at Lincoln's Inn Fields below me. Night has fallen. For the first time since I arrived in London the air actually feels cold on my face. I cannot make out the departing figure of Thomas Cade amongst the many moving shadows cast by the tall plane trees. Above us there is pale moonlight, but below just the shifting shades of black into which Cade has gone. It is too late.

'Thank you, Will,' I say. 'Yes, please bring me some ale. Why not?'

I am awoken early the following day. The sun rises at the same time here as in Essex, but the noises of the street scarcely cease all night – the watchman calling the hours, the rumble of cartwheels on the cobbles and, when there are no other sounds, the distant roar of the river as it rushes through the narrow arches of London Bridge. Now, with the first light of the sun dancing on the leaves of the planes, I hear a commotion in the gardens below.

Even as I am rising from my bed, Will bursts through the door.

'What now, Will?' I ask.

'They've found a dead man, sir. Down there amongst the bushes.'

I dress quickly, tucking my shirt into my breeches and thrusting my bare feet into my shoes. Will and I run down the stairs. I feel a sharp stab of pain in my leg as I do so – it has not yet recovered from yesterday's journey.

The warm sun strikes my face as I step into the green and well-tended grounds of Lincoln's Inn. There is a heavenly early morning scent in the air of roses and nicotiana. We follow the sound of voices and come across a small gathering of lawyers, gardeners and serving men clustered around something lying on the ground. The crowd parts respectfully as it notices me, and allows me to approach the body. I've seen men shot and I've seen them strangled and I've seen them with gaping wounds in their throats. This man has been killed with a blow – perhaps more than one – to the back of the head. His hair, neatly tied back, is matted with dark, congealed blood. When I touch it with my fingers, gently, though he will never feel the pressure of fingers again, it yields in a way that it should not. The skull is broken. Then, there amid the hair, I notice something. A splinter of wood. It is blood-soaked, but fresh and sharp. So he was struck perhaps with a wooden staff or club, and struck hard, a sliver of wood shearing off. And yet it need not have been a fatal blow. Some men receive such wounds and live. This one has not been so lucky. I do not need to turn him over to identify him, but I do anyway. Then I lower him again, very carefully, and allow him to rest.

'Mr Cade was right then,' says Will from behind me.

'Yes,' I say.

'His life was in danger.'

'The empirical evidence is in front of us,' I say. 'We can no longer doubt it.'

There is a silence during which Will does not point out how wrong I was. That's kind of him.

'We know he left us just after ten o'clock,' I say.

'At exactly fifteen minutes past the hour,' says Will significantly. I have to agree that I could have given him my attention for longer on his last night on earth.

'Indeed. Both that very relevant observation and the state of the body suggest that he was ambushed as he left the building. But ...'

I look at the exit from the building in which I have my chambers and at the gate that leads from the neat private gardens of Lincoln's Inn itself out into the more ragged public space of Lincoln's Inn Fields, where the parched grass grows long and pale.

'He didn't need to come this way,' says Will.

'No,' I say. 'Somebody must have lured him over to these bushes, then waylaid him here.'

'Or he mistook his direction in the dark,' says Will.

'But how would his assailant know that that was what he would do?'

'Perhaps he didn't know. Perhaps the killer simply lay in wait for the first person who would pass by, to attack and rob them.'

'This leads to nowhere,' I say. 'Most nights a robber could have waited here until dawn and nobody would have passed by. It would be poor business for a footpad, and risky. Afterwards, they'd have to walk out of Lincoln's Inn past the porter – or climb the wall and hazard being seen dropping down on the far side. Whoever it was, they crouched in wait for him by these bushes. They loitered patiently until Cade walked past, then jumped up and struck him with a wooden club, or something of the sort.' I kneel again and inspect the wound more thoroughly. 'It is a fatal hurt, but only one blow, I think. Perhaps whoever struck it did not mean to kill him.'

'To warn him?'

'Or rob him. He mentioned some jewel – a ruby, I think. If somebody knew he had it with him, or thought he did, then the risk of following him and attacking him might have been worthwhile.'

I feel in Cade's pockets. His purse is there. It contains some pennies and several Shillings. He also still possesses his silver fob watch. There is no gemstone of any sort. I feel the hems of his garments, where such things may be stitched, but the hems are just hems, neatly stitched.

'A common thief would surely have taken the watch,' says Will. 'Even if there were also more valuable items in his pockets.'

'Unless the assailant was disturbed before he could finish the job.'

'We heard nothing last night, sir. And whoever it was who disturbed the killer would surely have stumbled over Mr Cade's body.'

'True,' I say. I recalled standing at the window, looking out. I would have heard any altercation or even a man's boots crunching on the gravel path as he ran. Somebody killed Cade silently and privily, as I enjoyed the cool night air, then crept away, at his leisure, undisturbed and undetected. A murder has taken place in this walled and well-protected garden.

'Did the gatekeeper see any stranger enter here last night?' I ask.

'No, sir,' says a voice from the back of the throng. Perkins, the porter, is thrust forwards towards me.

'It was only the residents – the lawyers, sir, and their families and clerks – who entered yesterday evening. At least through the main gate. An agile man could scale the walls, if he had a mind to. There was a woman who approached the gate, sir, but then went away again and stood under the trees in the fields for some time. I thought it odd, but not so odd as to challenge her. Unless he was killed by a lawyer of the Inn, then the killer must have climbed in and then out again.'

'Thank you,' I say. 'Well, that's helpful. But now we must call for an officer of the Law.'

'Robert has already gone to fetch the constable,' says one of the gardeners. 'We sent for him as soon as we found the body. He'll be here soon, no doubt.'

I look up. A tall man is striding through the gate alone.

'Maybe that's him now,' says Will. 'If so, he's prompt.'

I shake my head. 'That's one of Arlington's men,' I say. 'I know him. Did you tell Arlington I was visiting London?'

'No, sir. You told me quite specifically not to.'

But Arlington has ways of finding these things out. Nothing stirs in these streets without Arlington being aware. A rat couldn't climb out of a sewer without Arlington enquiring as to its intentions and its loyalty to the House of Stuart. That's his job, after all.

Chapter 2

Whitehall

Lord Arlington is up early. Or late. Like many courtiers he has to keep the same hours as the King, at least from time to time. The King will have retired to bed quite recently and, regardless of which lady he has been with earlier, he will have retired with the Queen. He remains a dutiful husband. Similarly, some of the courtiers still have tasks to perform before their own day is ended – orders that the King gave while drunk, which he may still recall when sober. Arlington is nothing if he is not punctilious in the King's service. If, as the candles finally guttered to their death, the King had asked a favour of Arlington, he would be eager to fulfil it before the King awoke.

It is over a year since I saw His Majesty's Postmaster General and Secretary of State for the Southern Department. Perhaps his real hair has grown a little greyer beneath the luxuriant false hair that cascades over his shoulders and onto the rich silk dressing gown that he has wrapped around him. But, on the surface, little has changed. The generous, open smile is as untrustworthy as ever. And the thing that he is most noted for, the patch on his nose covering some long-healed wound, is as black and glossy and elegantly curved as before. Voluminous white shirtsleeves billow from the arms of the loose chestnut-coloured gown. His hands are long and slender – the hands, you might say (if you didn't know him), of a thoughtful and sensitive man.

'I congratulate you, my Lord, on the birth of your daughter,' I say. For he too is now a father. 'I trust that she and your wife are well?'

'Thank you. Isabella and Lady Arlington are both in good health. Children are always a concern, are they not?'

'Their well-being?'

'Their future. Whom they should marry. It has to be considered.'

'Isabella is how old now?'

'Six months. But planning these things takes time. I would not wish her to be less than a countess. She would be utterly miserable as a mere baroness. And, more to the point, it would not reflect well on me that I had done no better for her.'

'There must be many eligible young dukes in their cradles at this moment, some as yet unspoken for.'

'Far too few, though when the King's bastards are all given dukedoms, they may become plentiful enough. A royal match, even with a bastard duke, is a prize worth having. That is to be thought on.'

He enquires about my own family – Aminta, whose plays and poetry he admires; Sir Felix, whose morals amuse him; my son, of whom he knows little and cares less. It is clear that he does not see young Charles as a potential husband for his daughter. He has not called me here in the early morning to ennoble me or my heirs. We speak briefly of my late mother, a loyal supporter of the King throughout his long exile – a fact that excuses in part my own past support for Cromwell and the Republic. He suspects that I still have some loyalty to the Good Old Cause, but that is not something that it would be safe to admit here, even to myself.

'You intend to bury yourself in the country? Away from the Court?' he asks.

'That is precisely my wish.'

'It would be a waste – a loss to His Majesty. And to your own ambitions. A great pity.'

'Not in my view, my Lord.'

Arlington looks at me curiously. For him, there is only one game worth playing. Nobody in his world denies being ambitious, unless by doing so they can gain a major tactical advantage.

'You intend to spend your time managing your estate?' he says.

'There is much work to be done. The estate was mismanaged by my stepfather because he wanted it only to give him position in society and by my mother because mismanagement was a family tradition that she wished to keep up. My stepfather's and my mother's mismanagement were completely different, but both potentially ruinous. So, I give my attention to putting things in order and to sitting as a magistrate.'

'You are content with so little?'

'Yes,' I say. 'I also occasionally assist my wife in her work. Writers ask for honest criticism in the hope of receiving undiluted admiration. Within my limited ability, I give a little of both.'

'I am pleased your wife is still writing plays. I can't tell you how much I enjoyed the last one. I assume that Lord Rabblerouser was a portrait of that fool Ashley?'

'I wouldn't presume to know that. You must ask her.'

'She has a sharp pen to prick pomposity. She portrays the manners of the town more cruelly than anyone I know.'

'She does indeed. But she has found she can write of London when in the country. Better in some ways. From a distance, she says, it all comes into focus. She needs to be here only when her plays are being rehearsed. And then only for a short time. The presence of authors is rarely of much value to people. Their names do not even appear on the playbills with those of the actors and actresses. The public is happy that they remain obscure.'

Arlington rubs his thumb against his lower lip. He is wondering how best to say what he has to say, now he is about to get to the point.

'But, in spite of your strange retirement, your gratitude and loyalty to His Majesty is undiminished?'

'Like all of His Majesty's subjects, I hold him in the utmost respect and reverence.'

Arlington nods, as if this could actually be true. 'Good. Then you will be happy to help him with a small problem that he has.'

'If it can be done from north Essex, then I am at his service.'

'That's a pity. It can't be.'

'So, you will allocate the task elsewhere?'

'No, you'll have to spend some time in London.'

'Surely there are others you can ask?'

'The King thinks not.'

'The King has men who followed him loyally all the way

33

through his exile. There must be many amongst them whom he would trust with his life.'

'He doesn't want them. What man with any sense would exile himself in Bruges or Brussels, when he could have a career under Cromwell in London, as you did – work that he might actually be well paid for? The King needs somebody sensible, pragmatic and reasonably honest.'

He smiles again, but he wants me to understand that remaining in England under Cromwell was, for all that, in no way creditable. He himself crossed the Channel with the King and languished there until the Restoration. Those of us who stayed here and served the Republic are forever indebted to the King for his mercy and forgiveness. And that forgiveness could still be revoked. We former Republicans have no right at all to run off to Essex. Not if we want to keep our heads and our guts in the usual comfortable place.

'What exactly does the King wish me to do?' I ask.

'What do you think the King's income is each year?'

'I've no idea,' I say.

'To fund all of the functions of state, one million two hundred thousand Pounds a year is required, and most years we succeed, through taxation and other much resented measures, to raise that. It should be adequate to finance the Navy and all that it requires. But for some reason it never is. It is like trying to hold water in a sieve. Do what you like, it seeps through. There is never enough left inside. So, where does the money go?'

'Various people take their share of it as it passes through their hands,' I say. 'The King knows that, surely?'

'Of course. But how do we stop them?'

'Sack the corrupt ones and appoint new men. There are

many poor but clever clerks who could do the job instead of those whose rich friends have bought them their places.'

'Many of the current crew hold their offices by hereditary appointment – or almost. The Petts have controlled shipbuilding on the Thames for generations. The great Phineas Pett, who served King James. Joseph at Limehouse. Christopher and Richard at Woolwich. And, of course, Peter at Chatham on the Medway. Their appointments are as good as a freehold.'

'If there is proof of wrongdoing . . .'

'Precisely, Sir John. *Proof.* That would enable us to act. That would cut through the knot of entitlement. And that is where you come in.'

'You want me to provide the proof?'

'Me? I don't want anything of you. I'd be happy to let you return to Essex and look after your pigs or whatever you keep there. It is what the *King* requires that must be considered by all of us. And he wants an investigation. A silken enquiry that will make no sound, but which will securely tie up the culprits hand and foot.'

'That isn't the sort of work I've done for you in the past.'

'True. But it is free of the dangers that you have faced for the King previously. You need merely to travel to the various dockyards, speak to the officers there, interview some of the contractors.'

'That is all?'

'You may need to speak to some servants of the Crown in London.'

'As you wish.'

'As *the King* wishes. And he would like your report promptly – I can give you a couple of weeks.'

'That's very little time.'

'I have every confidence in you. You might also wish to speak to some of the King's ministers and mistresses.'

'Powerful people, then.'

'They won't be after the King has dealt with them. You have nothing to fear from them. Or very little.'

'A man was killed last night at Lincoln's Inn,' I say.

'There are footpads in all parts of London. He was a lawyer?'

I have to disappoint Arlington.

'He was a shipbuilder,' I say, 'with a yard near the Tower. He had come to me to raise exactly the same matter as you have. He said he had evidence of corruption in the royal dockyards and elsewhere. He said his life was in danger. I assured him that nothing could be done. I assured him he was completely safe and had no cause to fear.'

'You were clearly wrong in one respect. I hope you were wrong in the other as well.'

'I should have listened to him. His death was my fault.'

'Really? I think he must bear a large part of the blame himself. You didn't ask him to come to you, did you? Of course, you have carelessly lost a witness who might have been of great use to us. The King will not be pleased, *if I were to tell him*. But there will be other witnesses. And, now we are working together so helpfully, the King need not know. His death should sit lightly with you.'

'Would Samuel Pepys have been aware that the King was thinking of this enquiry?' I ask.

'He is in the confidence of the Duke, the King's brother. The King would doubtless have told his brother of his plans.'

'I'll need to watch my back,' I say.

'Yes,' says Arlington. 'Thinking about it, that might be prudent after all. I'd do that if I were you. Oh, there's no payment for this task, by the way. Your reward will be the King's everlasting gratitude.'

'I never imagined it would be otherwise,' I say.

I have returned to my chambers and am closeted with Mr Sparks, my new partner, who has arrived at his usual hour of nine o'clock. He walks here from his house over towards the Strand every morning. Unlike me, he has not taken up residence at Lincoln's Inn, nor does he plan to. It is unsuitable for a man with a young family. The walk takes sixteen and a half minutes in the summer, eighteen and a half in the winter when the road is more slippery.

Sparks is a neat little man, who never seems to get ink on his fingers. His clothes are as plain and precise as he is – a long black waistcoat that fits tightly round his slim body and descends almost to his knees, a black coat of similar length over it, black breeches more or less hidden by the flaps of the waistcoat, white woollen stockings, a plain cravat. And a periwig, of course. That is black too, and might as well be his own hair for all the good it does him. There is no attempt at excess here. Nothing for show. He has removed his hat, out of respect for the four or five years by which I am older than he is. If it were the other way round, he would take it much amiss that I did not remove mine. His is an orderly world with many pleasant rules and few surprises. I doubt that he has ever run anyone through with his sword in a dark alleyway. I doubt that anyone has ever shot him from behind, having only a few minutes before assured him of their everlasting goodwill. It might puzzle him that such a thing was possible. For some years he and I have lived in different worlds.

'Mr Atkins is not here?' he asks.

'I sent Will out to buy bread and cheese,' I say. 'I was up early. I haven't had time to eat yet. A man was killed in the gardens last night.'

'So I heard. I shall demand that the watchman takes greater care to protect us all.'

'I think Thomas Cade would have been murdered somewhere even if his killer had not been able to gain admittance to the grounds.'

'Ah, then that is another matter. Still, we wouldn't want Lincoln's Inn to get a reputation for that sort of thing. Bad for business.'

'No, of course not. But the porter thinks our killer may have got in over the wall and left the same way. If so, it is the wall we will have to strengthen rather than make our watchman more vigilant. In the meantime, you may take comfort in the fact that we have Will to protect us here in our chambers. Nobody gets past him. You will find that vexatious clients are kept firmly in the outer room.'

'I think that Mr Atkins will soon make an excellent lawyer,' says Sparks.

'Lawyer?' I say.

'Yes. He is very quick to learn. He now does a great deal of my drafting of wills and contracts.'

'Truly?' I say.

In all the time that Will has worked for me, I have employed him to fetch and carry and wake me in the morning and cook and pour my wine and clean my boots and prepare my dinner and receive the fees due to me and enter everything in his ledger. Oh, and to carry a pistol and watch my back sometimes when I was working for Arlington. That seemed more than sufficient for what I paid him. It had never occurred to me that he might be capable of drafting contracts – it had never occurred to me that he might want to draft contracts. And yet, in a few months, Sparks has discovered that he is and he does. How did Sparks do that?

'You must have trained him well,' says Sparks.

'Evidently,' I say.

'He is a credit to you, Sir John.'

'I am pleased to hear it,' I say.

There is a noise behind us. Will is laying the table. He entered without our noticing. There is warm crusty bread, butter, cheese, apples and small beer.

'I took the liberty of purchasing victuals for Mr Sparks as well,' says Will. 'I thought that you gentlemen might wish to discuss matters over your food. I spoke to the porter again, by the way. I thought that it was odd the woman waited so long outside the gates on a dark night. He says the light was not good by then under the trees, but he is certain she was quite short, and well dressed as far as he could tell. She seemed to be watching for somebody. He doesn't recall if she was still there at about quarter past ten when Mr Cade left your chambers, but thinks she might have been. Certainly, she waited a very long time for somebody or something. There are several places, he says, where a man might climb in, though not a woman in long skirts. He's warned the Treasurer and the Master of the Walks, he says, that the wall should be made higher. Of course, the killer could be a lawyer who has chambers here. That is a possibility you may need to consider.'

'Cade knew no lawyers,' I say. 'He said so. Even if one wanted to kill him, which is unlikely, why should any lawyer here know Cade was coming to see me at that moment? The woman might have been a useful witness, but I doubt we'll find her with so little to go on. Cade feared he would be harmed by Pepys. Our efforts would be better focused on those benefiting from naval contracts.'

'True, sir. Very true. Well, I think you have everything you will need on the table, sir. I'll be outside if you need me.'

'Is there by any chance food enough for three?' I ask.

'Yes, sir. That is to say, if viewing the body earlier hasn't sharpened your appetite more than usual.'

'Good. Then I'd take it as a favour if you joined us, Will. I need some advice.'

I have recounted my interview with Arlington. Sparks is thoughtful.

'I've never met this man Pepys, but I've heard of him. He frequents the theatres a great deal. He has a liking for the actresses. And other men's wives. Still, there is no hurt in that. The King is fond of other men's wives too. He has made the thing modish, like periwigs and long waistcoats.'

'And you?' I ask.

'I find one wife more than adequate,' says Sparks primly.

'Me too,' I say. 'I was born in the wrong age. The King's father never had a mistress. He wasn't allowed one. Cromwell never had a mistress. He hadn't the time for it. The present King makes up for them both.'

'Pepys isn't a man to cross, for all that,' says Will.

He has eaten modestly and insisted on fetching the food from the serving table and pouring our beer.

'Pepys would bear a grudge for ever,' I say. 'But his natural caution means that most of the time that is all he does.'

Will shakes his head. 'But from what you say, sir, Pepys could face ruin. Disgrace. Poverty. He's a proud man. I think he would do almost anything to avoid returning to the obscurity from which he came. As for any lack of courage on his part, men can be hired with little risk to do dirty work.'

'But,' I say, 'the King has only recently decided to take action. Would Pepys have really discovered his intentions so soon, let alone decided the only way forward was to have Cade killed?'

'Unless Cade had already tried to blackmail Pepys,' says Will.

'You think he would?'

'I spent some time talking to Mr Cade, on the various occasions that he came here looking to meet with you. At first sight he strikes you as an honest enough fellow, but his story varied a little each time he came. You heard the final performance. I was at the rehearsals. He has sharpened up the script and given himself some brave lines.'

'A playwright then, like my wife.'

'An actor certainly,' says Will. 'One of the parts he played was the betrayed husband.'

'Betrayed by Pepys?'

'Yes, sir. For a long time Mistress Cade had dealt with Pepys as a customer for frigates. Cade knew Pepys would offer a better deal to a pretty woman, so he let her act as she thought best. But then he began to grow suspicious of the true state of things. For years she's complained about having to live by the Tower Yard. Then a good post became vacant – commissioner at the royal dockyard at Deptford. Cade thought she'd be happy if he applied for that and they sold the yard and moved downriver. But she said no. That puzzled him a lot. Then he worked it out – if they moved to Deptford, she wouldn't be able to carry on behind his back with Pepys. Or not as often.'

'So, he had something of substance to blackmail Pepys with? And Pepys may have known he might do so?' says Sparks.

'Cade said nothing of that to me,' I say. 'He just told me that he had done wrong in the past, but now wished to rectify matters. He hoped for a pardon if he gave evidence, which he might well have obtained. I believed him. Not beyond reasonable doubt – just on the balance of probabilities. But I can see a desire to revenge himself on Pepys might have motivated him too.'

'This is a case of some complexity,' says Sparks thoughtfully.

'The way I see it,' says Will, 'none of us is wholly honest or dishonest. It depends on the circumstances. He may not know himself whether he's a rogue, seeking to score off his enemies, or a true Christian who, after wandering in the marshland of deceit, has now rediscovered the path of true righteousness and seeks to gain the high ground of pure conscience.'

'You should be a poet, Will,' I say.

'Thank you, sir. I try to please, and you always seem to enjoy allegorical flights of fancy of a Puritan nature.'

'So, what am I to do?' I ask. 'What role, if any, does Arlington play in this allegory that Will has kindly set before us?'

Sparks frowns. 'I don't know much about allegory,' he says, 'but I know you become a lawyer because you have a love of justice.'

I laugh. 'I know many who became lawyers because it offered a good income,' I say.

'But not us,' Sparks insists earnestly. 'We have spent little time together, Sir John, but I know you well from talking to Will – maybe better than you know yourself. You've taken unprofitable cases when you believed in the man in front of you. And you've turned down cases that would have made you money when it wasn't in the interest of your client to take it forward. Sometimes you have risked your own safety.'

I raise my eyebrows. 'This is some mythological character that Will has dreamed of after eating old cheese and told you stories about when he awakened with gut ache. A lawyer with the head of an owl and the heart of a lion and the voice of a dove. Now that is a true nightmare of allegory.'

'I've never known you do the wrong thing if there was a right thing to do,' says Will. 'Or not usually. I've sometimes wondered if you had the brain of a dove, it's true, especially when it came to accepting work from Arlington. But you've always come right in the end. And you're still alive, so your judgment can't be that bad.'

'I wouldn't hesitate to accept Lord Arlington's latest commission,' says Sparks. 'Indeed, I should not. I would regard it as an honour to be chosen to serve the King.'

I think back on all of the assignments on which Arlington has sent me. None, with hindsight, was an honour. Still, they made me a better swordsman than I was before. And they taught me to lie in a way that I never knew was possible. That, however, is in the past.

'Lady Grey is expecting me back in Essex in a week's time,' I say. 'I promised I'd be there without fail.'

Sparks, a married man, nods sagely.

'Perhaps that's all it will take, sir. A week. Or, if you're later home than you promised, then I'm certain she'll be understanding,' says Will, an unmarried man.

'I don't know,' I say. 'I need to be back in Essex.'

'You can blame me, sir,' said Will.

I sigh. 'I might just do that,' I say. 'So start sharpening up the script, Will. You'll need a good one.'

Chapter 3

From a Diary

Up very betimes and by water to White-hall where I was to meet with the Duke of York, but he being closeted with the King I was put off until another time. So I walked in the park, in case I should still be called for presently, the King having no taste for long discussions at this hour, and did meet again with Sir G. Carteret, who remains much taken up with the business of the Commissioners of Accounts. I told him that I had no fear that my selling calico flags to the Navy would be seen as contrary to the rules that govern these matters. Indeed the King has gained in that I sold them at a lower price than I might have done and at less than I had paid for them almost. I tried to discover from him whether my sale of cork to the Navy was also known, but he pretended not to have heard of it, which worried me more than the business of the flags, for at least he and I are in that together, but his feigned ignorance of the cork, which he must surely know of, may mean he intends to abandon me if the matter is raised and say that I did it without his knowledge or consent.

At this point a man came running from the Duke and I was summoned back to the Palace. There I was questioned on the contract for the new frigate and the Duke told me that the master of the Tower Yard, Thomas Cade, had been found dead this morning. This troubled me that he should know of it, but I dared not ask him for more. I enquired whether the Commissioners of Accounts had the support of the King in their present business. He thought that, as with so many things, the King would lose interest, and that this slender sapling would be cut down long before it bore any ripe fruit. He had heard, however, that my Lord Arlington had been ordered privily to look into some related matter, though it was not clear to what end. He thought Arlington had no great desire to see it through, but would do so for form's sake and his own hold on the King.

I left very fearful indeed, especially in view of the possibility of Cade having revealed to somebody the extent of our previous dealings, which *nota bene* he can no longer do and which he could not have done without much harm to his own condition, but I now cannot easily discover whether he has already spoken to the Commissioners of Accounts. Cade was loose-tongued, especially when drunk, and his wife is not a jot better than he. Indeed she is worse and more doltish.

And so to bed with a troubled heart, my wife remaining up until Mid-night to teach foolish words to her new parrot, which I verily wish she had not accepted.

Chapter 4

By the Tower

The house in front of me is two storeys high and resembles many of those that made up the City before the Great Fire three years ago. Its timber frame is black. The infilling has been repeatedly whitewashed over the years, but each time it has quickly turned grey again in the London air. Only the glass of the upper windows shines, the June sun having climbed high enough to squeeze down that far into the narrow street. The fire never reached this side of the Tower. St Paul's was destroyed along with the Guildhall and many fine buildings, but the conflagration spared this modest residence, built in all likelihood when most of London was contained within its City walls and the street I am in was grass and trees.

I knock on the door. A maid, dressed soberly in dirty, ill-fitting black, answers it. Yes, her mistress is at home. Where else would she be, her poor, long-suffering husband being stone cold dead? I am shown into a low-ceilinged parlour.

It is a comfortable place with bright, cushioned chairs and tapestries on the walls and silver on the dresser. The windows are small and leaded and speak of a time when glass was rare and wonderful. The floors are stone flags, covered with rushes. At midday, the summer heat in here may be inconvenient, but not at this hour. Thick walls and heavy oak doors still hold the morning warmth at bay.

Mistress Cade bustles in, wiping dough from her hands with an old cloth. Perhaps she does not employ a cook. Though she has dressed her maid in the first black dress she could lay her hands on, she wears a very becoming dark grey gown, covered with a clean linen apron, trimmed with lace. She has a small lace cap on her head, tied under her chin. She is short, plump and no longer young, but pretty enough. In her grief, she has rouged her cheeks and newly curled her hair. She smiles at me uncertainly, the purpose of my being there still unclear to her.

'You are Mr . . .?' she says.

'Grey,' I say.

She nods. 'Mr Grey. The girl said "Mr Brown", but with no great confidence. She can't keep an idea in her head for more than a minute at a time, that one. Except for the idea of next door's footman, of course. If she's got time to waste with footmen, then she's got time to clean the silver properly, that's what I tell her. I don't pay her to talk to footmen.'

'Grey, Brown, Black. They're common enough names,' I say. 'Easy to confuse.'

'Well, we're all who we are,' she says, as if citing the words of Socrates or Descartes. 'And what can I do for you, Mr Grey?'

'I wanted to talk to you about your husband,' I say. 'I was one of those who found his body at Lincoln's Inn this morning. I came to offer my condolences.'

She nods. She's had condolences already. She's not sure whether she really needs any more. But one part of what I have said worries her.

'You're a lawyer?'

Lawyers clearly do not rank highly in her estimation. Probably much the same as wasps or woodworm. Their existence is undeniable but you definitely don't want them in the house.

'Yes,' I say. 'I'm a lawyer.'

'Well . . .' she says, in a tolerant way.

'I am sorry for your husband's death, Mistress Cade. It must be a great loss to you.'

'Oh,' she says. 'Cade left me adequately provided for. I'll say that for him. He had money enough. More than I ever suspected, now I have his keys safe in my pocket and access to his papers. I find myself a wealthy widow, Mr Grey.'

She looks at me significantly, in case that commends her to me, lawyer though I am.

'I am glad of it,' I say. 'What will happen to the yard? Will you run it yourself? I understand you had dissuaded your husband from moving to Deptford. You preferred to remain here.'

'Who told you that exactly? Deptford was just one of Cade's fancies. The commissioner's post has been vacant for some time but whoever wants it will have to pay well to get it. As for remaining here, I've no love of ships. Or of this stinking river. We've no son to succeed us, unlike the Petts, where son has followed father and nephew has followed uncle in the yards lower down the Thames and on the Medway. For the moment my husband's deputy, Harry Truscott, is managing things. He wants me to continue here, but I think it may be the end of days for the Tower Yard. Though they've built ships here for hundreds of years, the river's getting too shallow to launch the big ones – merchantmen or men of war. Lord, to think of the pains I went to, to persuade Pepys that he should put work our way and keep the miserable yard running.'

'And did he agree to do so?'

She laughs. 'I think he would have done, given time. The King needs another ship. My husband had discussed the design with the King, and the King had sketched what he wanted on an old sheet of paper. It was just a question of which yard it went to, which was Mr Pepys's decision. And Mr Pepys is very susceptible to any request from a pretty woman,' she says, with no trace of false modesty. 'I have my ways, Mr Grey. Indeed I do. You're fortunate there's nothing I want from you, for I should have it.'

'Your husband approved of your . . . methods?'

She laughs. 'You seem shocked, Mr Grey. That is how things are done nowadays. It isn't as it was under the Republic, with those sour-faced Puritans telling us what we should do and what we should eat and drink. Perhaps Cade would not have approved had I told him every little detail. But no wife tells her husband everything, does she? I doubt Mrs Grey would be so foolish as to tell you all she does. Otherwise how would we women have any fun?'

'You weren't afraid that Mr Cade would find out exactly what you were doing? Was he not at all jealous?'

'I did nothing improper.'

'Really?'

'Well, only a little. Cade was not a man of any great imagination. He'd be the last one to realise what was going on behind his back. And, if he had found out, business is business after all. Or that's what Cade always said. It's no crime to make money – not in London. And you could do good business with Pepys.'

'I met your husband,' I say. 'I mean I met him last night. Just before he died. He came to me to denounce Pepys for taking bribes and trading in Navy stores, improper conduct for an officer of the Crown. He wanted me to speak to the King about it. That's why he was at Lincoln's Inn last night.'

'So it was you . . .' she says. 'But do you know who killed him then? Did you see anything?'

'No,' I say. 'I merely spoke to him.'

She lets out a long sigh, then shakes her head. 'He said he was thinking of going to see somebody – a lawyer. I told him not to. The fool. Why couldn't he leave well alone? Where was the profit in that?'

'He wanted to put things right.'

Mistress Cade looks out of the window at the dingy street, then turns back to me. 'Right? Right for who? We'd had a falling out with Pepys, that's true. He was slow to agree the last contract. But all was not lost – not by a long way. Cade had no need to come to you in such a manner. Pepys has been a good friend to us over the years, Mr Grey. I would have been very sorry to denounce him for corruption, I would indeed.'

'So, Pepys did gain from his association with you?'

'Of course he did. It was his right, as Clerk of the Acts. When a man buys a post like Clerk of the Acts, or has it bought for him by a rich patron, he expects to make money from it. When people think of ships they think of the oak that makes up the hull and timber for the decks, but there is so much more to them than that. Ships need sail cloth and rope and blocks and flags and masts and nails and anchor chains and oakum and guns and gun-carriages and gunpowder and shot and ramrods and rum and biscuit and salt pork in barrels, each one an opportunity for honest gain for somebody. It's always good business selling to the King, but you need to be friends with one of the officers of the Navy Board or you'll never sell so much as a bent nail. But Pepys wasn't unreasonable. He knew that any profit had to be shared round fairly.'

'So why should your husband seek to spoil that?'

She pauses and bites her lip.

'Well, like I say, they'd had a disagreement about the price of the next ship. Pepys said it was dear, which was true enough, but Cade told Pepys he had agreed the price with me and should stick to his word.'

'That was all? Are you sure he couldn't have been suspicious about you and Pepys?'

'Well, if he was, it was on account of nothing *I* told him. And Pepys would never have dared . . .'

'When your husband spoke to my clerk he implied he knew.'

'Then that footman-pestering maid of mine must have let something slip to Cade . . . That must be it. I'd have employed somebody better, but I didn't know how much money we had then. I'll turn her out on the street when I leave here, which can't be soon enough. I can go and live with my brother in Kent for a while. Until something better presents itself, as I hope it will, for my brother's temper is always uncertain. I don't mind his rough tongue myself, but others do and so there is little good company at his house. Perhaps I'll become the mistress of some nobleman and strut around in Court. I've had offers, I promise you. You would be very surprised if I told you who. But I have other admirers too, closer at hand. I don't plan to be a widow for longer than is decent. As for Cade and what he knew and what he thought ... it was difficult to tell much of the time. It's not the same with me. If I have a view on something I speak my mind. I'm sure Mrs Grey is the same.'

'Your husband thought he might be in danger. He thought he might be killed.'

Mistress Cade stares at me. 'He *knew* somebody was going to attack him? I can't see that was possible ...'

'He thought he was in danger from Pepys. If your husband did know about you and Pepys, could he have tried to blackmail him?'

Mrs Cade's expression suddenly relaxes. She actually laughs. 'I don't think so, sir. Even if he had, Mr Pepys is not a reckless man. He plans carefully. He always made sure that Cade was well out of the way when he visited me – or he always thought he was. Young Sam was ready to jump out of bed at the first hint of a footstep on the stairs. And his fear that he might get a child on me ... Lord, that man worried about everything except a lady's virtue and good name.'

'But Mr Cade knew about more than Pepys's infidelities. He knew about the bribes he took too. Clerks expect to make money on the side, as you say, but that doesn't mean they won't be dismissed if they get caught.'

'I suppose so. He was like to be-shit himself whenever he thought on the Commissioners questioning of him.'

'Commissioners?' I say. 'Which commissioners? The Navy Board Commissioners? The dockyard Commissioners?'

'No, sir, the Commissioners of Accounts. A parliamentary committee. They are enquiring into naval contracts.'

'Have these Parliamentary Commissioners been investigating for a long time?'

'Not that long. A few months I think.'

'Why then would the King start a new enquiry of his own?'

I realise that in asking this question out loud I have revealed more than I wish, but Mrs Cade does not take it in any way amiss.

'How would I know what the King thinks of anything? I'm one of the few women in London who's never had the King in my bed, though I should not refuse him, for a man with so many mistresses must know what he's about, don't you think? Perhaps you should seek an answer from my Lady Castlemaine. She knows the King's mind and much else.'

I nod and ask no more foolish questions. But what is the meaning of this new Commission and why did Arlington say nothing of it to me? Of course, we are dealing with a King who has had two of his ministers negotiate the same foreign treaty in ignorance of his instructions to the other. Who is he now playing off against whom? And when would I have been told?

'Your husband said that he had papers that might be used in evidence against Pepys and others.'

Her eyes open wide in a protest of innocence.

'I've been through such papers as he left, sir. He wasn't a great writer or reader. I have seen nothing that might be used in such a way.'

'Could I perhaps view them anyway?'

'They are locked away at present,' she says very quickly. 'And I have mislaid the key. I shall look through them again when I find it and let you know at once if I discover anything. At once, Mr Grey. You may rely on me for that.'

She smiles, daring me to call her a liar.

'Thank you,' I say. 'Please do let me know if you find anything. Pepys had dealings with other dockyards?'

'Well, he'd have been in and out of the royal dockyards all the time – Deptford, Woolwich, Portsmouth, Harwich, Chatham. That's his job after all. As to the private yards – yes, of course he'd have dealt with others, but mainly us, I think.'

'Then your husband would have been an important witness against Pepys? And he was not unwilling to give evidence?'

'Unless I could have stopped him doing something so foolish.'

'And Pepys could afford to employ an assassin?' I say.

'He's a wealthy man is Sam Pepys, and we made him wealthier. We like to pay money to the wives where possible – it's less noticeable, so long as the wives are discreet. But Pepys would have none of that. He doesn't trust Mistress Pepys, any more than she trusts him. Only gold coin in his own hand would content him. Still we sent Mrs Pepys a parrot. It was Cade's idea. I took it there myself. Pretty looking bird, it was – all blue and yellow – though it swore something terrible because it came from a sailor. That's why we got it cheap. She tipped me a Shilling when I delivered it. Must have thought I was a servant. "Take this for your pains, my good woman." Stuck up cow. My pains? A Shilling doesn't even cover mild discomfort. I sometimes felt sorry for Pepys, I really did.'

'I don't,' I say. 'Strangely, I never feel sorry for Samuel Pepys.'

Chapter 5

Seething Lane

Pepys is not a difficult man to find. He lives and works at the Navy Office, here in Seething Lane. It is no great journey from the Tower dockyard and he must have found visiting Mistress Cade very easy. Returning by boat from Westminster, as he must often have done, he could have alighted at Tower Stairs and turned left to duty or right to temptation, as the spirit moved him.

The Navy Office is a large, old building of reddish brick, streaked as everything is in London by soot. I am told it possesses 180 windows, though I do not have the leisure to count them now. At the porter's lodge I am asked, very politely, to wait, and then, after a short enquiry to Pepys, I am admitted to his office.

He greets me as an old friend, which I am not.

'Sir John!' he says. 'I am pleased to see you looking so prosperous. I congratulate you on your knighthood.'

I have not seen him since Arlington obtained the title for me in lieu of the money I was owed and would have preferred.

'Thank you,' I say. 'I was gratified that my years of service to the King were thus valued by him.'

'A well-deserved testament to your loyalty to His Majesty. And your loyalty to my Lord Arlington, of course.'

This last remark is barbed enough. Pepys still regards me as Lord Arlington's creature. It explains my knighthood in a painless way. Arlington tossed it to me as you'd toss a scrap to a cur. Pepys himself has yet to be knighted, though he would very much like to be so. You would have thought that one or other of his patrons – Lord Sandwich or the Duke of York – might have worked this for him. Knighthoods are handed out freely enough. But they have not done so.

'Loyalty is often its own reward,' I say.

'Indeed,' says Pepys bitterly, 'it is. And to what do I owe the pleasure of this visit, Sir John?'

I decide it is time to tell him.

'Do you know Thomas Cade?' I ask.

'The owner of the Tower dockyard? Of course I know him. He carries out repairs for us and builds some of the smaller ships.'

Any pretence at amity has vanished at the mention of Cade's name. That is no surprise, if anything that Mistress Cade told me is true.

'You are aware that Cade was killed last night? At Lincoln's Inn?'

'I had heard that . . . there was a rumour . . . I mean nobody has confirmed until now that it was so . . . but you tell me that it is, and I am most sorry for it.'

'I am sure that you will visit his widow and offer her what comfort you can.'

'Of course. As soon as my duties permit. You tell me he was killed at Lincoln's Inn – that is where you have your office?'

'It's where I live when I am in London. You have not been to Lincoln's Inn recently yourself?'

'Me? No, why should I? I have no need for legal advice. I have not been to Lincoln's Inn for ... oh, a very long time. How did the poor man die? Is that known?'

'He had been struck a blow on the head.'

'Ah ... A robbery?'

'No, not a robbery. I think he was killed for what he knew.'

Pepys's face betrays nothing at all but he grips the arms of his chair tightly with his hands.

'And what exactly did he know?' he asks.

'Cade had visited me the night he died to tell me that he had evidence of corruption in the procurement for the Navy – he had documents, which I have so far been unable to discover, but still hope to.'

'Hope to? You mean that you are investigating his death? That is surely a job for the London magistrates?'

'I have been asked by Lord Arlington,' I say, 'to make enquiries into the sale of goods to the Navy. Had Cade not died he would have been a witness. In that respect his death is very relevant. It is, as you say, for the London magistrates to discover his killer. I am sure they will do so.'

I have not made Pepys happy, but then I did not intend to. He frowns.

'But the Commissioners of Accounts ...' he says. 'How does this enquiry dovetail with theirs? I do not understand Arlington's design.'

Well, nor do I, for that matter. I can only hope Arlington will tell me.

'It will all become apparent in good time,' I say.

'But another enquiry . . . I hope that your master realises that these interruptions in our work do little to ready the Navy to fight the Dutch?'

'I can tell him that, but I doubt that it will help you materially.'

'I am of course willing to assist you in any way I can,' Pepys says. 'About the supply of goods to the Navy or anything else. I have no secrets. I can, if you wish, give you a full account of the processes that we use to ensure that we obtain the lowest possible price for all goods.'

'Thank you,' I say. 'But perhaps we can begin with Cade. Did you give his yard much work?'

'Some. In the past. As I say, mainly repair work at fixed rates. Rates approved by the Navy Board. You will find that it was all properly recorded. And there was a proposal for a new frigate, which had the King's blessing in principle. He had taken a great deal of interest in it, as he does with all his ships. Now Cade is dead, however, I cannot see that it will proceed.'

'And if Cade had lived?'

'That ship would probably have been the last they built. Most of our vessels – and all of the larger ones – are built in the royal dockyards. Chatham, Deptford, Woolwich, Portsmouth. But some are still built in private yards, as they always have been. Cade's was one of the smallest. In past times it had been very valuable to us, but ships have grown larger and the Thames shallower. If the King were to have his way, we would build only the largest ships – the first raters. He wants vessels that are terrible to the enemy. He wants high quarterdecks, with enough gilding nearly to blind any man who dares look upon them. He wants three gundecks, all bristling with massive bronze cannons. He wants virile ships that embody the power and majesty of the English nation – ships that personify the King himself.'

'So that's what you build?'

Pepys shakes his head. 'You might suppose, Sir John, that a big ship will always beat a little one, and so it usually will. Our great ships unleash a thousand pounds of iron balls every time they fire a broadside. Within minutes they can hole an enemy vessel in twenty places and reduce masts to matchwood and sails to rags. But burden a ship with large cannons, the way the King demands, and it sits mighty low in the water, sir. The nethermost gunports are no more than three feet above the waves. In rough weather those gunports must be closed or sea floods in. Thus a full third of the ordnance cannot be used without risk of sinking the ship. The powder and shot required takes up so much space that there is little room for other stores – stores that would be needed to cross an ocean without too many of the crew dying of hunger and thirst. In short, our largest ships dare not venture out of port until May brings calm waters, and must be safe home again by September. Nor can they stray far from the Channel and the North Sea. If we wish to defend our shores during the winter, if we wish to protect our plantations overseas, then also we need smaller, faster, more lightly armed craft.'

'And that is what Cade built?'

'Yes.'

'Did he do it well?'

'Of course not. Like all shipwrights, he was a lazy, drunken, gouty illiterate. He was incapable of drawing up a plan that any other man might understand. I never saw a draft of his that made any sense. He was wholly without art and, having no ability to make proper calculations, depended on his eyes alone to determine the proportions of the ship.'

'But you considered Cade a friend in spite of that?'

'A friend? Indeed not, Sir John. I visited the yard often, when it was building for the King. But I visit all of the yards where we build ships. That is my job. To neglect that would be to ignore my duty wholly. You seem to think that the Navy Board is lax in ensuring that the King is not robbed. But we work long hours for very little money.'

'I'm surprised that honest men can be found to do the work,' I say.

'Honest, true and loyal,' says Pepys. 'No king was ever better served – something that I shall prove if called upon to do so.'

'Do you know Cade's family?' I ask.

'I have met his wife once or twice,' he says cautiously.

I make no response. There is a long and promising silence, then Pepys adds: 'Does she claim I was a friend of hers? What she says is not to be trusted. She has strange ideas.'

'She speaks well of you,' I say.

'Really? There was nothing improper in my dealings with the Cades. Nothing at all.'

'I never said there was,' I say. 'But since you mention it, did Cade ever offer you any inducement to approve work at the yard?'

'I have never accepted a bribe of any sort,' says Pepys indignantly. 'I have already told the Treasury Commissioners that. Occasionally a contractor will give me a small gift, which it would be churlish and ungentlemanly to refuse, but I have never accepted a penny unless it was to His Majesty's advantage. In all my time in the Navy Office I have added scarcely a thousand Pounds to my estate. And set against that the fact that I am owed four hundred Pounds by the King in unpaid expenses. Four hundred Pounds, sir. That is a great deal of money for a poor man such as I am. Tell Arlington that it will all be in my evidence to the Brooke House Committee. He can read that if he chooses. I flatly decline to answer to him as well on such petty detail. It is monstrous that I am harassed in this way.'

He pauses, aware he may have said too much.

'Did Cade ever threaten you?' I ask.

'Threaten to do what exactly?'

'Threaten to reveal the nature of your dealings with him.'

'There was nothing to reveal, Sir John, as Lord Arlington must surely know. My evidence to the Commissioners will show clearly that I have done everything in my power to reduce irregularities in the payments for the King's ships. I hope you, as a gentleman born and bred, will be able to distinguish between the truth, as I have clearly set it out, and the lies you may be told by others.'

'I make no claims to gentility any more than I asked for a knighthood.'

'Tush! You are both a gentleman and a man of learning,' says Pepys. 'We were at the same college at Cambridge, as I recall: Magdalene.'

I shrug. This is not the first time that Pepys has drawn my attention to this purported reason for our being allies.

'What sort of man was Cade?' I ask.

'I've told you already. A drunken illiterate.'

'But no fool,' I said. 'I've met him, don't forget. What he told me made sense. It would have made sense to the Committee too. And Cade was as sober as you could wish when he died.'

'There are many different types of fool. Not all wear caps and bells like the King's jester, Thomas Killigrew.'

'Still, not quite good enough for Mistress Cade?' I say. 'She wanted something better as a husband?'

'You must make your enquiries of the lady concerned, not of me.'

'Where were you the evening that Cade was killed?' I ask. 'You claim you were not at Lincoln's Inn, but you have not told me where you were.'

At first I think that Pepys will die of apoplexy before he can answer. I wait patiently to see if he will. Of course, if he does die and it is my fault, Arlington will not be pleased I've lost a second witness. Eventually Pepys spits back at me: 'I was dining with Lord and Lady Sandwich. You may ask him if you disbelieve me.'

'Lord Sandwich, your patron?'

'My kinsman, and the hero of many sea battles. I can assure you that he would not tell lies on my behalf.'

'Wouldn't he?' I say. 'How unfortunate for you.'

'I wish you well in your enquiry, Sir John,' he says. 'If you will excuse me, I have work to do. The King's work.'

I pick up my hat, which, for all that I am a knight and he is not, I have chosen to remove in Pepys's office. 'Thank you,' I say. 'I am much obliged for your good wishes, Mr Pepys. I may need to speak to you again. It depends what other people have to tell me.'

I pause again, but this time Pepys says nothing. That's the wisest thing he's done this afternoon.

Chapter 6

Lincoln's Inn

'Well,' I say, 'that is what I have discovered so far. I have no doubt that Pepys was taking bribes from the Cades, but Mistress Cade has conveniently mislaid the papers that Cade was to let me have. She may wish to sell them to somebody who pays better than she thinks I will, but more likely they incriminate her as much as Cade and Pepys. I fear she will burn them, now I have generously told her how dangerous they are. Pepys denies emphatically taking anything from the Cades or anyone else. And he seems to have an impeccable alibi for the evening that Cade died. But that doesn't mean that he didn't pay somebody else to do it, while he drank Canary and flirted with Lady Sandwich. As for Cade, I now think that his denunciation was influenced as much by his discovery of how far his wife had been prepared to go with Pepys as anything. Cade may have already threatened to blackmail Pepys for one thing or the other. So, Pepys could have been aware that Cade was a threat well before he heard that he intended to come to me.'

Will Atkins and Mr Sparks both nod thoughtfully. I have given them a full account of my discussions, though I think I have discovered little of any real weight.

'I've been asking around, too,' says Will. 'I know one of Pepys's clerks and took him to an inn to share a jug or two of ale, for which I will bill you in due course, if that is acceptable. Mr Pepys is not quite as impoverished as he would like you to believe. He's recently bought a new carriage, for example. And the Commissioners have questioned him about his sale of flags to the Navy. I don't know how much he made on the deal, but there's no doubt he's broken the rules for procurement.'

'Did he tell you anything about the Commission?' I ask.

'I've discovered a little about that from one of the lawyers at the Inner Temple,' says Sparks. 'The Brooke House Committee was set up by Parliament after the disaster of the Medway. The Commissioners, and their clerks, have been investigating the whole management of the Navy for some months, and are likely to take several months more. My friend thought that their work might run into next year or even the year after. They've already spoken to Pepys and to his colleagues on the Navy Board.'

'I still don't understand,' I say. 'You say the Committee is already in place, apparently well-staffed, restricted to the work of the Navy Board and given many months – perhaps years – to complete its investigations. I apparently have a fortnight to undertake a much wider enquiry into corruption across the whole field of public expenditure. Why doesn't Arlington at least await the findings of the Brooke House Committee?'

'Perhaps he doesn't trust it?'

'Even so, why not see what they have to say before he conducts his own investigation?'

'Because it's urgent,' says Sparks. 'Because it won't wait.'

'But what won't wait? Courtiers have been making money out of the King ever since the Restoration. Another few months will make no difference. What has changed?'

'That would be beyond the knowledge of my friends at the Inner Temple,' says Sparks. 'And *a fortiori* outside mine.'

I sigh. 'Perhaps it will be clearer when I speak to Arlington again.'

'I'd speak to him soon then,' says Sparks.

I shake my head. 'I've nothing to report back yet. And he guards his own time as carefully as he fritters away other people's. I'm going to the Tower shipyard tomorrow morning to talk to Cade's deputy, Truscott. Hopefully I'll learn something from him.'

Chapter 7

From a Diary

Up and to work at the office early, having quarrelled last night with my wife, who felt the need to remind me of my amours with her maid Deb, long past. She accused me of having tried to contact her again, but I said I knew not whither the poor wretch had fled, after she had thrown Deb out of the house. So we parted still on bad terms, which troubled me greatly, she to start the preparations for dinner, Sir W. Penn and his wife being invited today, and I to work on preparing my defence for the Brooke House Committee. But at eleven o'clock comes Sir J. Grey, the puffed-up creature of my Lord Arlington, and asks me the most strange and impertinent questions concerning Cade and the contract for the new frigate. I put him off with soft words and told him that I and the other members of the Navy Board have already detected many abuses, to the great benefit of the King, and that I had already answered the immediate charges raised by the Committee, though I know there may be others. He seemed content, but for all that I could not discover Arlington's design in sending him, the Brooke House Committee already sitting and its enquiries well advanced. He sought to blame me for Cade's death. I told him that I was dining with Lord S. when Cade was attacked and doubt that he will dare to question my Lord to contradict it, though I shall speak to my Lord urgently in case he does. Yet Grey has proved adept at prying into my affairs before, and I am uncertain whether it would be better to make him my good friend or to undo him as best I can.

I returned home still much troubled, to find myself and my wife friends again and dinner prepared – a great venison pie, a sturgeon and an apple tart and strawberries newly come from Kent. And we were very merry all four of us. Then to Westminster by water to see the Duke, but he was away at Hampton Court, so returned home again and spent much time in the boat pondering Arlington's true purpose, which cannot be to my advantage. But what is it?

Chapter 8

The Tower Dockyard

The ship sits in dry dock, looming above us here on the wooden quay. The hull is complete and the masts are in place. Now carpenters and painters finish the fitting out. A man sits on a narrow plank suspended on ropes, swaying gently, gilding the wreaths above the single row of gunports. There is an elegance to the ship that even I can appreciate. Its lines are fine and well proportioned. It is designed to cut through the waves like a dolphin. This is not a ship to overawe the enemy but a workmanlike craft that will serve the King well, summer and winter, in the cold North Sea or the palm-fringed Caribbean. There is a clean, sweet smell of sawdust that hangs in counterpoint above the base notes of pitch and tar. The air buzzes with the noise of sawing and the crack of wooden pegs being driven home.

'I congratulate you,' I say to Cade's deputy. 'You are about to launch a fine vessel.'

Harry Truscott shakes his head. 'This isn't how it should be done,' he says. 'Not at all. When we're busy, we launch once the hull is complete and watertight. The fitting out can be done on the river. This one still sits in dry dock because we have nothing else to replace it. In a few weeks' time I shall have to lay off the shipwrights and the carpenters and the painters. There will not be anything for them to do.'

'The contract for the new frigate hasn't been agreed?'

Truscott shakes his head again. 'It was never signed and I can't say whether the build will go ahead now Mr Cade is dead. I'm running things now with Morgan – he's the head carpenter – and we can shift well enough with the men we have to complete this vessel.'

'Mistress Cade spoke of selling the yard,' I say.

He shakes his head. 'I hope I've persuaded her otherwise,' he says. 'Or may yet do so. I've waited a long time to be master of a yard. She won't deny me the chance to make a go of it. But it isn't going to be easy. Mr Cade was the one with contacts. He was the one who would go out looking for new work. So long as the contract is unsigned, the danger remains that the order for the frigate will go to another yard further down the river – one with an owner who knows somebody at Court. Or the King will arrange for it to be cancelled in favour of a giant first rater. He likes his women witty and compliant and his ships as big and nasty as possible.'

'Mr Cade's death was sudden and unexpected,' I say.

'Yes,' Truscott says.

He seems uneasy, but then few of us are entirely comfortable with death, even other people's.

'Can you think why anyone would have wanted to kill him?' I ask.

'Cade was a good master,' he says, looking away and towards

the river. 'The best I ever had. You could rely on his word. He paid us when he could.'

None of those things seems to be a motive for murder.

'But he must have had enemies?' I ask.

'Everyone has enemies,' says Truscott, looking at me grimly, 'but I should say Mr Cade had as few as it's possible to have.'

'Mr Cade came to me the night he was killed. He said that he had proof that there was misappropriation of the King's money.'

I am making Truscott uncomfortable again. He looks at me doubtfully.

'Did he, sir?' he says.

'I am afraid I failed him. I might have assisted him, but instead I sent him out into the night and to his death.'

Truscott swallows hard. 'I . . .' he says. 'I could have stopped him coming at all. I bear part of the blame for this.'

'Had he said to you that he might be in danger, then?'

'No, sir. Not that exactly. Only that I knew he was troubled. I should have done more. I just wasn't sure . . .' He shakes his head.

'Did he mention Samuel Pepys at the Navy Office?'

'Pepys?' Truscott breaks into a smile in spite of himself. Like Mistress Cade, he finds it strange that I should accuse Pepys. He clearly does not know the whole story.

'Yes,' I say. 'Mr Cade wanted to expose corruption and bring Pepys down. He believed that Pepys would kill to avoid this. I think he may have done so.'

Truscott considers this for some time. 'Is that so?' he says eventually. 'Then I am much surprised by it. But Mr Cade was not one to harbour fancies. He was a practical man of business.'

'Do you know anything of Cade's dealings with Mr Pepys?' I ask.

'I know only that Pepys could approve the contract we needed.'

'Would Cade have needed to pay Pepys to get it?'

'Yes, of course. That's the way these things are done. All offices of the Crown are remunerated more or less well, but their occupants expect to double their salaries at least with the fees and presents. And, provided they don't overstep the mark, it's winked at. The Navy is the biggest item of expenditure for the King and so offers some of the biggest rewards. Posts such as Pepys's are much sought after and sell at a high price.'

'You don't think that's wrong?'

'Look, Sir John, every office, every post under the Crown, high or low, has its own opportunities, its own perquisites. That's why they are so valued. Do you happen to know how wide a staircase is in Chatham?'

Now it is my turn to look puzzled. 'I have no idea,' I say.

'Two feet eleven inches,' says Truscott with grim satisfaction. 'And all because of chips.'

'What are chips?' I ask, because Truscott is expecting me to. That is the way these stories are told.

'When you're building a ship,' says Truscott, 'cutting timber to shape leaves heaps of wood chips everywhere. They can't stay there. They get in the way and there is a risk of fire. So the carpenters are allowed to sweep them up and carry them off to use as kindling in their hearths at home.'

'That seems a reasonable thing to do. A small perquisite that benefits everyone.'

'Indeed. A small perquisite for a poor man. Of course, some chips are larger than you would need for kindling. A piece of planking might repair some wainscoting at home. A block of wood might be shaped into a stool and sold to a neighbour.'

'I suppose that there must be a lot of chips,' I say. 'How large can a chip be?'

'As you might guess, the men sought to take home larger and larger offcuts of timber. That is in the nature of things. The larger the chip, the more amenable it was to become something more marketable. To avoid entire ships being dragged out of the yard and sold for firewood, a limit was placed on them. A wood chip must be under three feet long.'

'Hence staircases in Chatham all being two feet eleven inches?'

'Precisely. Stairs, doors, windows. All must conform to dockyard standards if they are to be built of chips, supplied free of charge by His Gracious Majesty.'

'And are there often chips of that size?'

'It depends entirely on how they cut the timber, doesn't it?'

'That is an abuse that should be stopped.'

'The alternative is that their wives and children starve, the King being somewhat in arrears with their wages – sometimes as much as two or three years behindhand.'

'That does, of course, put a different complexion on things.'

'Precisely. When you are carrying out your investigations for Lord Arlington, Sir John, before you form too many judgments, just think on the staircases of Chatham, and be charitable in your judgments. Your first impressions may sometimes be wrong. Did you have any further questions, Sir John?'

Did I? If so, this story has for the moment made me forget them.

'Thank you,' I say. 'If I see the King, I'll suggest he starts paying on time.'

Chapter 9

Goring House

My Lord Arlington's London residence sits at the western limits of the City, with St James's Park on one side and open farmland beyond. It is a grand building in the new classical style, named after a former owner, Lord Goring, but soon doubtless to be retitled Arlington House, because who would wish to live in a home named after somebody else? This is the centre of Arlington's web, to which he retreats when he is not at Court and where he and his wife, in the steady glow of a hundred wax candles, entertain anyone likely to be of use to him. I have never been significant enough to be invited to one of the Goring House soirées, but I have been redirected here now by my Lord's clerk at Whitehall Palace.

There is a delay before Arlington appears, wrapping himself in his silk dressing gown. He is unshaven. It would seem that he has been attending late on the King again, and I have caused him to rise too many hours before noon.

He may not be pleased with me when I tell him how little I have discovered.

'You have something to report, Sir John?'

'I have spoken to Pepys,' I say, 'and to Mistress Cade—'

'Who is that?'

'The wife of the owner of the Tower shipyard.'

'Ah, yes, your late witness. Please continue.'

'I have also spoken to Cade's deputy at the dockyard. I have no doubt that Pepys has been accepting bribes, from the Tower dockyard and elsewhere, and that there are more men involved in naval contracts who are pocketing the King's coin than are not. Pepys has grown rich – or richer than he would have the world believe. I shall look further into that. But much of the corruption in the dockyards seems so deeply ingrained that it would take years to correct it.'

'Is there proof concerning Pepys?'

'I have as yet nothing in writing.'

'And will you obtain it?'

'I would think that both Pepys and Mistress Cade will destroy everything they can, if they have not already done so. Truscott, Cade's deputy, might be able to help me find evidence – he seems honest – but I fear that he and Mistress Cade have already formed an alliance of some sort. She has appointed him to run the yard, and he likes doing it. He wants her to keep him on. His loyalties will not be with me.'

'Well, that cannot be helped,' he says more tolerantly than I had expected. 'What do you plan to do next?'

'I shall hire a boat and visit Deptford dockyard this afternoon,' I say. 'I intend to discover more about bribes paid by contractors. I hope also to uncover the murderer of Thomas Cade.'

'I think you need not expend too much effort on that. From our point of view, he's simply dead and of no further use. The magistrate and coroner will produce their report in the fullness of time. And I imagine that he will have to be buried. None of that need trouble you. You have other things to do.'

'But do you not think that his death is related in some way to what you want me to investigate? He would, as you say, have been one of our most important witnesses. Now, coincidentally, he is found dead, shortly after he left my chambers, having threatened to expose Pepys for embezzling the King's money.'

'And you suspect Pepys of killing him? That seems unlikely.'

'Mr Pepys has the alibi of a dinner with Lord and Lady Sandwich. Do you wish me to check that he was really there?'

'I would suggest that you concentrate on your visit to Deptford and forget Mr Cade. There will be other witnesses.'

'Of course,' I say.

'Excellent,' he says. 'One excursion to the dockyard should be adequate. After that, you should start to make enquiries at the Court.'

'As you wish,' I say. 'There is only one thing that troubles me, my Lord.'

His face does not want to smile but he obliges it to do so. 'I should be delighted to clarify matters if I can.'

'The Brooke House Committee is sitting, is it not? Surely that would produce all of the information that you need in another few months? You do not need me to do anything.'

Arlington nods thoughtfully. 'That is a question that I should have anticipated and perhaps answered earlier,' he says. 'You are correct that the Committee's remit overlaps with your own. But, it is slow – indeed, it may never report anything to anyone. And unlike you, it is far from impartial. It is moreover a Committee of Parliament, which gives it cause to cry itself up in its own ridiculous importance. You should understand that things have altered at Court since you last visited it. The fall of my Lord Clarendon has changed a great deal. A mighty oak has toppled and, in the now empty and broken ground, puny seedlings vie to establish themselves in its place. Many are harmless and will shrivel in the sun ere long, but others grow poisonous and thorny, and must be pulled up by the roots. It is the sort of work that requires many hands. Thus it is that some who were not friends formerly – myself and the Duke of York, for example – have reached an understanding on how we might labour side by side. With Clarendon gone, the Court is a less acrimonious place than it was once. Or it would be if it were not for the Duke of Buckingham, who seems determined to stir up trouble.'

'He is a thorn?'

'A large and well-established one with deep roots. A common thorn who believes that he might grow one day to be the rose of England – a crowned rose.'

Arlington clearly enjoys allegory as much as Will does.

'Surely he was once your ally?' I say.

'My only true loyalty is, and always has been, to His Majesty the King. My allies are the King's allies. My enemies are the King's enemies. But you are right that Buckingham was once more obliging than he is now. Even in Essex, you must have heard that he has become very ambitious of late. He is gathering about him a Presbyterian party. Some claim, I cannot say with what truth, that his purpose is to depose the King, just as the King's father was deposed by Cromwell, and to set up a new Commonwealth with himself as Lord Protector, or whatever title he chooses to assume. To that end he is picking off the King's friends one by one. He has had Sir William Coventry, the Duke of York's secretary, sent to the Tower on wholly trumped-up charges. You've heard the story?'

'I've been in Essex,' I say. 'I'd heard only that Coventry had retired.'

'That's the short version of it. First Buckingham conspired with Sir Robert Howard, who wrote a play, *The Country Gentleman*, with Sir Cautious Trouble-All sitting in the centre of a circular desk. Coventry has an identical desk. Indeed, he has the only desk of that description. Coventry heard about it and threatened to cut off the nose of any actor who impersonated him. Then he wrote Buckingham a letter of complaint that was taken as a challenge to a duel. Buckingham showed the letter to King, who disapproves of duels and put Coventry in the Tower. Coventry's out now but, as you say, he's wisely decided retirement is the safest option. Now Buckingham has the Duke of York in his sights. He will try to use the Brooke House Committee to his own ends, feeding it lies. If it can be persuaded to condemn the Duke, as Lord High Admiral, for the defeat on the Medway – condemn him and perhaps have him exiled like Clarendon – then the King will have lost his greatest support.'

'Is that likely?'

'It is almost certain that is his intent. We need to know, and to know urgently, what the true facts are: what accusations we can easily refute and what presents a real danger to our party.'

'You could have explained that before.'

Arlington pulls his gown more tightly round him, though the day is already warm. 'How would it have helped you? The facts that we require are the same. And you could have answered any questions honestly: that I had told you that the King required the information in order to reform the administration of the Navy.'

'I still like to know what job I am doing and who I'm working for.'

'Well, now you do. You are seeking the truth. The plain, unvarnished truth. For the King.'

'Thank you, my Lord,' I say. 'I am much obliged to you. Otherwise I might have thought I was doing something else entirely.'

Chapter 10

Deptford

Abel Symonds is amiable enough. He is tall and thin, with a ready smile. He wears a leather jerkin over a grubby woollen shirt. There is a bright bunch of steel keys suspended from his belt, a symbol of his authority as head of the yard, though not commissioner, that post – as he explained almost before I could disembark from my boat – still being on the market. He has provided me with some new piece of information every ten yards or so on our walk from the river to the warehouses. His keenness to help me stems from the fact that it takes him away from less congenial duties on a pleasant June afternoon. He might have been checking bins of nails of various sizes or surveying heaps of sailcloth in a dark store. Instead we are strolling along the waterfront with the sunlight dancing over the wavelets. There is a fresh breeze off the water.

Here at Deptford there is none of the unassuming efficiency that I saw at the Tower. Planks lie stacked in irregular heaps.

Men sit around smoking their pipes on coils of rope. There is occasional bustle but little evidence of progress. A large shed that runs the length of the quay is completely empty.

'That's the ropewalk,' says Symonds, with an unaccountable hint of envy.

'There's no need of rope now?' I ask.

'No, there's a great shortage of it, but the rope makers claim that they are employed by the yard, not by the hour. Once they have completed their agreed quantity of rope for the day, they put their tools down and go off to the alehouse for the afternoon, to drink away the profits of the morning. There's nothing I can do to stop them. It's a tradition. If you could gather together all of our traditions and stack them like timber, they would occupy a whole warehouse.'

'I'm surprised that everyone doesn't become a rope maker,' I say. 'Perhaps I should too.'

'Was your father a rope maker, sir?'

'No, Mr Symonds, he was a surgeon, late of the King's army.'

'Then you'd have little chance of being accepted as an apprentice yourself, sir. Nor would most of the others in the yard. Tradition dictates a long apprenticeship for all of the trades employed here, and tradition also dictates that the sons of rope makers should become apprentices before the sons of anyone else. And nobody may work as a master craftsman here who has not served his time as an apprentice. So, I'd take up some other less profitable trade if I were you, sir.'

'You served as an apprentice yourself?' I ask.

'Yes, sir, as a shipwright. It's one of the longest. You need to know how wood is worked and the different types used in different parts of the structure. You need to know how the proportions of a ship are calculated and how the plans are drawn up and how the quantities of timber needed are calculated.'

'I had understood much of it was done by eye.'

Abel Symonds laughs. 'You've been talking to our Mr Pepys then?' he says. 'To be fair to the man, he tries to understand how a ship is built and he asks us questions all the time but, Lord, we're not going to reveal the mysteries of our craft to him. Why should we? If we're truly guessing our measurements, as he supposes, how does he think we ever produce a ship that will sail? Sometimes the smallest change in a plan can ruin a ship. We've had ships back in the yard and have moved the main mast forward a couple of feet to gain a few extra knots or make her more responsive to the rudder. Two feet – that's all the difference between a ship that will outrun the Dutch and one that will be left trailing in their wake. If masts were placed by eye, the vessel wouldn't get out of the Thames, let alone engage the enemy fleet like a true Englishman. Everything is measured down to the last inch. But we don't tell him that. We let him listen to Sir Anthony Deane at Portsmouth, who imagines he's the only scientific shipbuilder in the country, but who is in fact merely a better talker than he is a constructor.

'To be fair to Pepys too, he knows what he wants. Building a ship, you see, is a matter of making compromises. You'd like a ship that is large and fast and stable and strong and carries as many guns as possible. But it can't be all of those things at once. If you build the way the King wants us to build, then you'd have a monstrous machine of war, broad so that it is stable when the guns fire, made of heavy timbers that will take the punishment when the enemy fires back and with a massive hull that will accommodate the guns and the men to fight them and the stores that both men and guns require for a long campaign. And we could build them, but they would be slow and low in the water, and would not respond well to the rudder. Or we can make them sleek and narrow and fast, but such a ship does not provide a steady platform for the guns and may be sunk by a single broadside. Or we can build something in between the two – hence the many ratings that the Navy has. You'll have seen the first raters that go out only in fine weather but which can blast a smaller craft off the water in an instant. Sometimes, sir, you row past such a ship, skimming through its cold, wet shadow, with the vessel towering over you and its three rows of guns all pointing right at your chest, and your bare arms tremble at the oars, sir. I wouldn't want to be a Dutch sailor or a Frenchie on the wrong end of that broadside. And neither nation has anything to match it. Mr Pepys would have us build nothing larger than a second rater, and he'd place fewer guns on them, as the French do, to keep them higher in the water and enable them to go out in rough conditions. He doesn't like us wasting good money on gold paint either. But the King wants grandeur. The King wants majesty.'

'Did you know Thomas Cade?' I ask.

'Yes,' he says, looking out across the broad, muddy river at the dark green marshes on the far side. 'Yes, I knew him. A good man. Sad business, sir. Sad business. He was a rival, in a manner of speaking, but I was sorrier than I can say to hear of his death.'

'Pepys was thinking of giving him a contract for a frigate.'

'No need,' says Symonds sharply. 'We've scarcely got enough work here at the moment, in the royal dockyard. No need to pay a private contractor to build for us when we have men idle ourselves. The four royal dockyards can handle all of the new ships that have been approved.'

'So why would Pepys consider it?'

'It depends how much Cade was paying him,' says Symonds. 'Cade . . . well, I don't want to speak ill of the dead . . . but he was little better than a common thief, sir. He'd overcharge on every little item, and he got away with it because he'd pay some officer of the Navy Board to get him the contract. That's how the private yards get the work, but Pepys could have got a better deal almost anywhere else and from us best of all. It makes you wonder, doesn't it, sir – how much Cade was paying him?'

I look round at the yard. Perhaps Pepys simply preferred to deal with somebody who was efficient and likely to get the job done.

'I heard that Cade was interested in the vacant commissioner's post here,' I say.

Symonds smiles. 'That wouldn't have suited Mr Pepys,' he says. 'Some yards have resident commissioners and some not. Where there isn't one, the Navy Board manages things and Mr Pepys has just that bit more control over who gets the contracts for what. He won't want to see a commissioner appointed – not when he can get me to do the work for half the money and have none of the influence with suppliers of masts and ordnance.'

I nod. That sounds like Pepys.

'Do you know why anyone would wish Cade dead?' I ask.

'If you mean do I happen to know who killed him, then the answer is no, sir. I don't. How could I? But, as I say, he had no business taking work from the King's own dockyards and food from the mouths of our children. If contracts were handled honestly, then he wouldn't have been able to do it. But Cade knew how to grease palms, and dishonesty of that sort always comes back on a man. I had to lay off some carpenters only a few days ago. Told them why – too much work going to private yards, I said. Don't blame me. Blame that thief down at the Tower. His wife's a flighty piece too, as you may have already discovered. I hear Truscott's taken over the yard now. That's no surprise either. He's been angling for that for a long time. Everything comes to those who wait, eh?'

A bell rings. The sound comes lightly but insistently across the yard.

'That's to muster the men,' says Symonds, looking towards the warehouses. 'We carry out a muster at least once a day, to establish how many men are working here. And nobody is to know in advance when we'll do it, or how many times, otherwise they'd all be here for that ten minutes alone and in the alehouse for the rest.'

Men are sauntering out of various sheds and workshops. Like Symonds, they seem happy at this interruption of their routine. Some seem very old. One or two do not have all of their limbs. I comment on that to Symonds.

'It's difficult to dismiss anyone,' he says. 'Unless we catch them doing something more than usually illegal. If a workman has nowhere else to go, then he remains here on our books until he's dead, and sometimes for a while after that if his family is clever or is willing to share the money they receive with one or other of the clerks. And we take on ships' carpenters, of course, when they can no longer go to sea, even if the reason for not going to sea is a missing arm or leg.'

'Are they fit to do much work?' I ask.

'Very little, sir, very little. How could they? You look at this yard, sir, and see it as a business – a place for making ships as cheaply as may be. But we're more than that. Where would a legless carpenter go except here? We care for them, sir, long after the King has forgotten them, and the King has a short memory. Would you care to take a glass of Canary before you return to London? Now you've asked all your questions.'

I haven't, but I suspect, like Truscott, Abel Symonds has given me all his answers.

We pass a very grand house, which Symonds tells me belongs to the commissioner of the dockyard, when one is in residence. We stop at another, scarcely much smaller, which Symonds proudly identifies as his own. It is set in neat gardens. Under the pleasant shade of a mulberry tree, some men are constructing new shutters for the windows.

'We don't have work for them on a ship at the moment,' says Symonds, 'so I'm keeping them busy here. They're our very best carpenters. A couple of years back they made some fine bookcases for Mr Pepys. Beautifully carved, they were, from the rarest walnut and rosewood. Took weeks to make them. You should get him to show them to you.'

I don't think it's worth enquiring whether Pepys was asked to pay for them. I am beginning to understand how the naval yards operate.

'You all make yourselves very comfortable,' I say. 'One way or the other.'

'The work of the Navy is very important,' says Symonds with a wink. 'The country would want nothing less for us, would it?'

I take a boat from Deptford to just below London Bridge. The incoming tide is flowing strongly now, washing Londoners' orange peel and turds back towards them again. We make good progress as we work our way up the broad, smooth, winding river to the point where the water rushes through the pinched arches of the bridge in a noisy torrent of white foam. Here I pay the boatman and, not wishing to drown just yet, I decline his invitation to shoot the bridge under his expert control.

I begin to make my way on foot through the City. Even now I find my shoes covered in ash after half a dozen yards. London is a strange sight, still more than half in ruins from the fire three years ago. All that is left of the churches are the broken walls and gaunt towers, sentinels over heaps of rubble that were once naves and chancels. From the thick layer of dust and ashes and fractured stones, dark green ivy and vines now grow up and over the ruined window tracery. The floors of the churches are carpeted with grass and wild flowers – pimpernel, ragged robin, buttercup. The organs are decayed and silent, robbed of their brass pipes and their ivory keys, but the bees hum in the warm air. From the heaps of detritus, you can (if you wish) pull thick, irregular slabs of glass that were formerly windows, until they melted, ran and cooled again. Once you could also find lumps of lead and even gold, but they have long since found new homes. Out of the same powdery desolation, new houses now also rise in ones and twos. In between are dirty wooden shacks, covered with tarpaulins. Everyone who lost a home in the fire is at least staking their claim to the land it once sat on. The City is shaking off the disaster as a snake sheds and slithers away from its old skin. Soon this will be London again, though not the ancient half-timbered City we once knew.

I leave the wall-encircled central parishes by Lud Gate, then cross the sluggish, stinking Fleet River by one of its surviving bridges. The river did not check the course of the flames, but the fire burned itself out a short distance beyond.

I have another few yards of trudging through ashes until, just beyond Fetter Lane, everything becomes verdant and hopeful again. And, when I reach Lincoln's Inn, a pleasant surprise awaits me.

'I see that you have got your shoes and stockings in a terrible state with dust,' says Aminta. 'I can't even leave you for a few days or you revert to being a grubby schoolboy.'

I hug her in spite of this unjustified slur on my behaviour.

'I was the cleanest schoolboy in Essex,' I say.

'Not according to your mother and she claimed to have known you quite well.'

'Have you come to London just to check on the state of my stockings?' I ask.

'I would have been more than justified in doing so. Good woollen stockings are not cheap. But I decided to visit after Will wrote to me explaining that any delay in your return was entirely his doing. There is nothing that excites a wife's suspicions more than an assurance on the part of one of her husband's friends that something is not her husband's fault. It runs contrary to her whole experience of him. I came at once.'

'There was no need. Lord Arlington asked me to undertake some work for him, that's all.'

'So Will has already explained to me. But you have not so far lost a leg or an eye, so you can have scarcely begun.'

'Arlington expects the task to be completed in two weeks. I would have been back in Essex before you knew it.'

'I doubt that very much indeed. Arlington's weeks are longer than other people's. Still, it's as well I'm in London. I have to keep an eye on Killigrew – in his role as the manager of the King's theatre company rather than as the King's jester.

I don't trust him to recompense me properly for my new play, in spite of his many promises. You are aware that the size of my payment as author depends on the size of the audience at the third performance? I need to be there, that afternoon, to count the takings myself. Killigrew's adding-up is not as good as Davenant's used to be, though unlike Davenant he possesses a complete nose, never having had the pox, for reasons I do not entirely understand. And Killigrew can't keep his actors. The first thing that I heard when I arrived in town is that two of them have just quit, scarcely a week before the play is to open.'

'Who told you?'

'Will.'

'Does he know that sort of thing?'

'Yes.'

'Killigrew is one of the King's drinking companions,' I say. 'As well as being his jester in office. I am surprised he has time to run a theatre.'

'I'm not sure he does, and if he doesn't pay more attention to his business then I may have to manage things until he sobers up. Otherwise there will be no third performance at which the takings can be counted.'

'You don't need the money,' I say.

'That shows an aristocratic contempt for gold coin that almost no aristocrats would share. If you wish to pass yourself off as more than minor gentry, which is honestly all you are, then you need to be a little more rapacious. Think back to your days as a practising lawyer. Or exchange a few polite words with my Lady Castlemaine.'

'I have no wish to pass myself off as anything,' I say. 'I am content in plain black wool and my own hair.'

'Yes, that reminds me: we'll need to get you a periwig while we're in London. The vicar had one made in Saffron Walden and now he looks like a demented sheep in it. Better than he looked before, of course, but still not good. No, you need a London periwig. Don't worry, they'll have used up most of the hair taken from plague victims, so you'll probably get the flowing mane of some brute hanged for murder or for stealing a Shilling from a shop. You get longer credit and a better class of fleas from a London periwig maker. A man can go around in Essex in his own hair, but he needs something more genteel and pretentious if he wishes to enter polite society.'

'I don't want a periwig,' I say.

'That's a pity,' says Aminta, but she says it in the same way that Arlington does.

I explain what progress I have made for my Lord, to reassure Aminta and to divert the conversation away from dead men's hair.

'I find his second explanation even less likely than his first,' says Aminta. 'How does the Commission threaten the Duke of York, and how could your mission be of any use to him? Arlington sends you to the dockyards, but everyone knows how inefficient they are and how the officers there feather their own nests. Peter Pett at Chatham has already been made the scapegoat for the defeat on the Medway. I think it may be rather late for the Commissioners to try to blame the Duke of York. That can't be the real reason for Arlington's enterprise.'

'You seem well informed.'

'I've been talking to Will.'

'And does Will think Pett deserved to take the blame?'

'Pett has made himself more comfortable than most, but more tellingly he's the least clever of the Navy Commissioners.

The more intelligent members of the Navy Board, like Pepys, were very happy to see him blamed. Pett's evidence to the committee, especially his claim that his plans and model ships would, if captured, have been of more value to the Dutch than the real ships, caused him to appear ridiculous. That he actually gave priority to saving them rather than moving the King's warships upriver to safer moorings has been made to look like treason.'

'Will is well informed,' I say.

'You should have noticed that before.'

'Perhaps,' I say.

'Will's only fault is his complete loyalty to you,' says Aminta. 'I would have been happier if he had been willing to break a few more confidences – at least to me.'

'I shall speak to him about it,' I say. 'I shall advise him to go behind my back more.'

'Thank you,' says Aminta. 'I would find that very helpful.'

'Are you saying I should ask for Will's advice on Arlington's investigation?'

'His advice is always good, but in this case you also need something else. Whatever Arlington's real purpose is, it is clear that you will need to gain the confidence of some courtiers close to the King. But you are, as we have already agreed, only minor gentry. A real aristocrat can spot minor gentry a mile off and stop them in their tracks. I, on the other hand . . . well, I am the third or possibly fourth cousin of Sir Thomas Clifford, Comptroller of the royal household and bribe-master general. And related in some way that I can no longer recall to the Duke of Buckingham. They may tell me things they would not tell you. I think I shall need to spend an extra day or so in London to ask questions that nobody could fault coming from me but that would be simply impertinent coming from a country magistrate with no periwig and horse-shit on his boots.'

'That is very considerate of you.'

'I merely wish to ensure that we can return to Clavershall West as soon as we can.'

'And you know who you need to speak to?'

'I shall find out. The balance of power has shifted at Court since you were last there. Clarendon, as you know, is gone – fled to avoid impeachment. Buckingham is on the ascendant. But your friend Arlington is losing ground, whatever he may tell you, and my good friend Sir Thomas now has the King's ear, being a real Catholic rather than a Catholic-of-convenience, as my Lord Arlington is.'

'Did Will tell you that too, by any chance?'

'No, that was my friend, Lady Harvey. If you want to know what's going on at Court, ask a woman. The wives of the King's ministers know weeks before their husbands who is in favour and who is not. The King tells his mistresses things that he does not tell his ministers or even his drinking companions. His mistresses tell their friends in the very strictest confidence. Eventually the husbands may also hear of it.'

'You don't need to explain to me how the King conducts his business. It's not only that he tells his ministers no more than they have to know. The whole system of royal finances is utterly corrupt. Officers of the Crown expect to receive gifts and bribes as a normal perquisite of their employment. Suppliers expect to pay them. The King surrenders monopolies and the proceeds of taxes to mistresses and favourites rather than use the money to pay for the defence of the country. Everyone who works for the King, or hangs around the Court eating his food, knows it. They take their example from His Majesty. If any part of Arlington's purpose really does involve reforming the royal finances, nothing I am likely to achieve in two weeks will make any difference.'

'Reform has to begin somewhere,' says Aminta, 'and it requires somebody with a conscience to begin it. Like Arlington, I doubt that the Brooke House Committee will achieve much. It will proceed slowly and cautiously, as committees do, and conclude that all that is required are a few very small changes that will inconvenience nobody of any importance. I have no idea what Arlington's real intention may be, but it may give you a chance to say some of these things to the King.'

I shake my head. 'The King already knows that if he paid his workmen on time then they might need to steal less. If he didn't fritter away his revenue rewarding worthless favourites, others might be less inclined to help him impoverish himself. Things are as they are. If the King doesn't mind, why should I?'

'You wouldn't have said that once.'

'That's what Will tells me too.'

'And the death of Thomas Cade? Have you forgotten that?'

'I can't make Cade out,' I say. 'If you listen to Pepys, he's an illiterate drunk, incapable of designing a ship. According to his deputy at the yard he's an honest, skilled shipbuilder with an eye for the well-being of his men. If you listen to his wife, he's a fool with no head for business. At the royal dockyard they accuse him of sharp practice – of being a clever thief, who could put them all out of a job. Will's view is Cade might have been one thing or the other, but that we should have helped him anyway because, in the end, he was trying to do the right thing.'

'Well, you met him yourself,' says Aminta. 'What do you think?'

'He spoke like an honest man, though many rogues have learned that trick well enough. But his dockyard couldn't lie. It was efficient and well run. It hummed with activity. The royal dockyard, on the other hand, was a haven for the idle and incapable, and so tied up in tradition that it could scarcely move. I pity Symonds trying to manage it – his job might truly be one of the labours of Hercules – but if the King had visited both on the same day, as I did, then he'd have noticed the difference.'

'And you think Pepys had Cade killed? Will says Cade had a lot of useful information about him.'

'Pepys guarded his words as soon as I mentioned Cade's name. Cade would have been able to blackmail Pepys over his handling of Navy contracts or his handling of other men's wives. Or Cade could have gone to the King and informed on Pepys about the bribes he had been taking or simply shown up how inefficiently the royal dockyards were being run under Pepys's management.'

'You don't think he would have just bought Cade off? All he had to do was sign a contract and that should have shut Cade up.'

'Perhaps. Anyway, Pepys was dining with Lord and Lady Sandwich.'

'Really? Are you going to find out if that's true?'

'Arlington says not to bother. That alone makes me suspicious.'

'You don't like Pepys, do you?'

I nod. She doesn't have to tell me that I've made that mistake before. Disliking somebody proves little. Liking them proves even less. If I've learned one thing in my work for Arlington, it's that I should never trust a friendly smile.

'If it is Pepys,' I say, 'there's nothing to be done. Sandwich will tell me whatever Pepys asks him to tell me. Anyway, the Duke of York will protect him; and Arlington, as he has told me, is now the friend of the Duke. It will take more than me to bring down Samuel Pepys. I'll do what I undertook to do for Arlington. Though he rarely returns favours, it will at least do us no harm. I'll report back to him whatever I discover. Then, once we have taught Killigrew how to count, we shall return to Essex.'

Of course, the more evidence I can assemble against Pepys the more difficult it will be for him to escape entirely unscathed. I doubt Mistress Cade will have spent much time hunting for the documents that her husband promised me, because she already knows that she's destroyed them, but it is worth speaking to her again, just in case she has set a few aside for her own purposes.

I descend the stairs and emerge into the shady gardens of Lincoln's Inn. The evening sun is low in the sky, but I have still an hour and a half before a cooling dusk descends on the City. I take out my gold watch to confirm this. Then I hear a voice behind me.

'Sir John! A moment if you please, sir.'

I turn. A tall man, plainly dressed in a faded black suit, has been waiting for me. His features must once have been pleasingly even, but a broken nose now gives them a certain asymmetry. He smiles briefly but long enough for me to count how many yellow teeth he has left.

'How can I help you?' I ask.

'My master wishes to speak to you, sir,' he says.

'About what exactly?'

'A matter of business.'

'I'm afraid I no longer practise Law,' I say. 'But my partner will see him tomorrow if he presents himself to our clerk, Mr Atkins. Our chambers are on the first floor.'

'It's you he wishes to see, Sir John. Nobody else can help. Unfinished business, you might call it. Business with you and you alone.'

'Very well. Let him call at eight tomorrow. If he is already a client and the matter is a simple one, I shall see what I can do. What is your master's name?'

'Tomorrow will not serve. He wishes to speak to you now.'

'That is wholly impossible. Please go home and explain to him that I can see him for a few minutes tomorrow.'

'He is here in the garden, Sir John. Just over there.'

I look towards the line of shrubs that the man is pointing to. I can see nobody. But there may be a man concealed behind them. Or many men. I wonder which it was that Cade encountered, one or many? Of course, this may be a completely innocent request to go to a little-frequented part of the garden on a summer evening. It is perfectly possible that it is no part of the plan that I should be waylaid and killed within the next few minutes. But I would still rather know who wishes to see me so urgently and secretly.

'I don't talk to my clients in bushes,' I say. 'Other lawyers may, but I don't. Tomorrow, at my chambers, would be more convenient. Your master can tell me his name then if he chooses to do so, or not if he doesn't. The Law and the fee will be the same either way. We'll see then what, if anything, I can do for him.'

I check my pocket watch again. I should still be able to get to the Tower and back before night falls. But when I look up the tall man is holding a large, heavy pistol. Not three tiers of cannons, but adequate for his purposes.

'Walk just in front of me, if you please, Sir John. We're going a few short steps. My master, as I say, is close by. He can explain when we get there.'

I wonder whether to employ my sword. Perhaps not. Not yet. I imagine that, if I allow my hand to stray towards the hilt, then I shall not live long enough to make much use of the blade.

'On second thoughts, I should be delighted to meet him now,' I say.

'No more words,' he says. 'Just walk as silently as may be. Keep a sword's length in front of me, if you will. That's it. A little further, Sir John – beyond the bush and over by that windowless wall. Now, please turn to the left.'

So, this then is his master. I do not recognise the man facing me. I don't think he's ever been a client of mine. He is shorter than his servant and better dressed, in blue velvet and a broad-brimmed feathered hat. There is a sort of cavalier swagger about him. He also seems to have taken better care of his teeth. He wears his own sword on a wide embroidered sash, another new fashion. A narrow moustache adorns his upper lip. Though I have come out of my way to see him, he does not appear in any way grateful.

'I'm in a hurry,' I say. 'I don't know you. What business do you have with me?'

'This,' he says.

I stagger back from the force of the blow that he gives me in the gut. The brick wall provides some support as I recover my breath. There are muscles beneath that innocent blue velvet coat. He advances on me, then stops. People often do when they get a proper look at the scar on my face. They can see I've been in a fight before. They know they'll have to do quite a lot of damage if they're hoping to impress me.

'Who are you?' I ask, but the words are more effort than usual.

In reply he strikes me hard again. I need a bigger scar. Or maybe a nose patch like Arlington's. But this time I am prepared. I twist my body and the blow glances off. I'll have a bruise there later, but I'm still standing. He takes a step back, as if to admire his work.

'Clearly I have done something to offend you,' I say, rubbing my ribs. 'Do you intend to tell me what?'

'Your recent enquiries are inconveniencing certain people,' he says. 'People whom you would do well not to annoy. Go back to Essex, Sir John, or next time we meet I may have to slit your nose, or your throat.'

'Am I allowed to enquire who these inconvenienced people are?' I ask politely. My chest aches where the blows fell, but I'm not going to let him know that. 'The crudeness of your threat suggests they are courtiers.'

'They are powerful men. That is all you need to know.'

'I am acquainted with some powerful men myself,' I say. 'You may not hold as many cards in your hand as you believe.'

He laughs. 'Don't think that Lord Arlington can protect you,' he says.

I look from him to his servant and back again. The gentleman's sword still hangs easily on the elegant sash. I have no way of knowing how well he would use it if I chose to draw mine. Possibly worse than I do, but probably better in a fair fight. I have used my sword a great deal, but I have used it fairly only in the last resort. I could be at some disadvantage if I had to do so now. His companion is still holding the pistol, which I note is not yet cocked. I think I could kill one or other of them almost certainly, but probably not both. Killing the gentleman in blue will give the other more than enough time to cock the pistol and, if it is properly loaded and primed, put a ball into me from close range. Killing the man in faded black will give his master the leisure to draw his sword and run me through before I can extract my own blade from whichever part of his servant's body it has lodged. I could slash the servant's face, as close to the eyes as I can get, and still be ready to defend myself against the master, but then we come back to the question: am I then going to have to fight fairly? I prefer not to.

'Arlington never protects me,' I say. 'That's the one thing we can both depend on.'

'Then don't be a fool like Cade. London's a big city, but not too big for us to find you. You'd better run now, Mr Lawyer. You and your play-scribbling wife. Go back to the Essex mud you both crawled out of. Because there's nobody protecting your son at the moment, is there?'

He has advanced again while giving me this advice and is now standing only a foot or so from me. I hadn't expected him to make that mistake. My fist sends him staggering back onto the grass. He regains his feet quickly, but not before I have drawn my sword. I haven't gained as much of an advantage as I'd hoped, but I have at least caused him a little pain. His servant struggles to cock the pistol but the man in blue grimaces and shakes his head at him. Whatever his instructions are from his easily offended patron, they are not to kill me on this occasion. Or even to add to the scars I already have. He takes another deep breath then straightens up and smiles. 'I'll repay you for that, Sir John, as soon as the opportunity allows.'

'Please do,' I say. 'In the meantime, I'm much obliged to you.'

'For what?'

'For helping me make up my mind. I thought that my enquiries had had no effect. Clearly they have. I am grateful to you for clarifying that point. You can tell your master that, whatever it was troubling him, you have made things slightly worse.'

'Think of your wife's safety, and your child's, if you don't care about your own,' he says.

'If you believe that threatening my family helps your patron in any way, then again I have to correct you,' I say.

'You have no idea who you are dealing with,' he says.

I decide that he may as well have the last word. I don't want it much anyway. And, to be fair, he's right: I have no idea who I am dealing with. I hold his gaze for half a minute or so, until he gets bored with it all.

He turns and stalks off towards the gateway. His servant looks on open mouthed, then follows him at a trot. I think the man in black doesn't care to be with me alone, in spite of the weapon in his hands. It's always a mistake to give a gun to somebody who doesn't understand how to use it.

So was that a warning from Pepys? It lacked the finesse that I would have expected from the Clerk of the Acts to the Navy Board. There is no plan behind it other than to give me a mildly unpleasant five minutes in the gardens of Lincoln's Inn, without regard to the possible consequences. I think that the person who commissioned this affair had little knowledge of me, or indeed of my wife.

Still, I have clearly made a powerful enemy. The only question is: who?

Chapter 11

The Thames

I hail a skiff at Temple Stairs. I feel a stab of pain in my leg as I jump aboard and another in my chest as I fold myself into the seat at the stern. At the moment the new injuries trouble me slightly more than the old ones. The sooner I can resume my duties as a rural magistrate the better.

'The Tower,' I say.

The boatman nods and pushes off into the stream. It is high water and the current flows neither one way nor the other. The surface of the river unnaturally still, as if covered with a layer of oil. The stink of the Thames always seems a little less when it is full, but a scent of ashes still hangs over everything, high tide or low, especially when the wind is from the north. Those who live here the whole time say they do not notice it, but, coming from the country, I do.

'Sad sight – I mean the City, sir. Near three years now since the fire time and it's still dust and ruins as far as the eye can see. Meanwhile, all they do is argue whether it should be this plan for rebuilding or that.'

'They've left it late if they want to realign the streets,' I say. 'Householders have already started to rebuild on their own account. They won't be shifted just because Sir Christopher Wren wants to put a road through their new sitting room.'

'True, sir, they won't. London is the hardest city in the world to rule, so they say. The French bow down to their King and do his bidding, and the Chinese prostrate themselves in front of their Emperor and lick the ground he walks on, but we Londoners are no slaves. We threw off the King's father and we'll do the same with the new King if we choose to do.'

'Careful who you say that to, if you want to keep your head.'

'That we sent the old King to the block is already in the history books and no treason to say it. Nor was it treason to serve under Oliver as I did at Naseby and Langport. As for the current man, I haven't said what I've chosen to do, so that is no crime either. In any case, a fellow may say what he likes on the free River Thames without fear. That's the Law, sir.'

'You know the Law well, then?'

'The river is both a highroad and a university, sir. As to pulling down the King, bless you, sir, I have Republicans in this boat every day. London is full of them now. They say that my Lord Buckingham has thousands of men who will rise at his command and set up a holy government again.'

'Buckingham's no holier than you or I.'

'It's still what they say.'

'We haven't heard it in Essex,' I say. 'Now, look to your oars as we pass under the bridge. The water is slack but the arches are narrow.'

At high and low tide, the passage through the arches can be made without danger. For a short time, twice a day, the brackish water surges neither upstream nor down. As we approach them, there is no more than a dark, sinister swirl round the jutting wooden starlings that protect the stonework. The splash of our oars echoes as we glide out of the sunlight and into the deep shadows. It always feels cool and damp here, even on the hottest day. Water drips from gaps between the green stones high above us – hopefully, but not necessarily, rainwater. The hollow sound that the falling droplets make forms a ragged counterpoint to the regular splash of the oars.

Then we are out again and into the late afternoon sun. I look back at the bridge with the untidy mass of houses and shops that lines it. On the short stretches without buildings to obscure it, traffic can be seen proceeding across the bridge at a leisurely pace. Men on foot shuffle in an overheated mass of humanity behind carts and coaches. Every now and then they all stop completely as wagons travelling in opposite directions try to squeeze past each other. Nobody crosses the river that way unless their load is too big or they cannot afford the small price of a skiff.

'Do your passengers say that Buckingham has many supporters at Court?' I ask.

'Buckingham is the leader and champion of the common man,' says the boatman. 'He despises the Court and its frivolity. But the great Lord Dartford is of a mind to help him – so they tell me.'

'Is Dartford ever sober enough for his support to be of value?'

'He is a wit with a sharp tongue, sir, and a rich man since his marriage.'

'I'm surprised that any respectable heiress would wish to marry Dartford.'

'She didn't, sir, but he carried her away by force and so the lady had less choice in the matter than she might have wished. She'd have been better off if she'd been poor, sir, and beneath his notice. Much better. He'll have spent her inheritance and given her the pox by the year's end, mark my words.'

'May God protect her,' I say.

'Amen to that, sir. But Dartford may have other ideas.'

I pay him his sixpence for the journey, and a penny for his somewhat doubtful legal opinions, and disembark.

The Cades' house is locked and shuttered. There is no smoke from the chimney. At first I think that everyone has gone away, then I see a forlorn figure sitting on the doorstep. She still wears the faded black dress into which her mistress put her on hearing of Cade's demise. Her straw-coloured hair is partly over her face. She has an untidy bundle beside her on the step. There is an almost empty brandy bottle in her hand.

'Good day,' I say to her. 'Mistress Cade is not at home?'

She looks up and tries to focus her gaze on me, but everything is blurred for her by hair or brandy.

'Gone,' she says. 'First that nasty trollop dismissed me – just for speaking my mind and telling her the truth – then she threw me out of the house. She was going to Kent, she says, and didn't need no servants there. That's gratitude. Look at me. Scarcely a penny to my name and nothing to eat or drink.' She takes a swig of brandy in proof of this.

'I'm sorry,' I say. 'And you have no way of getting back into the house?'

She winks and removes a key from her apron pocket. 'How do you think I got the brandy then? Got this cut for myself, didn't I? Betsy's not so much of a fool as she looks. I pretended to go, then came back half an hour later. House was locked up and empty, so I slipped inside for a moment. If the mistress ain't back by nightfall, I'll sleep in her feather bed tonight, fart in it until dawn and be on the King's highroad at sunrise. But I doubt the lying cow really has gone to Kent and I don't want her to report me for breaking and entering if she does come back this evening. Then some slimy, poxy magistrate, begging your honour's pardon, will just sentence me to transportation to the pissing American colonies to work in the tobacco fields. Here in the pleasant English sun suits me for the moment.'

'Where do you think she's gone, if not to Kent?'

'Now the master's dead? To one of her gentlemen friends, no doubt.'

'She has many?'

'There's that smarmy clerk – Pepys. He was round here a lot when the master was away – God rest his poor deceived soul.'

'He never found out?'

'Not till I told him.'

'When was that?'

'A few days ago. When the mistress first threatened to sack me. I went to him and told him everything she was up to – with Pepys and with the others. Had to, didn't I?'

'Others?' I say.

She taps the side of her nose. 'Give him all the names, I did. Some surprised him, I can tell you. He'd never suspected a thing. He thanked me. Gave me a Shilling.'

'That was very honest of you.'

She looks at me suspiciously. 'Yes,' she says. 'It was. I know my duty to my master. He was a good man. He was kind to me. Not like her.' A tear runs down her cheek, leaving a line of clean skin in its wake. She takes another gulp of spirit then wipes her mouth with the back of her hand.

'Of course,' I say, 'now he's dead, there would be no harm in telling me the names you gave him. It can't hurt Mr Cade and it may be that one of them killed him. It would be to your advantage.'

She shakes her head. But she has told me her price already. I take out a Shilling from my pocket, then, to make sure, a second one. They both bear the head of King Charles, crowned with laurel, looking like one of the more untrustworthy Roman emperors. I think the artist has captured his subject well. I hold the coins out, but not so close that she can reach them.

'There was Harry Truscott from the shipyard,' she says quickly.

'Mr Cade's deputy?'

'That's the one. He always knew when the master would be away from home. Him and the mistress – ideas above his station. Of course, he's younger than she is. In one sense, he could have done better for himself. A lot better. But he always wanted to run the shipyard. And now that's what he's doing.' She spits in the dust. 'Do I get the money now?'

'I'd like all of their names.'

'Well, you've had the first, so you can pay me for that one.'

I hand her the first Shilling. She takes it without comment. I wonder, at a Shilling a lover, how much this will cost me. Hopefully Mistress Cade will prove relatively chaste.

'Then there was Mr Pepys.'

'I know that,' I say. 'I'm not paying you a Shilling for him.'

'Sixpence?'

'No.'

'Penny?'

'No.'

'Please yourself. Then there was a very grand gentleman. Only saw him once, but most attentive. They closeted themselves away, where I couldn't hear what they were saying. Up in her chamber. And her poor husband's body scarcely cold.'

'When was that?'

'Yesterday. Quite early. Maybe a couple of hours before you came.'

'You hadn't seen him before that?'

'No. I'm not saying it was his first visit, mind. In fact, I'd wager this Shilling it wasn't, knowing her. Just I didn't see him before.'

'And his name was . . .?'

She frowns. 'Can't recall. I did hear him say it. It was a place.'

'Lord somewhere or other?'

'Yes. That's right. Somewhere. Lord Somewhere.'

I wonder whether to suggest a few names, but I know she'll just say 'yes' to the first one in order to get the Shilling.

'Can you remember nothing?'

'It was a place I'd heard of – that the master used to go. Can I have another Shilling now?'

'Not for that, you can't. The peerage is relatively large and many have houses in London. We'll need to narrow it down a bit. What was he? Duke? Marquess? Earl? Viscount? Baron?'

'One of those, probably. What's the difference?'

'Not a great deal unless you are one. Then which you are is a very important matter indeed. Any other men?'

She looks longingly at the silver coin in my hand. 'No,' she says eventually. 'That's all.'

So that's three lovers, including one member of the nobility. It seems a modest total, but I'm not really in a position to judge. I'll have to ask Aminta how many is usual at Court. And Truscott is not quite the loyal servant he appeared. He kept that quiet, though Cade apparently knew before he died that he'd been betrayed. Did he confront Truscott straight away? Maybe not. The shipbuilder seemed to me the sort of person who'd consider his options carefully before acting.

From this doorstep you can smell the river and hear it – the boatmen's calls, the creak of the waterwheels, the crack of the wind-filled sails as a boat tacks across the river. You can also hear hammers and saws at work in the boatyard, now under Truscott's careful direction. It's a fine place to be if boats and the river are your life, less so if they're not. Mistress Cade needed other diversions. I don't blame her. Men have more choice than women where they are to live and where they are to work. Women live where their fathers live and then where their husbands live, unless they prefer domestic servitude or prostitution. The afternoon sunshine is hot on my thick velvet coat. A warm smell of tar drifts in on the breeze. For a moment I envy the men at the dockyard, able to divest themselves of coats and waistcoats, without needing to maintain the public dignity of being minor gentry. At least I don't have on my head a covering of other men's hair, though that may soon be unavoidable.

She looks up at me. 'This won't buy me much of a supper,' she says, holding up the single Shilling that is newly hers.

'You'll have to steal one, then,' I say. 'You have the key to the front door.'

'That's right enough,' she says. 'And I know where the mistress keeps her other keys when she goes out.'

'Do you?' I say.

She nods. Perhaps my journey is not as wasted as I was beginning to think.

'Why don't we go in and refill your brandy bottle?' I say. 'I'd like to take a look round the house anyway.'

She is not yet so befuddled that I haven't raised her suspicions.

'I can't let you in the house, sir. It wouldn't be right. You might be a thief.'

'I'm a lawyer,' I say.

'That's what I meant.'

'Five Shillings,' I say.

She finds that argument more convincing.

'Ten,' she says.

'Five,' I say.

'Seven.'

'Five.'

She rummages in her pocket and takes out a large key. I offer her my hand and help her to her feet. She staggers against me, bringing with her a mixture of odours – brandy mainly, but with hints of the kitchen she will no longer inhabit – sour milk, rancid butter, animal fat, sweat. For a moment she leans soft and heavy on my shoulder, then she is upright, swaying gently. On her third attempt she gets the key into the lock. It turns smoothly and in a moment we are into the cool, shadowy parlour with the heavy oak door closed and locked behind us.

'Where does Mistress Cade keep her keys?' I ask.

'In that oak cupboard yonder,' she says. 'In the wooden jug. I'll have my five Shillings now, if it's all the same to you.'

I walk over to the cupboard and open it. It contains various household items, including a wooden jug. There is a large bunch of keys in it.

'Do you know which key is for what?'

'Some. What do you want to steal?'

'Nothing, probably. Where would your master have kept his papers?'

'In the chest in the bedchamber, if they weren't at the yard.'

'Is this the key for the chest?' I hold up the largest one.

She shrugs. I'll just have to try each of the keys in turn.

'Five Shillings now and you can take what you like. I don't care,' she adds.

'Is there a back door?' I ask.

'Through there.' She points in the direction of the kitchen.

I go through. The kitchen is in some disarray, as might be expected when a drunken maid of all work departs on bad terms with her mistress. I do not need to locate the back-door key. It is in the lock. I turn it and open the door. Outside is a yard with a hard-baked earth surface and a wall that can be climbed easily enough. That may be the way I leave if we are disturbed. I close the door but do not lock it.

I return to the parlour. The maid has not moved at all. She seems almost asleep on her feet. Still, she's all I have as an accomplice.

'Watch the street,' I say. 'If you see your mistress returning, call and warn me.'

'Watching is extra,' she says.

'No it isn't,' I say.

'Then I'll have my money now,' she says.

I wonder how long she'll remain at her post if I pay her.

I wonder how long she'll stay awake. But I need her. I can't jump out of windows the way I used to.

'When I'm finished,' I say. 'You'll get your money then.'

She nods uncertainly, perhaps recalling that I am a lawyer and likely to slide out of our contract citing some obscure statute of Henry I. 'Five Shillings,' she says, 'and don't try to cheat me. I know your sort.'

I leave her where she is and start up the wooden stairs.

The bedchamber is low-ceilinged and the doorframe is even lower. I have to duck as I enter. It is sunnier up here. There is more blue sky visible through the leaded glass than there was at street level. The bed is unmade and a dress lies crumpled on top of it. By the window there is a table with various jars and pots. Two contain red paste, another white powder, all three open. Whoever Mistress Cade has gone to see, it would appear that she changed her dress and painted her face. Did she leave in a hurry or was she counting on her maid to tidy things away? I pause and listen for sounds downstairs. It is silent.

By the fireplace is a large chest. I select the most likely-looking key from the bunch – the one I suggested to Betsy. It fits, but the chest proves to be unlocked anyway. An overpowering smell of rosewater and lavender meets my nose as I open the lid. This is where Mistress Cade keeps her dresses and the bottom half of the chest seems to be taken up with them, but on top of the clothes there is, carefully rolled, what seems to be a contract for the construction of a third-rate man-of-war. It is unsigned.

Voices in the street make me break off and hurry to the window, but it is just a party of young men and women taking a short cut through the narrow street, stepping over the slimy cabbage stalks and pea husks, on their way to somewhere better. I watch them go, wondering if my watch-woman in the room below is still awake. There is at least no sign of the mistress of the house returning.

I apply myself again to the task in hand and rummage through the clothes, but can find nothing else of interest. An iron strongbox under the bed yields to a much smaller key. It contains two or three hundred Pounds in gold coins. Very pretty. Cade was not a poor man then – that might have been enough to buy the commissioner's post at Deptford. I lock the box again and return it to its proper place.

The fireplace next catches my eye. There are ashes in the grate, which is unusual for a bedchamber in June. The material in the hearth is well burned, but appears once to have been paper. Only kitchen fires usually burn on through the summer, but the daily care and cleaning of all fireplaces would be part of the maid's work. Unless she decided not to even glance at a hearth between May and October – not impossible in the light of my dealings with her so far – then it is likely that the fire was lit after Betsy had made her rounds this morning. I examine the remains carefully, because a word or two can sometimes be made out on the least promising material, but they are silent as to what they once said. Mistress Cade has ensured that the fire burned well and left nothing behind, which is in itself of interest.

So, she has gone out of her way to tidy up her husband's paperwork, but the contract has been retained. Then she has departed, sacking the maid and locking up, but she cannot have gone far because she has left behind a large quantity of gold under the bed.

There are voices in the street again, but this time they stop beneath the bedroom window. I have stayed too long. I hear a key in the front door, then the back door slamming. My watch-woman has decided that it's not worth alerting me to the return of her mistress – better not risk transportation to the tobacco fields of Barbados or Maryland just for the sake of a few extra Shillings. There are voices in the parlour below.

'I'm sure I heard a noise,' says Mistress Cade very clearly.

'I heard nothing,' says a man's voice. I do not recognise it, but I don't think it is anyone I wish to meet. Not Truscott and certainly not a duke or marquess. Another Shilling's worth that Betsy was unaware of? 'Let's get whatever you still need to get and be gone. You've spent long enough in this place. You were a fool to ever come here.'

'Hush! I tell you, somebody is in the house. In the kitchen, I think.'

'How would they have got in? The front door was locked. Anyway, why should I hush? If there's an intruder I'll face him like a man.'

'What makes you think it's only one of them?'

'I'll check the kitchen,' he says.

'I'll come with you,' says Mistress Cade. 'You may need brains as well as brawn.'

Unless the maid has paused to lock the door, which I doubt, then I know the outcome of that investigation.

I hear footsteps as she returns. 'Door open. Two bottles of brandy taken,' says Mistress Cade.

The removal of the second bottle suggests that the maid was more alert than I thought as she made her final exit.

'It looks as if we came back just in time,' he says. 'You've lost nothing of value.'

'The gold!' she exclaims. 'The gold, you idiot!'

'What do you mean? We've just reclaimed all of the gold your husband had out on deposit.'

'No, there's more under the bed. If we've lost that . . .'

She has a point. If I were a thief, the first place I would look for something of real value is under the bed. If I were the owner of the house, that's the next place I'd check to ensure all was well.

There is the noise of a cupboard door opening. They will be looking for the key to the strongbox, which was until recently in a jug but which now rests in my pocket.

'The keys - they've gone!' The alarm in Mistress Cade's voice is clear enough.

'You've mislaid them.'

'Or that maid of mine has stolen them. Not that she'll know one key from another.'

'Do you have a spare?'

'To the strongbox? Yes, of course.'

'Then find it and get the gold.'

'But what if . . .'

The conversation that follows is short and whispered.

Again, I can foresee how the next few minutes will play out. I could, of course, force my way back down the stairs as they attempt to come up, but I may still need cooperation and information from Mistress Cade, and I am more likely to get these things as an honest lawyer and magistrate than as a scurvy house breaker. And, more to the point, my unsanctioned presence here will confirm beyond doubt that I have suspicions about her own honesty. I would rather she did not know this. Not yet. I hear the first step on the wooden stairs – the careful tread of one who is not sure who or what awaits them in their most private room. But only one. The other is, wisely, waiting below, perhaps to cut off some other escape route.

Indeed, on the far side of the bedchamber I notice that there is a second, smaller door. It must lead somewhere. I pray that the hinges do not squeak, and God rewards me by allowing the heavy oak plank to swing silently open and then closed behind me. Cade maintained his house well. I give thanks to St Joshua, patron saint of spies and informers, whom I have had to trouble in this way before.

I find myself in a small closet, large enough to take a child or servant's bed, but currently empty. A tiny window provides a little light for the child or servant in question and a view over the garden. On the far side of the room there is yet another door, which may lead, via the back stairs, down to the kitchen or somewhere else. I could try that, and walk straight into whoever has remained below, or I can stay where I am. I stay and listen.

The door I have passed through is very thick but it remains open a crack and I find I can hear a little in the bedroom I have just left. The cautious footsteps reach the top of the stairs, then I hear a man's voice calling out that the room is empty. Lighter steps follow as Mistress Cade ascends in her turn. They converse. The voices that come to me are indistinct, but there are definitely two of them, which means there is nobody downstairs now, if I wish to make a run for it. On the other hand, by staying I may learn a lot more than I had hoped for.

There is more discussion that I cannot quite make out, then I think I hear the strongbox being dragged from under the bed and the large chest being opened and then closed with a bang. Finally, there is silence. I think they have retreated downstairs, having concluded that no self-respecting thief can have visited the bedchamber and left the gold intact. I allow a quarter of an hour to pass according to my gold pocket watch. I open the door cautiously. The bedchamber is empty. I check under the bed. The box is gone. I open the chest. The contract too is gone.

I creep carefully down the stairs. That I don't expect a trap doesn't mean there won't be one. The parlour is silent. There is no sound of anyone trying but failing not to breathe. There is no telltale rustle of a skirt from behind a cupboard. I move silently across the floor to the front door. It is locked.

I think nobody will be returning to the house today, so I inspect the room more freely. The only surprise is the discovery of a few books of poetry on the dresser – Shakespeare's sonnets, Spenser's *Faerie Queene*, Samuel Butler's *Hudibras* and a bright new copy of Milton's *Paradise Lost*. Whose are they? Cade's? I had not expected this of him, but I have been shown so many sides of his character that another does not astonish me. The volumes are tucked away so neatly that I almost missed them. Just for a moment I am tempted to rescue *Paradise Lost*. I have not yet bought it and I am sure this copy will languish here completely unread in the damp river air. No, there is a thick bookmark of some sort in the volume, so not entirely neglected. The book pleads with me, but I find I am still too much of a lawyer to steal poetry from an empty house. I go into the kitchen, where the back door is now locked but the key is easily accessible. I let myself out into the sad, neglected garden, and thence, without needing to climb the wall, via a door guarded only with a bolt into the street. A large red sun is setting over the river, but I have time to get back to Lincoln's Inn before night falls. The streets of London have become more dangerous of late and daylight is my friend.

Chapter 12

Lincoln's Inn

'I'm sorry, sir, that I have brought this upon you,' says Will. 'If I had not told Mr Cade that you would see him—'

'I would probably have seen him anyway,' I say. 'If a man loiters in my waiting room long enough, then I shall encounter him sooner or later. And if you had driven him away, then he would have found me out in some tavern or other.'

'That I do not doubt,' says Aminta.

'Your husband seems to me to be the most sober of men,' says Sparks.

'I have known him since he was six,' says Aminta. 'And he isn't. You may accuse him of being a Puritan if you wish. That is always amusing. But in the interests of fairness, I cannot allow you to condemn him for being sober.'

'Thank you,' I say.

'It is my pleasure to ensure that the truth is known,' says Aminta. 'The question, however, seems to me not one of blame – though I do, of course, blame John absolutely for his lack of caution – but of identity. Who commissioned the attack upon my husband?'

'Surely it is the same man who had Thomas Cade bludgeoned to death?' says Sparks. 'The two ruffians who accosted you almost certainly murdered him. It was in the identical place, almost.'

Will shakes his head. 'They would not take the risk of returning here, Mr Sparks. Sir John says that they had no intention of killing him, so he would be able to identify them to the magistrates. If they had already killed a man here, they could not risk that.'

'Precisely,' I say.

'Unless they are desperate men indeed,' says Sparks.

'That's also possible,' I say.

'You should report them to the magistrates, in any case,' says Sparks, for whom the Law is a very simple matter. 'As Mr Atkins says, you would be able to provide a good description of both men.'

'They clearly do not think you will do that,' says Aminta.

'Or, more likely, they believe that, if I do, then they will be protected. So, who would think that?'

'Somebody close to the King,' says Aminta.

'At first I thought it must be Pepys,' I say. 'But it lacked the finesse I would have expected from him. And the men claimed their master was powerful – suggesting a senior courtier rather than the Clerk of the Acts.'

'The same person as the nobleman who visited Mistress Cade?' says Sparks. 'But that, you implied, could be almost anyone. The field is wide open.'

Aminta shakes her head. 'Those who could expect protection from the King as a right are few in number – Buckingham, say, or Dartford.'

'Lord Dartford is known for that sort of thing,' says Will. 'He's had at least one enemy killed, and got away scot free. He's as close to the King as you could wish.'

'Lady Castlemaine,' says Sparks. 'You're investigating corruption and she benefits from the King's mismanagement of funds as much as anyone. And there is nobody closer to the King than her, surely?'

'Lady Castlemaine's star is waning,' says Aminta. 'The King has generously given her Berkshire House to live in.'

'I can't see that she is out of favour, then,' says Sparks. 'The house is a noble gift, even for one as rapacious as my Lady.'

Aminta shakes her head. 'The gift means she has ceased to live at the Palace as she did before. He no longer wants her close to him. She is struggling to maintain her hold on the King. Of course, the King will do no more than he has to. He will not drive her away entirely unless she forces him to do so. But Lady Castlemaine has never liked sharing the King with others, even with the Queen. There are stormy days ahead.'

'The problem is why any of them should wish to send me back to Essex,' I say. 'Other than Pepys, I have evidence so far concerning none of them. Buckingham may be plotting the King's death, but even the Thames watermen seem to know that.'

'But could Mistress Cade's noble admirer be Dartford?' asks Sparks.

'I wondered that myself,' I say. 'But I had no wish to lead the witness on this occasion. I wouldn't have trusted the answer. The maid said the place from which he took his title was somewhere Cade used to visit. I believe that anyway.'

'Well, the charming village of Dartford is certainly close enough to London for frequent visits from Cade,' says Sparks. 'We don't have your witness to cross-examine but, in her absence, I'd put money on it being Dartford, both as Mistress Cade's visitor and the originator of the attack on you. He's a bruiser in velvet and lace, with a taste for writing obscene verse. As Mr Atkins says, the assault on your good self was very much in his style, though to have slit your nose would have been even more so.'

'The man sent to give the warning promised to do that on some convenient occasion in the near future.'

'My Lord Dartford as Mistress Cade's lover is improbable, unless her charms are much greater than one might have expected of the wife of a small dockyard owner,' says Aminta.

'Her charms,' I say, 'are very much as you might expect. Pepys found her compliant – he asks for little more than that. Truscott's motives are yet to be discovered, and may relate to his wish to run the shipyard – perhaps after marrying Mistress Cade. But it is odd that Dartford should have troubled her – a young and pretty actress would be more to his taste.'

'She certainly would be,' says Aminta. 'But Dartford may have had other reasons for being there.'

'If Arlington wants me to speak to courtiers, perhaps I should begin with him. I'll pay Dartford a call. Not now but in the morning.'

I doubt that he sees much daylight in the normal course of things. Like a night-hunting owl he will be at a disadvantage when exposed to the bright sun. I think I shall have the advantage of him then.

Chapter 13

Dartford House

A lesser man may hide in London pretty well, but the nobility cannot resist advertising their presence. Unlike Arlington, Dartford has wasted no time in renaming his residence – there is no doubt who owns the house I have come to.

Dartford does not greet everyone who arrives at his door, but I ensure that his man reports to him that I come on Lord Arlington's business, and I am admitted and led up a wide, curving staircase to a panelled withdrawing room on the first floor. I am told to wait there. I am not invited to sit. So, I stand for some time, admiring the tapestries on the wall. They are new and bright and show events in the life of Julius Caesar, his overthrow by Brutus and the accession of Augustus. Doubtless they send some political message, but what they show above all is that, since his marriage, Dartford has five houses, farmland stretching across seven counties in England and three in Ireland, and chests full of gold coins. I think he may also have a sore head.

When he arrives he is wrapped in a dressing gown and without his periwig. His short, bristly hair is covered by a soft cap, made of velvet and embroidered round the edges. He wears Turkish slippers. His eyes are bleary. He has not shaved. I've met with larger men, but there's a hardness to him that you wouldn't want to cross. He has a reputation for learning, though. He'd stab you through the guts and then go off and compose a sonnet about it.

'What the Devil does Arlington want at this hour?' he demands.

'It is eleven of the clock, my Lord,' I say. 'The sun is long up and will soon think of beginning its slow descent towards Whitehall Palace. Cobblers have been at their benches and grocers at their counters for nigh on four hours.'

'Grocers? What's any of that to do with me?' he asks. 'Buckingham may choose to dine with such men, but I have no need of their support. I have ambitions to lead no party of my own. My shoemaker is content to wait upon me at such hours as are convenient for his customers. He does not look to me to lead him.'

'I am pleased to hear it, my Lord.'

'Who are you anyway? My man simply said that your master Arlington had sent you.'

'I'm John Grey. I'm a lawyer. Of Lincoln's Inn.'

Dartford's face reveals nothing. 'Never heard of you.'

'Lord Arlington has asked me to look into certain matters pertaining to the Navy.'

'I have as little to do with His Majesty's ships as I do with His Majesty's tailor.'

'Nevertheless, it would seem, my Lord, that you would prefer that I did not carry out the investigation,' I say.

'I've never said that.'

'No, the men you sent to waylay me said that, though I said some sharp things to them as well.'

'Why should you imagine I've sent men to Lincoln's Inn?'

'I did not say you had. I said that I have my chambers there. Though, by some strange coincidence, that was also the place to which somebody sent two ruffians. They were apparently sent to discourage me. They haven't succeeded, but they probably told you that.'

He rubs his eyes. If he realises he's made a false move, it doesn't bother him. Perhaps it's intentional – he wants me to know who my enemy is. He certainly makes it clear that he doesn't need to concede anything to somebody as insignificant as a Lincoln's Inn lawyer.

'You came here to tell me so little? You have wasted your time, Sir John. If you've been told rather forcefully not to work for Arlington, that seems to be very good advice. You'd do well to follow it. But I say again, I've never set foot in Lincoln's Inn. The men who attacked you might be working for anybody.'

'You've set foot in a house by the Tower though.'

'Who says?'

'The maid of the lady you visited.'

For the first time Dartford looks disconcerted, but he quickly recovers himself.

'That is certainly no concern of yours, damn your impertinence.'

'Her husband died recently. He was killed in much the same place as your men attacked me.'

He shrugs. 'What's his name? If I'm intimate with his wife, I may recognise it.'

'Thomas Cade,' I say.

His face betrays nothing. 'And you think I arranged the death of this Thomas Cade? Was that before or after I'm supposed to have attacked you?'

'I think you recognise the name very well. I can think of how you might have arranged his death. I can think how you would have managed to cover up any involvement on your part. I don't yet understand why.'

'You realise, Sir John, that I could run you through now with my sword then have my men take your body, wrapped in a carpet, to Tower Stairs and thrown into the river? You wouldn't be missed.'

'Yes,' I say. 'I do realise you could arrange that. But I would not wish to put your servants to so much trouble. Not after having to visit Lincoln's Inn on my account. I do, however, intend to discover who killed Thomas Cade.'

I wait to see what his response may be.

'This is nonsense, Sir John. Is that really what Lord Arlington has asked you to do? To come here and waste my time?'

'No,' I say. 'As I said, he wants me to ask about naval contracts. But you tell me you know no more about those than you do about the men who make your shoes. And one shipbuilder more or less – I doubt that troubles you much.'

'Go back to Essex, Sir John,' he says.

'Where were you three nights ago when Cade was killed?' I ask.

'This is an outrage! Lord Arlington shall know of your disgraceful lack of manners.'

'He already knows, in general terms. I doubt if this specific instance will trouble him greatly. It may amuse him. What do you think, my Lord?'

'You're mad if you think I had Cade killed. There was no need to kill him. None at all.'

'I thought you knew nothing about Cade?'

'London is a dangerous place, Sir John. I'm sure you would find Essex safer.'

'Hunting? Shooting?'

'If you enjoy those things.'

'I don't think that I do. I'll probably stay here for a while.'

'You're a fool, Grey.'

I smile, bow and turn on my heel. Always let them have the last word. It costs nothing and saves a great deal of time.

He's right, of course. Essex would be safer. Especially after this morning. But Dartford knows about Cade all right. I think he knows a lot about Cade.

Chapter 14

Berkshire House

Berkshire House has not yet been renamed Castlemaine House. Perhaps Lady Castlemaine hopes to be restored to the Palace. Perhaps out of modesty she does not wish to attach her name to the building, though that is unlikely. Perhaps she is awaiting a greater title that she can employ in its place. If her sons are going to be dukes, then the least the King can do for her is to make her duchess of somewhere that doesn't yet have a duchess. She can rename the house when she knows exactly what she's duchess of.

The house is on the far side of the park from the King, almost in the country. But it is large and comfortable. It is no ignominious exile. But it is exile for all that.

This time I am kept waiting in the hallway on the ground floor, while the mistress of the house is informed of my arrival. I hear her long before I see her – a rustle of heavy silk gliding across the polished wooden floor. Even here on the outskirts of London, even for a mere lawyer like me, she knows that it is important to make an entrance, that it is worth having two footmen to fling open the doors before her so that she can advance effortlessly towards her objective. She looks me up and down and I return the compliment.

Barbara Villiers, Countess of Castlemaine, is dressed in a shimmering silver-coloured gown. The bodice is tight and the skirt simply cut, but the sleeves cascade down to her elbows in two flowing extravagances. Her dark hair is curled in many ringlets, contrasting with her white skin. A double row of large creamy pearls adorns her neck. A small lapdog follows her, unnoticed, stumbling over her silken train in its eagerness to discover what his mistress is up to this time. He must have seen a lot in his short life and formed a strange idea about the human race and its habits. As for his mistress, I would say that she has not aged at all since I last saw her in the plague year, but there is one great difference. She is not with child by the King. She will bear no royal bastard this year. No amount of silk and lace can disguise that shameful fact. She holds out her hand to be kissed. I do so, knowing how most men in London would envy me.

'I am very pleased to see you, John,' she says, taking my hand in hers. 'To what do I owe this pleasure?'

She has the ability to make you feel, albeit you have been left standing in her entrance hall for some time, that she has been looking forward to this meeting all morning. Her grip on my hand tightens imperceptibly as she draws me a little closer to her. 'It's too long since I last saw you. I was so pleased to hear of your marriage to Lady Pole. I never liked her first husband. She made a *much* better choice the second time round, didn't she? She's a clever woman. Very witty. I wish that I could write plays and verse, rather than merely being lampooned in them. I hope she and your family are well?'

I give her an account of my living relatives, which fortunately are few because I think she is not really interested. In response she says that three of her children are living with her here, two are in France. She appears vague as to which are where. I do not ask about her husband, Lord Castlemaine. He is the least visible man in England.

'Are you comfortable in your new house?' I ask. 'It must be pleasant to be able to escape from the constant activity of the Court.'

'Oh, I have not given up my rooms at the Palace,' she says, 'and the King comes here daily. Do not pity me, John, whatever you may have been told, do not pity me.'

'It would never occur to me to do so,' I say.

'Don't think that I don't know what they say,' she says. 'That poor popish whore – cast aside by the King and made to live amongst her puking bastards a good ten minutes' walk from the Palace. Well, I'm not finished yet. The King will never persuade Frances Stuart to join him in bed, and he'll soon tire of that common strumpet Nell Gwynn. She probably still tries to sell him oranges every night. He'll come back to me. Of course, in the meantime, I am free to do as I choose. I've always liked you, John. If you have come here to seek some favour, you have only to ask. It is always a pleasure to grant requests to those whom you like. It's one of the privileges of power, and I can assure you that I am still very powerful indeed.'

She smiles at me. She has not yet released my hand.

'There is something that you can help me with,' I say. 'Lord Arlington has asked me to investigate the handling of naval contracts. I don't understand why. The Brooke House Committee is already looking at it. What am I missing?'

My hand is finally dropped abruptly. Her mouth freezes in mid-smile.

'How would I know that?' she asks.

'You are his friend.'

'You spend little time at Court, John. Friendships – friend-ships with men like Arlington – are temporary things of convenience. I shall count you as a friend always. A true friend. But you are one of the few men in London I would trust with my secrets – one of the few I would trust totally not to betray me. Nobody trusts Arlington with their plans for dinner.'

I nod to show that I have understood entirely. She does not wish me to continue with this line of questioning. A bit like Dartford, Pepys and Symonds. On the other hand, that's what I've come to do. 'Arlington thinks that members of the Court are making money out of the contracts,' I say.

To her credit, she does not slap my face. Not yet. You need a lot of self-control to stay at the top for as long as she has. 'Yes, of course they are, John. How else would a poor courtier live?'

'I have no idea how courtiers live and no plans to find out. But I still don't understand what Arlington thinks I shall discover.'

'Nothing,' she says. 'Nothing at all. As you say, the matter is already being investigated. Your time is being wasted, my dear John. There are many things to do in London – many pleasant things and many diverting places to go. Witty people to talk to . . . and maybe to do other things with. Wouldn't you prefer that? We could spend the day together so pleasantly. Don't waste your time on dreary naval accounts. What does it matter to people like us what the Navy pays for rope?'

'A man has been murdered,' I say. 'A man who might have been a key witness.'

'Who?'

'A shipbuilder. He has a yard at the Tower. His name was Cade.'

She shakes her head.

'Do you know him?' I ask.

'Why should I know a shipbuilder?'

'There is money to be made from building ships.'

'The King makes adequate provision for me. And who killed him, may I ask?'

'Perhaps Lord Dartford. He felt the need to send men to threaten me and then to deny that he did so.'

'Lord Dartford? Surely not?'

'He has a reputation for that sort of thing.'

'Well, that at least is true. If you wish to kill somebody, Sir John – I mean kill them and escape punishment – then I would advise you to be of ancient lineage, a wit and a hard drinker. Or pretty, female, of no lineage at all and readily available at all hours. These things will endear you to the King. Of course, you will be arrested and tried, because the King does not wish to appear to be a tyrant who flouts the rule of Law. But once you have been tried, if the Judge has not already been sufficiently influenced in your favour and found you not guilty in spite of the evidence, then you may sue for a pardon in full confidence that it will be granted before the hangman has a chance to get his hands on you. Dartford is the fourth earl of that name – as ancient as it needs to be – with wit enough for half a dozen men and an unequalled capacity for claret and brandy. He could kill with impunity, if he wished, unless . . .'

'Unless?' I say.

She places her hand very softly on my arm. Whatever she

tells me next, she tells me as her friend. Her very good friend, who will not repeat a word of this conversation.

'Unless, John, he loses the King's protection. Dear me, that would be a pity, would it not?'

'Is that likely?' I ask.

'You don't listen to Court gossip?'

'We hear little of it in Essex.'

'How dreadful for you. Perhaps that's why I never go there. Well, my dear John, the story running the corridors of Whitehall Palace is this. Dartford, as you know, is a poet as well as a wit. Most of his poems are written privately – for friends. Most are scandalous. He wrote one about the King that circulated for a few weeks, clandestinely. Our loyalty to the King dictated that we should inform His Majesty at once, but nobody wished to be the *first*, if you see what I mean. So nobody did.'

'I can understand that,' I say.

'Then Dartford made a mistake. The King had heard that his Lordship had written a truly filthy satire on the Earl of Clarendon, and, seeking pious and high-minded diversion, asked him for a copy. Dartford, not entirely sober, selected what he thought was the manuscript in question and sent it to the King. Later he checked and found that he still had the satire on the Earl of Clarendon, but lacked the one he had penned on His Majesty – the one that compared the King's privy member to his sceptre. It also called me a whore, but that is no insult in this Court.'

'And the King's reaction was ...'

'Nobody knows. Dartford waited, trembling, for some days. Each day he entered the King's Presence Chamber expecting to be admonished, chastised and dismissed from Court, but met only with smiles. He concluded that the King had the poem but had not yet read it. The King … well, he does not read very much, for business or pleasure.'

'I know,' I say.

'Or perhaps he did read it and liked it, though that is improbable. The King will laugh at any insult to other men, but feels that criticism of the monarch should be avoided on constitutional grounds. Anyway, Dartford questioned Chiffinch, the King's doorkeeper, and Chiffinch agreed, for a small consideration, to search the King's papers and retrieve the poem, but he reported that it was not there. Dartford of course offered Chiffinch more money to try again, but Chiffinch assured him that the poem would still not be there however much Dartford paid, which was very principled of Chiffinch, don't you agree? So has the King read it and hidden it somewhere, but nobody knows where, or has he lost it, or somebody taken it? If it has been removed, I think Dartford would pay a great deal to the man who had it.'

'Would he also kill to retrieve it?' I ask.

'The same thought occurred to me. Only if that was easier than payment. He would do whatever least disturbed his lace cuffs. Are you saying that your shipbuilder might have possessed it? That seems unlikely.'

'He had an interest in poetry, but I think he did not collect material of the sort you describe. He preferred Milton.'

'Not Dartford's verse? Then your shipbuilder was missing the very best. Nothing twists the knife like pentameters.'

'And is Dartford still looking?' I ask.

'I believe so. In which case he clearly did not retrieve it from the dead shipbuilder. But how would a shipbuilder lay his hands on that sort of thing anyway?'

'I've no idea,' I say. 'Though he had visited the Court and met the King.'

'And stolen the poem?'

'I doubt it.'

'As I say, a waste of your time. You have enough duties in the country. A man like you should come to London for pleasure and nothing else. Will you at least stay for a glass of wine? And just talk to me? Please? Good, intelligent conversation is so rare at Court and I have some excellent claret in the cellars here.'

Again, a hand on my arm. We've dealt with business and have the rest of the day to do as we please.

'I must return to Lincoln's Inn,' I say. 'Thank you, Lady Castlemaine. I'm most grateful for your time.'

'And what will you report back to my Lord Arlington?'

'I think,' I say, 'that you're right. It probably matters very little what I tell him.'

Chapter 15

From a Diary

Slept but ill, worrying about the Commission and whether they have been told of my selling cork to Pett for the ships, though I know he will say nothing. I heard the watchman pass by at one o'clock and two o'clock and three o'clock, each time calling out that it was a fine clear night. Fell at last into a slumber, only to be woken by my wife, who was rising early to begin washing the linen with the maids before the heat of the day. She consented that one of the maids should assist me in dressing, the boy still being sick, but not until the soiled sheets were soaking in the buck tub. So, I lay for a while, my mind going over my troubles again, then in comes Abigail saying that her mistress had told her to go to me and enquiring what I wished her to do. I asked her to bring me hot water and a towel, then brush my coat and comb my hair, which last thing she was doing when my wife came into our chamber and flew into a rage saying that here I was at my old tricks again. Then she turned on Abigail and called her a whore and a slut. I protested that the poor girl was merely seeing to my hair, which I have allowed to grow too long, but she would have it that I would use Abigail as I had used Deb before, and bring shame on her and myself. In all this Abigail was struck dumb, not knowing how or why Deb had left our service and being unable to account for my wife's anger towards me or her. Now I was wrath also, my wife having gone from washing one basket of dirty linen in front of the servants to washing another. Thus I accused her of having sent Abigail as a trap and of having entered the room for no purpose other than to spy on me. I swore a most solemn oath that I had not seen or spoken to Deb since she left the house, which is untrue but my wife has no way of knowing that. She said that she would find Deb and slit her nose and many other things not fit for a lady to say in the presence of her maid or for me to write here. Through all this Abigail was in tears and swearing that she would not stay in a house where she was treated thus and called a whore for fetching hot water, and that my wife was no better than her former mistress with accusations such as these, which made me wonder how she came to leave her last position and whether the girl might be persuaded to do more than comb my hair on some future occasion. After a while Elizabeth went out, slamming the chamber door, leaving me and Abigail to do as we wished, and I was left to comfort the poor girl, except that I knew not whether this was a further trick of Elizabeth's and that she was waiting outside, listening and ready to return at any moment. Thus I told Abigail to go back to my wife and that I could manage well enough on my own, which I did before we had servants and which most men do still I suppose.

So to the office but after a while comes a man from Lady Castlemaine asking me to go with him to Berkshire House on a matter of great urgency, he having her Ladyship's carriage outside the door and waiting upon me. So I went in her coach, having no time to get my own ready and my coachman being engaged in wringing lye out of the linen for my wife.

My Lady received me graciously, alone in her bedchamber, in a robe of Indian silk, which I admired greatly. She told me that Sir J. Grey had visited her and asked her questions, though she knew not his aim and he did not reveal it, pretending that my Lord A. had not made his true purpose clear. I said that he had also visited me and that I did not trust him, but thought that he would return soon to Essex. She asked if he had enquired into the matter of the Ruby and I said God forbid that he should do such a thing and that he appeared not to know of it. This comforted her, but troubled me, for I had clean forgot that Lord A. might ask him to ask about that too. I said that it was too long ago and that nobody now need fear Parliament's discovery of it, and that the King must surely know already and have decided to do nothing. She permitted me to kiss her hand and I walked back to the office through the City, my Lady having need of her carriage and there being fewer cut-throats now amongst the ruins, so many buildings going up again, with workmen all around during the day, though I should still not dare to do so alone after dark.

Home for dinner, the wash being done and Abigail and my wife friends again and no talk of her leaving, which pleases me strangely. After my wife and I had eaten we repaired to the leads of the house, Elizabeth, I and the servants, where I played upon my flute for everyone and Abigail sang a pretty ballad, and were very merry, though my wife said that Abigail sang ill and that I looked at her too much. Later to my study where I consulted my papers on the Ruby and gave thanks to God that we all conducted ourselves with such discretion. All except that fool Cade.

Chapter 16

Goring House

My Lord Arlington views me suspiciously. He has failed to supply me with precise instructions as to what I had to do and now he fears that I may not have done it.

He pulls himself up to his full height – not tall but taller than the Earl of Clarendon – and fingers his glossy nose-patch. 'Well?' he says.

'I have carried out my investigations as you requested, my Lord,' I say. 'The dockyard at Deptford is as inefficient as anything I have ever seen, the men there steal all they can easily carry away. I think Mr Symonds would run the yard well if he was allowed to do so, but he is so tied down by precedent and custom that he has no opportunity. Pepys could appoint a commissioner to run the yard, and he might do it better than Symonds. But that might stop some of Pepys's own games. So Symonds remains in place as acting manager and feathers his nest whenever he can. But the yard builds good ships for the King when they have no more pressing use for the timber and rope and tar. I assume that you know all that, however?'

'You found out nothing more than that?'

'What was I supposed to discover?'

'Did Symonds say nothing else to you?'

'Symonds resented Cade's efficiency. He called him a common thief for taking work away from the royal dockyards, merely because he could build ships more cheaply and faster.'

'As you say, being less bound by tradition, Cade had an unfair advantage,' says Arlington. 'He said nothing else?'

'He might have done if I knew what questions I was supposed to ask him.'

'Perhaps you should go back then. It is after all a pleasant trip to Deptford. I said that this work would not be arduous.'

'Except that somebody doesn't want me to complete it,' I say. 'Two ruffians attacked me in almost the same spot that Cade was killed.'

'You don't know who it was?'

'I'd recognise the two men. They didn't say who had sent them. But the message was clear enough: I should return to Essex and not trouble myself with naval matters. I think they may have been sent by Lord Dartford.'

'I'll ask him,' says Arlington.

'I already have,' I say. 'I paid him a visit. He said they were not sent by him. I don't quite believe him.'

'You were rash to show your hand so openly.'

'Rash but not altogether wrong. I think he revealed more than I did. He knew Cade and knew Mistress Cade even better. Mistress Cade's maid said that a nobleman visited the house the day after Cade died. I think that was Dartford.'

'What interest would he have in Mistress Cade?'

'I have no idea.'

'Dartford is dangerous.'

I nod. 'He told me in the clearest possible terms that you would not be able to protect me.'

'The arrogance of the man!' Arlington snorts. 'The . . . the . . .' But he can find no words to neatly summarise his indignation that Dartford would think thus. Of course, Arlington hasn't actually said that he would have protected me, even if he could.

'If I were an earl of moderately ancient lineage,' I say, 'rich from my recent marriage, and if I knew as many of the King's secrets as Dartford does, then I might be a little arrogant myself. My Lady Castlemaine believes however that Dartford can no longer be as sure of the King's support as he once was. Do you know anything of this poem that he sent to the King?'

Arlington laughs. 'The whole Court knows about that. Chiffinch told Lady Castlemaine, because, like everyone except the King, he is in her thrall, and my Lady told everyone else, because she wouldn't wish to lose an opportunity to be unpleasant.'

'She told them even though the poem disparages her?'

'Though it calls her a whore and a tyrant, it also calls her the King's mistress in chief. She'll settle for that.'

'But the King is still not aware of the satire?' I ask.

'Nobody dares tell him and admit they knew all along. Or perhaps everyone is simply enjoying the thing too much to want it to end. In the meantime, Dartford creeps round the King as if he were walking on a gravel path in bare feet.'

'And the poem is now lost?'

'Who told you that?' asks Arlington.

'Lady Castlemaine.'

'Has she asked you to find it?'

'No,' I say.

'Could you find it?'

'What do you think such a poem would be worth?' I ask. 'A whole book of them can be bought for a few Shillings – even Milton.'

'I was not offering to purchase it – merely enquiring if you knew where it was. Well, that need not concern us now. It is more important that you continue your investigation.'

'But I have clearly not discovered whatever it is you wish me to discover. I do not know how I am to do it. Perhaps after all I am the wrong man for the job. I have made too little progress. I have been threatened. My wife and son have been threatened indirectly. I think I should follow Lord Dartford's good advice and go home. Or perhaps I should follow Lady Castlemaine's counsel and enjoy myself while I can. Both seem better than another visit to Deptford. I am happy to be released from this task.'

Arlington is not happy. He knows I am right. But he doesn't have time to get somebody else to do the job in my place. Whatever it is I am supposed to discover, I am close to discovering it. I think he will try bribery next.

'Are you content to be a knight and no more than that?' Arlington enquires.

'Perfectly,' I say.

'The title will not pass to your son.'

'He has expressed no desire for one.'

'Your wife might like to be a peeress.'

'She despises new titles,' I say. 'She was a viscountess by her first marriage and it didn't live up to expectations. You could offer her a parrot, I suppose.'

'A parrot?'

'Cade tried to bribe Pepys with a parrot for Mrs Pepys.'

'And you think your wife would like a parrot?'

'No. She just wants me to go back to Essex. You could try bribing her with that.'

'Well, you can't go back to Essex. I am asking you to continue – for the good of your country.'

'But why, my Lord? Just consider – I uncover inefficiency and corruption at the dockyard, only to find that it is well known. I learn that most officials regard it as normal to accept bribes, but I think that also is nothing new. I should be grateful if you could make it clearer what it is that I am supposed to be discovering on your behalf.'

'Go back to Deptford,' he says. 'Ask Symonds about the Ruby. The Ruby – understand?'

'The Ruby?' I say. 'Cade said something about a Ruby. What does it signify?'

'I've no idea,' says Arlington. 'I never mentioned any such thing.'

'I'll go tomorrow,' I say. 'I have to go to the theatre next.'

'Pleasure?'

'Business.'

'Of course, I was forgetting you were a Puritan. I hope you have a most unpleasant visit.'

'Thank you, my Lord. I fully intend to.'

Chapter 17

Drury Lane

Inside the darkened theatre it could be almost any hour. Outside, it is not yet midday but Killigrew is already drunk – perhaps 'still drunk' would be a better description, because I think he has been drinking continuously since yesterday. Like many heavy drinkers he has the ability to continue imbibing indefinitely while appearing no drunker than he was before. And as the King's jester, as well as a theatre manager and playwright, drinking is an important part of his job. You could be the King's jester and stay sober, but you wouldn't enjoy it much. He sits on a stool on the stage, his periwig spread between his feet like a sleeping lapdog, his long coat draped over a painted wooden tree that formed part of the scenery of whichever play they acted yesterday. *Macbeth* perhaps. He rubs his lined forehead and scowls at us. He must be almost sixty years old and looks seventy. His hair is grey and his wispy, once-blond moustache is now white, stained wine-red at the edges. He wears a green velvet waistcoat, which even in this light is also clearly stained. His shoes are scuffed. One stocking is rolled down. He shifts uncomfortably on the low seat. He is beginning to realise that it was not a good choice at his age. But he is too drunk to stand with much dignity.

'This isn't acceptable, Killigrew,' says Aminta. 'If I am to write plays for you, I expect you to be in a fit state to produce them.'

Killigrew waves his hand, as if swatting away a fly, then belches loudly.

'Killigrew, nobody will write for you if you manage your affairs like this. All writers are feckless and idle or they would find honest work, but there are limits to what even we will tolerate.'

Killigrew shakes his head. 'I hate writers. I hate writers even worse than actors. God rot all of you. I have plays enough of my own that I can perform. I'll give them *Claricilla*. Now, there's a fine play for you. Can fill the house night after night with that. Comedy is all very well, and tragedy is very respectable, but tragicomedy is the pinnacle of the dramatist's art. Make them laugh. Make them cry. Make the men lust after the actresses and the ladies lust after the actors. Works every time. The old plays are better than the new ones anyway. Shakespeare's never in here complaining about his share of the profits.'

'Killigrew,' says Aminta, 'please stop rambling, just for a moment. We have agreed that you will produce my new play – merely a comedy, I admit – and that you will pay me the usual fee. If you won't rehearse the actors then I will. Where are they?'

'Where?'

'Yes, where?'

'I don't have any.'

'Even you cannot have upset them all. There must be some left.'

'And there you are wrong, my Lady. First one, then another. Then all of them. *Exeunt omnes*.'

'Mr Killigrew, the sooner you explain yourself clearly the sooner we shall be gone,'I say.'What has happened to the actors?'

'Attacked,'he says.'On the way home last night. My leading man. My wit. My villain. All waylaid by ruffians and told to stay away from this theatre if they didn't want worse to befall them. Ladies threatened too. God bless them all.'

'Who threatened them?' I ask urgently, because Killigrew has lapsed into the thoughtful silence that often precedes snoring.

Killigrew shakes his head as if to clear it, straightens his back and looks at me. 'A man in my position makes enemies, Sir John. You cannot be a wit and popular with all men, sir. The two things are like oil and vinegar – they bide together for a while but sooner or later they will go their separate ways in the salad. It is in their nature and they are not to be blamed for it. Somebody I have lampooned . . . or a friend of theirs. Someone I have speared with my wit. A man cannot be expected to remember everyone whom he has insulted. Not at this Court. And until I do remember, or he chooses to remind me, this theatre will be shut.'

'Which actors?' I ask.

Killigrew frowns. 'Michael Mohun, Charles Hart, Edward Kynaston,' he says, counting them off on his fingers. 'The cream of the London stage.'

'Where can they be found, Mr Killigrew?' I ask. 'Where are they now?'

'In some tavern or other.'

'The Royal Oak,' says Aminta. 'It is close by.'

The Royal Oak is indeed but a short walk. It is another of the ancient buildings that escaped the fire. I recognise Kynaston at once. I have seen him many times on stage. He was once a boy actor, specialising in women's roles at a time when women could not appear on stage. Now, in his late twenties, he plays the male lead and is a great favourite of the ladies of the town. There is still a feminine softness to him, as if he was reluctant to leave off playing the other sex entirely. His wit is said to be rapier sharp, but today he sits alone, staring into the distance, a tankard of ale before him.

'Killigrew said we'd find you here,' says Aminta. 'Are Hart and Mohun joining you?'

'They have run away,' he says, turning to us. His diction is clear and precise, the voice of one whose whole life has been spent on the stage. 'King Henry IV you see in front of you, but Hotspur is fled.'

'Killigrew says that you were all threatened,' I say.

'We were told politely not to appear on the stage for the next two weeks.'

'Who were the polite men?'

'I didn't recognise the lackey, but the threatener in chief was Robert Makepeace, a creature of Lord Dartford's. A nicely trimmed moustache and a new blue suit of clothes, with lace to the neck and cuffs of his shirt. Very genteel, but a ruffian for all that. I think he is nominally his Lordship's secretary, but he makes himself useful in any way he can, including work that might be beneath Dartford's dignity.'

'It sounds as if it was Makepeace who attacked me,' I say.

'The blue clothes, the moustache, the gentlemanly manner, the fist in the gut. So, it was Dartford, for all his denials.'

'Then Dartford's aim in attacking us was clearly to intimidate you,' says Kynaston. 'Thank you for the introduction to his Lordship. I'm sure we are all much obliged to you.'

'But, as you can see, my husband was not intimidated,' says Aminta, 'having a much exaggerated idea of his own ability as a swordsman. I'm surprised that Hart and Mohun were frightened off, though. They both fought for the King in the late wars. Hart was with Prince Rupert and was engaged in actions that were as pointless as they were dangerous.'

'It is one thing to fight to prevent Parliament tyrannising the country. An arm or a leg lost in such a contest can simply be put down to experience. It is another matter entirely to risk losing your looks and your career for a scurvy fortnight's work with Killigrew and a year of chasing him for payment. Of course, I was too young to have fought for anyone in the war and, not being in the habit of brawling in the street, the decision was, for me, a very simple one. With a blunt sword on stage, I am the nonpareil, but with a sharpened blade ... That is another kettle of fish. I am sorry, my Lady. I had clean forgot that we were to give one of your plays to the town. But without Mohun and Hart, there is nothing to be done. Killigrew has already offended so many actors and actresses that there is nobody he can use in their places – not while there is a Duke of York's company to offer employment to those leaving his service. Perhaps you should take your play to Betterton, who runs the Duke's Company.'

'I think we should just give Betterton the same problems that we have clearly given Killigrew,' says Aminta. 'No, we shall find a way of reopening the theatre and getting you all back on stage.'

'Well, I shall be there if the others are,' says Kynaston. 'Hart chides me for missing Marston Moor, so I must prove my valour in other ways.'

'You have acted the brave man often enough,' I say. 'You must understand what is needed.'

'Do not mock me,' he says firmly.

'I mock nobody,' I reply. 'As one of Arlington's agents, I have played many parts. I understand acting. The trick is to really believe you are who you pretend to be. Especially as a spy. You must not admit, even to yourself, that you were once somebody else. Not if you want to live. You must be the person others think you are from the moment you wake up until you fall asleep again. If you can, you must dream that person's dreams. Then perhaps you may wake up again, still alive and breathing, and start to play your part once more.'

'Do you actually have a plan for reopening the theatre?' I ask Aminta as we walk back down Drury Lane. 'Or are you saying that you hope we shall find a way of doing it in due course?'

'What I am saying, my dear husband, is that you got us all into this mess by allowing Mr Cade to be murdered. I am confident that you will find a way of getting us out of it again. I shall of course assist you. We have a name: Makepeace. I shall make it my business to find out more about him. In the meantime, you might like to find out what objection Dartford has to your investigations. As Arlington told you, you've been asking the wrong questions. I would suggest you go back and ask the right ones. Whatever they are.'

'I have to ask about the Ruby,' I say.

'Then ask about the Ruby,' she says. 'How difficult can that be?'

Chapter 18

From a Diary

At my desk all morning then home to dine, just my wife and I, upon a chine of beef, which she had prepared, though she had burned her hand in the making of it. And merry enough we were until her parrot flew across the room and shat on the table upon the new white linen cloth that she had spread there, though fortunately not in the dish as far as I could tell. I was forced to reprimand her for allowing the bird the liberty of the house, as she doth, and asked why it could not be kept in a cage as they are in other households, but she replied that it was wrong to confine one of God's creatures so, a bird or a wife. And so we fell to arguing about my not taking her to the play last week, though it was not fit for her to see and even I had blushed at some of the words that the players spoke. Then she accused me of not taking her so that I might better acquaint myself with the actresses afterwards, when they were in their retiring room and only half clothed. I said that I had stayed at the theatre only a short time after the play was done and merely to compliment

Mistress Knipp, whereat she called Mrs Knipp a harlot and a trollop, which I denied. She then produced from her pocket a note, which she presented me with and asked whether I was the 'Dapper Dicky' to whom it was addressed and whether the 'Barbary Allen' who had signed it was anyone she knew, though her producing the thing at that moment suggested that she already had the answer to both questions. I said that it must have been placed amongst my papers by chance, perhaps by one of my clerks who frequented the pit, and that I knew not who the writer or recipient might be and cared little what she did with it. So she smilingly replaced it in her pocket, from which I must find a way of retrieving it, lest she show it to Lady Penn or Lady Batten or somebody else who may guess the truth.

After dinner comes a man to the door, who introduces himself as one Truscott from the Tower Yard, whom I did indeed recall a little. He was ill at ease, and I took him to a nearby tavern, where we were unlikely to be overheard. I asked him if it was now known who had murdered Cade, but he claimed not, saying only that Cade had told several people that he intended to visit Sir J. Grey and that anyone almost might have lain in wait for him in the dark at Lincoln's Inn. I questioned him further, but if he knew he would not say. He then asked me about Lord Dartford and what business he might have with the Cades. I said that I knew not, telling him nothing of Cade being a party to the matter of the Ruby. He said that he had found some papers that had been in Cade's possession that mentioned Lord Dartford's name and mine together, but did not know what it signified, only that seeing our names thus he had hoped I might be able to help him. I asked to see the document, but he said it was but a list of names with the word 'Ruby' above, and he had found it amongst some papers that were in Cade's desk. I said that I couldn't guess what it might be, but that he should bring it to me if he wished, which he said was not necessary. This vexed me greatly, but I now could not insist I saw it without revealing more than I cared to, having denied all knowledge of it. Nor could I get him to say more about what he had discovered. I wondered greatly what his intention was but he next asked me whether I believed Lord D. was enamoured of Mistress Cade. I said I thought not, which seemed a source of comfort to him. I advised him, for his own safety, not to trouble his Lordship on the matter, which I feared he might do, and he left for the Tower, as he said, and I returned home, wondering whether I could obtain the list of names somehow, without exciting his suspicions or cupidity.

At my office, casting my accounts until it was too dark to see without a candle, which I would not have brought to me, my eyes being so painful to me and candlelight bad for them, then home, where the parrot is still at liberty. It landed on the table beside me and strutted around squawking (unless I am much mistaken) 'Dapper Dicky' over and over again, but flew away when I tried to seize it and throttle it.

Chapter 19

The Tower Yard

The great, grey mass of the Tower hangs above us, ravens circling it high in the leaden sky. The day is heavy and hot and moist, and we must have rain before sunset, I think, if London is to sleep tonight.

Truscott is talking to another man when I arrive. He is introduced to me as Morgan, the head carpenter with whom Truscott is sharing the duties of running the yard. Morgan is a solidly built man of middle height, more at home with wood than people. He excuses himself saying that he must go and oversee the gilding of the cabin. I think Truscott is happy to see him go.

'Things are clearly running well,' I say to Truscott, as the other man climbs the gangplank onto the ship and vanishes from sight onto the quarterdeck.

'Yes, but the job is almost complete. You must notice a slackening in the pace of everything. The men know once this job is done there will be no more. Everything is now done with great care and much remeasurement. It will be the most measured ship that ever set sail on the Tideway, sir.'

'Will you and Mistress Cade run the yard together if there is more work?'

He shakes his head sorrowfully. 'I thought that was her intention but there has been a misunderstanding between us. Somebody has been spreading lies ... She has left London in any case. I think she's in Kent ... with her brother ... I've tried writing to her there.'

'Your plans have come to nothing then.'

'What do you mean by that?'

'What I say. That things have not gone as you intended. Perhaps it would help if I said that I've heard you have been quite attentive to Mistress Cade in the past. I've also been told that you'd wanted to run the yard for a long time.'

He nods. 'Well, sir, if you know that much, then you'll know that Mistress Cade was not content with her house or her husband. She wanted to quit the house and the river. We had talked of her leaving Cade and our settling down together in Devon, where I come from. Of course, we would have had little money, but I could have got work. You said I wanted to run the yard here, and that is true, but I would have gone with her penniless to Devon rather than leave her with a husband that she did not love and who left her to deal with men like Pepys.'

'But better for you if Cade died and you had both the yard and the lady.'

'I didn't kill Mr Cade.'

'I haven't said that you did. Only that his death should have worked well for you. But you say you have now fallen out with her?'

'A minor misunderstanding. As I say, I have written to her.'

'And Cade suspected nothing of this – your dalliance with his wife?'

'I'm not sure ... He talked of taking a post in Deptford. I had no way of following them there. But she put him off with excuses.'

'And Cade never said anything to you?' I ask.

'He and I worked together as if I'd never set foot in his chamber. Nor did he complain to me of Pepys – or only of how it was wrong that we had to bribe him to get work. Of Pepys and his wife he said nothing at all. Perhaps he didn't know. Perhaps he preferred not to believe it.'

'The maid may have told him about Pepys,' I say. 'Certainly I think Cade knew how the land lay in that respect – at least by the time he came to see me. That may have changed his opinion on a number of things.'

'Then I see it all more clearly,' says Truscott, shaking his head. 'His attitude to Pepys changed a great deal towards the end. But everything Betsy says is not to be trusted, sir. Far from it. She's a stupid girl, with strange fancies, and Mr Cade wouldn't necessarily have believed anything she told him.'

'You said before that you didn't know Cade had decided to come and see me?'

Truscott looks at me. 'I didn't quite say that. You see, sir, his decision to denounce Pepys was, as I say, sudden. But he'd been troubled for some time, not quite knowing what to do. A couple of weeks before he died Mr Cade told me that he didn't think we should go on as we were, and we needed to do something about it. The defeat on the Medway troubled him a great deal – and the capture of the Dunbar. The Royal Charles was the greater loss to the Navy, but the Dunbar was ours – the finest we'd ever built. And it didn't go down fighting, with sails cut to ribbons and masts splintered to ragged stumps, which is no dishonour. It was towed away without a shot being fired. Not so much as a single drop of blood spilled. The crew did try to sink it to stop the Dutch capturing it, but the Dutch refloated it with ease once it had been deserted. Perhaps Betsy did tell him about Pepys, but I'm not sure that's why he came to you. The Medway was a bad business.'

'But he didn't ask you to accompany him to Lincoln's Inn?'

'No, sir.'

'His denouncing Pepys wasn't in your interest, was it? Because once everyone knew what was going on, it was the end of the Tower Yard? The end of your hopes of running it?'

'Yes, sir. I admit that.'

'Well, that's clearer anyway.'

'There's one thing I don't understand, though,' he says. 'Do you know anything about Lord Dartford and Mistress Cade, sir?'

'Only what Betsy told me. That he came to visit her.'

'Mistress Cade's attitude to me changed soon after that,' says Truscott.

I think of Mistress Cade's boast that she might become a nobleman's mistress, but dismiss it very quickly. 'I think it unlikely that he came to make a romantic proposal.'

'True, sir. Dartford has a new wife and, if that wasn't enough for him, he could have had as many ladies as he wished at Court. The ladies like a rakehell, sir, all lace and plumes and foul oaths and sweet endearments. He just had to smile at one of them. I'm sure he flattered her, sir, but I never did quite understand what it was he wanted. And, since men like Dartford are not safe to be around, I began to fear that she might be in danger from him. Then I discovered this. Does "Ruby" mean anything to you?'

Truscott goes over to the desk and picks up a sheet of paper. He hands it to me. It is headed: 'Ruby'.

> *Total value as estimated by TC: 6,230L 15s 4d*
> *1 share Lady Castlemaine*
> *1 share D of Bucks*
> *1 share ~~Lord Sandwich~~ D of Bucks*
> *1 share ~~Mr Pepys~~ Lord Dartford*

To this list has been added, in scribble: 'The man who unloaded and stored. One quarter of one share at the most – but offer him L100. Agreed with Lord D.'

'Two people have mentioned the Ruby to me,' I say, 'but one wouldn't tell me what it was and the other now can't. It looks as if it may have been profitable. And you think this may be why Lord Dartford came to see her?'

'I can't be certain, sir. I asked Mr Pepys about it, but he seemed not to know.'

'His share, whatever it was, seems to have been cancelled,' I say.

'As you say, sir. Still, I could tell he was worried by the mere mention of the list, though he pretended otherwise.'

'Have you asked Mistress Cade?'

'I did not discover the paper until after she left.'

'Perhaps she didn't know.'

'I think that the last line is in her hand,' says Truscott. 'So, what do you make of it all, sir?'

'I think that a decent man has died trying to do the right thing,' I say. 'You say Mr Cade was a good master to you?'

'True, sir.'

'And I could have prevented his death,' I say. 'The least we can do, Mr Truscott, is to bring his killer to justice.'

'And you think you will find him?'

'Yes, I think I shall. Where were you, by the way, the evening Mr Cade was killed?'

'Me? I was at home. I lodge close to the yard.'

'You didn't visit Mr Cade or Mistress Cade?'

'I . . . I did visit Mistress Cade, sir. Briefly.'

'Why?'

'To talk to her about Mr Cade's intentions.'

'And what did she say?'

'She said he would not be so foolish.'

'I'm not sure he was foolish exactly – but he was brave. I think he understood the danger very well. And I'm not sure the danger is past. I have been threatened and told to stop my investigation. It would seem I know too much – or somebody thinks I do.'

'And the rest of us?'

'Nobody knows you have seen this paper – except me and Pepys. And Mistress Cade is safe elsewhere. Don't worry, Mr Truscott. You may know some of the things that Mr Cade did, but I think you are in no danger yourself. I promise you I shall discover your master's killer. And then he will suffer the full penalty of the Law.'

Truscott looks at me for a long time before he speaks again.

'Thank you, sir,' he says. 'You are right, of course. And I know you will do the right thing.'

I slip the list into my pocket and smile at him. I smile at him in, it now occurs to me, much the same way that I smiled at Cade. Dartford's name on the list provides the reason for his visit to Mistress Cade and the reason for him wanting Cade dead. But Dartford cannot possibly know that Truscott has seen the list. So Truscott really is in no danger.

But I am beginning to understand why I have to enquire about the Ruby.

The fastest way to Deptford is a sailing boat, working its way down the river with a good wind and an ebb tide. This is the closest to flying that a man can get, the shore skimming past in the middle distance, the gentle splash of clean, brackish water on the bows. The boatman is no more talkative than I need him to be. I am allowed to sit and watch the world go by and think how to get the better of Dartford. The heat is not so great out here on the water, but the clouds are now gathering in force, dark and menacing over the flat, marshy Kentish shoreline, like the giant grey sails of an infernal Dutch fleet.

The boatman lands me at the dockyard and I tell him to wait until my business is done, for he will not easily find another passenger out here and I shall not easily find another boat to return me to the City.

I find Abel Symonds at a late dinner. He has had a genuinely busy morning with deliveries of timber and pitch to check. There are also rumours of a visit from Mr Pepys, and much precautionary tidying to be done, both of stock and paperwork. But Symonds is content that I see things as they are. He thinks he has nothing to fear from Arlington, who has no business interfering in naval matters, and who will be overruled by the Duke of York if he starts to raise objections to the way the yard is run.

'A glass or two of Canary, Sir John?' he enquires. 'We can take our wine in the garden. It is cooler there than here in the house. Truly I think we are in for a storm this afternoon, but not yet. If your business is brief you may get back to the City in time to avoid a drenching.'

I take a seat and sip the Canary. It is very good. Symonds does not need to worry about the cost of his wine. Of course, if no duty has been levied on it, it would be considerably cheaper than the price others pay. And the marshes round here are a good place to land all manner of cargo.

I put the glass down. 'I was wondering, Mr Symonds, whether you could tell me anything about the Ruby?'

'The Ruby, what's that then?' he asks, with such innocence that he can only be lying.

'I was told you knew about it,' I say.

He shrugs, then looks away across the river to the Isle of Dogs, so flat as to be scarcely visible. 'I know a bit about a lot of things. Why don't you tell me what you know? Then I might tell you a bit more, or I might choose not to.'

'I know Pepys was involved,' I say.

'You'll need to do better than that.' He grins a crooked smile.

'And Lady Castlemaine,' I say. 'And the Duke of Buckingham. And Lord Dartford. And you benefited too. But they gave you no more than they had to – they offered you a paltry hundred Pounds, in spite of your taking all the risk. I'd say you were robbed blind. Those lords . . . They don't give a fig for the working man, do they? Not even Buckingham.'

Much of this is a guess, but knowing Symonds I have no doubt that this is exactly what he'll believe too – whatever the Ruby is or was and however much he got. It will have been too little for whatever it was he did. In his view, people like him always get swindled. It's the way of the world.

'Well, that's the truth,' he says at length. He pours me another glass of Canary, because I am his friend and he is no more deceived that I am proper aristocracy than Aminta is.

'So, tell me about the Ruby,' I say.

'Of which I think you still know very little,' he says with a confidence that will shortly be undone. 'So, tell me, why should I help you? What's in it for me?'

'With luck, nothing at all. You may get away scot free.'

He looks at me through narrowed eyes. 'Is that some sort of threat?'

'Yes, of course it is. I apologise if I was in any way unclear in that respect.'

'You want me to incriminate myself in exchange for nothing at all? Go back to London. I won't do it, Sir John.'

'There I must disagree with you, because you will do it. You know Buckingham is involved. You know Lady Castlemaine is involved. I think you may be the man who arranged the storage of the goods.' I pause, because, honestly, even that last bit is a guess. What follows I am definitely just making up. 'You could have hidden a lot in a yard like yours, with wagons coming and going the whole time and nobody asking many questions. Arlington will wish to bring down his enemies – Buckingham and anyone who is his friend. But he'll look after his allies, whatever they may have done. Which side do you wish to be on, Mr Symonds? The side that lives happily or the side that meets with an unfortunate accident?'

'He can't make that happen.'

'Arlington has spies everywhere, Mr Symonds. It isn't a question of whether any of your men are in his pay – it is just a question of how many.'

Symonds looks at me. What I say could be true. Only Arlington would know for sure. But even Symonds knows that only a fool would make an enemy of Arlington. He's not much of a friend, but you still wouldn't want to be his enemy.

'You'll guarantee my safety? If I tell you what you want to know?'

'Arlington does not work on those terms, and if he did I'm not authorised to offer them. Not to you, Mr Symonds. But I'll report back to my Lord what I have found out. Then he can arrange to deal with you as he chooses. You can of course apply to the Duke of Buckingham for protection. I'm sure your safety will be his first concern. After all, he's dealt with you fairly so far, hasn't he?'

'You're the son of a whore, Grey,' he says.

'I've never claimed otherwise,' I say. 'Nor, to be fair, has my mother.'

He pours himself another glass of wine, then, on second thoughts, pours me one too.

'You know the Ruby is a ship?' he says.

Well, I do now. I nod.

'It was a prize ship – captured a few years ago when we were fighting the French.'

'Go on,' I say.

'And you understand how these things work, I take it?'

'Feel free to explain,' I say.

'When a foreign ship is taken, the captain and crew of the ship that takes it are entitled to a reward from the cargo it carries. But the prize must first be taken into port so that the King or his agents may view the contents and value them. Only then is it permissible to break bulk, as they call it, and start to distribute the goods between the King and the crew and anyone else that the King wishes to reward. So far, so good?'

'Yes.'

'Breaking bulk too soon is an offence against His Majesty and, to be plain, theft pure and simple.'

'And that's what happened to the Ruby?'

'Lord Sandwich, Pepys's patron, was the first to get his hands on the vessel, while it was still moored at the mouth of the Thames. Before the King even knew the ship was taken, Sandwich went on board and assessed the value. Claiming that the King had already given him permission to do so, as a mark of his utmost favour, Sandwich divided up the contents into lots and sold them off at advantageous rates to his friends. Lady Castlemaine bought a share, hoping to sell quickly for a profit. So did her cousin the Duke of Buckingham. But they needed somebody on the Navy Board to give the action some semblance of legality, so Pepys was offered a share too. Then Sir William Coventry, the Duke of York's secretary, got to hear of it and commented that the procedure adopted was "unusual". That was enough to scare everyone shitless. There was complete panic amongst those who had bought into it. Sandwich sold his remaining share to Buckingham for almost nothing. Pepys was almost as quick and offered his at some considerable discount to somebody or other.'

'The Earl of Dartford,' I say.

'So, you know that too, do you? Yes, it was Dartford that Pepys sold to. Still, the rest held their nerve and we managed to get most of the gear ashore by moonlight – it took us two nights, loading the sacks into skiffs and rowing them ashore, then storing everything in one of the warehouses under old sailcloth until we could get carts in to take them to London.

By the time the Navy Board arrived in an official capacity, the ship was empty and I was obliged to swear an oath to Pepys that the ship had been carrying nothing and that the reports of thousands of Pounds-worth of spices was no more than a tale told by ignorant French sailors. Of course Pepys knew I was lying and I knew he knew, but it was reported back to the Duke of York as a fact. It was the beginning of the end for the honest Coventry. Buckingham never forgave him and that's why, when he had the chance, he made sure that Coventry was arrested and sent to the Tower.'

'So I heard,' I say. 'And this is what Arlington was after?'

'He's your master. If you don't know then nobody does. But from what you say, he wants to use it to bring Buckingham down and maybe wants you to report in such a way that his ally, Lady Castlemaine, emerges smelling of lavender and roses.'

Well yes, of course. That explains everything. This was what I had to stumble on during my investigation. This is why he couldn't wait for the Brooke House Committee to report. They might have said too much. Better to pre-empt them. Arlington wants the guilty punished, but only some of them.

'So it would seem,' I say. 'Buckingham and his ally Dartford will suffer a defeat. Whether it is fatal, whether the King will pardon everyone in sight – these things remain to be seen. But Arlington will have scored a major victory. One thing still puzzles me – what did Cade know of it?'

'We needed skiffs from somewhere other than this yard to transport the goods. Otherwise word would have been all over the yard before the night was out. Cade supplied the skiffs. We also used his wagons for transport. But Pepys trusted Cade more than he trusted me. He was appointed to keep records of the whole cargo and see it was fairly divided up. He knew exactly what had gone where. I don't know what they paid him, but more than me.'

'Why should Dartford want to kill Cade?'

'Who says he did?'

'Unless . . . unless Cade tried to put the squeeze on Dartford, threatening to reveal what he knew.'

Symonds narrows his eyes. 'That was a long time ago. Cade was a fool. You don't try things like that on with Dartford. He sent Cade packing.'

'But that's why, when Arlington makes up his mind to ask me to investigate, Cade dies at Dartford's hand?'

'Maybe. Maybe not. As I say, Dartford wasn't too worried when Cade tried to blackmail him. The others might have been, but not Dartford.'

'Did the others know what Cade had tried to do?'

'The blackmail? Probably. Word would have got round.'

I look at Symonds. Is he trying to protect Dartford? Or place the blame elsewhere?

'Who else was involved in the Ruby business?' I ask.

'Some of Cade's men. But they were well paid to keep quiet.'

'Truscott?' I ask.

Truscott claimed not to know of the Ruby, but few people are making much effort to tell me the truth at the moment. Symonds reply may at least tell me whether Truscott is lying.

Symonds smiles. 'Truscott would've only just arrived at the yard then. Cade thought him too honest for his own good and ours. He was kept in ignorance – sent off somewhere that night so that he didn't see. Safer all round. He knows nothing – unless he's been doing a bit of digging since Cade died? Has he? That wouldn't be wise.'

I shake my head. There's no reason why Symonds should be told what Truscott knows. But who has Truscott already informed that he has the Ruby list? Symonds is right. That may not have been wise.

'Very well,' says Symonds. 'I've helped you and I expect something in return, Sir John. I want you to keep me out of it as much as you can.'

'I'll try, but I can't promise you anything.'

'Trying's enough. I trust you to do the right thing.'

I nod.

'I have to go and inspect a delivery now,' says Symonds. 'But my maid will get you some food before you travel back.'

'There's no need.'

'I insist. To show you there's no hard feelings on my part. To show we're on the same side now. I'd be honoured if you'd accept my hospitality, as part of the pact between us. Your boatman will wait.'

But he does not. When I return to the jetty I find that he has decided to forgo my fare and to take somebody else back to London. I wait an hour and a half on the quayside before another boat can be found willing to take me back.

The rain has so far held off, but the sky is almost black when I finally board the boat that will return me to London.

'I'll need to charge you two Shillings since it is so late in the day and the tide against us,' says the boatman optimistically.

'I'll pay the usual fare,' I say. 'A Shilling, and that's generous since we'll be back well before sunset.'

He shakes his head. A true gentleman would have concurred without hesitation.

'But you can have half a crown if we get back before the rain,' I say.

He laughs and looks at the sky. That concession will cost me nothing. Indeed, fat drops of water start to hit the river almost as soon as we are out in the stream. The boat has no tilt to protect passengers from the elements, and we are both very wet very quickly. The dark sky is soon lit up with brilliant white flashes. The boatman is not displeased. I am getting what I deserve for refusing to be imposed upon.

'Could be struck by lightning out here on the river,' he says cheerfully, the rain running off the brim of his hat. 'That's how it is, sir. Lightning always strikes the highest thing around. That's us at the moment, and you're a good three inches taller than I am, I'm happy to say.'

'It will strike the mast first,' I say.

'And leave us drifting out to sea,' he says cheerfully. 'With no mast and a storm raging, I doubt we'll ever come back to land alive.'

'If the mast goes, we'll just have to man the sweeps,' I say. 'Don't worry – I've done it before. But I'd prefer to get to London under sail if we can. You'll find the incoming tide's stronger if you steer closer to the Kent shore.'

'You've spent time on this stretch of river in foul weather then?' he asks sarcastically. 'You know all of the muddy creeks?'

'Yes,' I say. 'At least the ones where you might land contraband or a foreign spy.'

'And you rowed yourself?'

'Only after I had to shoot the boatman. He proved to be in the pay of somebody else entirely. You can't afford to be out on the river at night with a man you don't quite trust.'

My boatman looks at me, clearly wondering whether I am

armed. I settle back in my seat. The wood is hard but more comfortable than the saddle of a trotting horse. I am already so wet that a little more rain makes no difference. Things could be worse. I can, for a little while, forget Pepys and Arlington and Dartford and my Lady Castlemaine.

Suddenly the whole of the Isle of Dogs is lit up. The clap of thunder is deafening. The boatman jumps at the sound. Perhaps his nerves are not good.

'Steer her to port,' I say. 'I've told you: I'd like to be back before dark.'

With ill grace, he pulls the rudder round and we edge gradually towards Kent.

We arrive back at London Bridge with the sun low in the sky. The rain has ceased and the ground is drying. It has been a long day. I walk along the ruined shore, then out of the City, close to the Temple. Finally I skirt the walls until I reach Lincoln's Inn, where I stroll past the porter, who is huddling in his lodge and surprised to see me so wet and so cheerful.

I have, I think, a lot to report back to Aminta and Will. They, however, have news for me, and it cannot wait until I have divested myself of my dripping clothes.

'Mr Truscott has been found hanged,' says Will.

'How?' I ask.

'By his own hand, it would appear,' says Will.

'Who reported it?'

'Mistress Cade. She returned home from Kent, expecting to find Truscott waiting at her house. When he was not, she visited the yard and found him hanging from a beam in the warehouse. The men had gone home. She came straight here less than half an hour ago.'

'Not to the magistrate?'

'She doesn't trust them. She doesn't trust anyone. Too many people she knows are dying suddenly and violently. She has gone back to her house, where she will be waiting for you. She wants you to go with her to the Tower Yard as soon as you can.'

Too many people dying suddenly and violently. That's true enough.

'I'll go at once,' I say. 'This is my fault, Will, every bit as much as Cade's death was my fault.'

'I'll come with you,' says Will. 'I think it may be time to watch your back.'

'Yes,' I say. 'Thank you, Will. I think you may be right. I need a dry shirt and dry breeches and stockings. Then, if you'd be kind enough to load and prime a couple of pistols, we'll be on our way.'

Chapter 20

Amongst the Ashes

We have a moon to guide us, but we engage a link boy on the western edges of the ruins. Two are less likely to be attacked than one, and three are less likely to be attacked than two, even if one of those three is aged thirteen and a half and malnourished since birth. We cross the River Fleet, the link boy's torch reflecting red on its slowly flowing water. Then we enter the City through one of its great stone gates, and begin a steady but cautious progress through the wasteland that was once London. From time to time we stop, whenever the boy's experienced eyes catch sight of something he thinks is suspicious – or perhaps he sees nothing but seeks to increase our gratitude for a safe passage and augment the size of his tip. The light of the torch flickers on the grey shells of the buildings destroyed by the fire. Our boy uses the dark bulk of St Paul's as a landmark to steer by, as I have myself in the past. Houses can be rebuilt quickly, but this half-fallen giant will be one of the sights of London for many years to come. As with so many other things, there is no agreement as to what to do with the great cathedral – to attempt a repair or to start afresh. The King will decide, eventually, when more pressing matters have been dealt with. In the meantime ivy creeps up the walls and a small forest is establishing itself in the nave.

'If we're stopped,' says the boy portentously, 'then just hand over your money. Don't annoy them. There are some desperate men here.'

'We're armed,' I say.

'Then hand over your weapons first. You don't want to get shot by mistake. I don't want you getting me shot either.'

He holds up his torch so that he may see our reaction to his wise advice. For the first time, I think, he notices the scar on my face. His knowing smile fades. He swallows hard.

'But, of course, I'll get you to the Tower as fast as I can,' he says. 'This way, gentlemen. Be careful. The road is not as even as it once was and you're not as young as I am.'

Truscott's body is very still at the end of the rope. For some time he must have swung to and fro, less and less with each slow spin, until finally, perhaps while I was still waiting impatiently on the quay for a boat, it reached this equilibrium and stayed there. In the lantern light his shadowy face looks down on us, staring with permanent amazement at the world he has left.

I have already mounted a ladder so that I can look Truscott in the eye, feel his arms and legs and shoulders. The rope round his neck is thick and serviceable. It has marked his skin, but not cut into it. There is a pale furrow but there is no discolouration. His eyes are bulging. His tongue is swollen and hanging out. Even in this poor candlelight, I can see the small spots on his face that tell of death by strangulation. Now I am close to him, I am aware of a distinct scent of brandy. Looking down, I see an empty bottle, not far away on one of the benches. Truscott's limbs are starting to stiffen but are not yet rigid. I think I know the cause and time of death.

Back on the rough wooden floor, my shoes powdered with fresh sawdust, I survey the scene again.

'You've touched nothing?' I ask Mistress Cade.

She shakes her head.

There is an overturned stool a little way off. Truscott must have mounted it, tied the rope round his neck and then kicked it away. A good strong kick to send it that far. Yes, a very strong and determined kick. Nothing else is disturbed here. There is no sign of a fight. I examine Truscott's hands and the knuckles in particular. There are some slight abrasions – fresh ones. I have already examined the head. There are no signs of blows being struck there. His appearance is not all that you might wish, but he has not been beaten up. Not today. On the other hand, he may have been in a fight.

'He wouldn't have needed to tie a rope to the beam,' I say. 'There are plenty already in place for lifting things.'

'True,' says Will. 'He could have taken his choice of those already there.'

'Were the doors locked?' I ask Mistress Cade.

'No, they were not,' she says.

I shrug. It probably proves nothing. They would be unlocked during the day. Truscott would have told the men he would lock up.

'Has anything been taken?' I ask.

'How would I know?' she asks. 'Having to live in this godforsaken spot was bad enough. I did not frequent my husband's warehouses more than I had to. They are no place for a gentlewoman.'

'It would seem that the poor man hanged himself this evening,' says Will. 'I can smell the brandy even from here. He must have drunk some to steady his nerve. The rope was already supplied. He had merely to mount the stool and tie it round his neck.'

'Unless somebody else saved him the trouble of tying it,' I say. 'Perhaps somebody overcame him while he was drunk. He had no reason at all to kill himself, or none that we know of. On the other hand, like Thomas Cade, he possessed information that might have incriminated others. The abrasions on his knuckles suggest a recent struggle, albeit a brief one. I think he was surprised here in the warehouse, after the workmen had left for the day. He was quickly overpowered and strangled. Then he was strung up, as you see him, using a rope intended for lifting heavy objects. One man could have done that on his own. His killer, or killers, then tidied up as much as they needed to, placed the stool thus, for us to admire – but, I think, a little further off than he would have actually kicked it – and departed through the unlocked door. I think this is no suicide.'

'That is charitable of you, sir,' says Will, 'since suicide is a crime and the man's possessions could be forfeit to the Crown, to the detriment of his family.'

'He told me he had no family,' says Mistress Cade.

'Perhaps that is as well,' I say, 'since it will be the Coroner's decision rather than mine and he may not agree, unless and until I can prove it is Dartford's men who did this.'

'There's little here to show that,' says Will.

'Then I shall have to prove it in other ways,' I say. 'In the meantime, we'll need to send for the constable or risk being fined for not doing so. If Mistress Cade will give us directions, we'll report it on our way back to Lincoln's Inn. Then I shall return tomorrow to see if we can make out anything else by daylight.'

When I return in the morning, the coroner is already there. The body has been cut down and is lying on one of the solid woodworking benches. The coroner is in the process of washing his hands, in a basin that somebody has kindly provided. I introduce myself.

'So why did Mistress Cade send for you last night rather than go for the constable straight away?' he asks, picking up a towel.

'I had already questioned Truscott on a matter for Lord Arlington,' I say. 'Her husband was attacked at Lincoln's Inn and killed a few days ago. His death related, I believe, to Lord Arlington's enquiry – as did this death. I think there is a connection between the two events.'

'Between an attack on the other side of London and a suicide here in the yard?' he asks, rubbing his hands carefully on the cloth. He is not entirely convinced.

'Yes,' I say. 'This may not be a suicide as it appears to be. Did you see the abrasions on the knuckles?'

'I did, but the man works with his hands, does he not? Such minor injuries are common enough amongst working men. There are also some bruises on his arms. They might have been acquired in a fight, but equally it may have been some accident in the yard.'

I look at the bruises – they are quite narrow and straight, as if he had been struck repeatedly with a stick.

'He could have been attacked, then strangled and strung up.'

'Could have been. But equally he could have drunk the brandy in that bottle over there then hanged himself from a rope already conveniently in place. If he was in a fight yesterday, there's nothing to suggest that it took place here and the wounds are very slight. The blows to the arms are the sort of knock you might give to somebody to force him to drop a weapon – I'll grant you that – but they are scarcely intended to kill or even cause serious harm. He died by asphyxiation. There are no separate marks to indicate prior strangulation.'

'They could be hidden by the later marks.'

'Possibly.' The coroner is not convinced.

'But why should he kill himself?' I ask.

'Who can say? With many suicides I can find few good reasons why the dead man chose to end his life in that way. But what may seem a molehill to most of us is an intolerable mountain to others. The yard faced closure, did it not? He would have lost his employment. The empty bottle suggests a man drowning his sorrows.'

'He'd have found work elsewhere easily enough.'

'But perhaps not at such a congenial workplace. I understand from Mistress Cade he had some hopes of taking over the yard in due course. Those hopes would have been cruelly dashed.'

'He left no note – no explanation,' I say.

'As is often the case,' says the coroner. He lets the towel fall back on the bench, next to the body. 'Perhaps what you say is true. Perhaps he was surprised and attacked while drunk and unable to defend himself. Perhaps a weapon was knocked from his hands. Perhaps he was strangled, or half strangled, and then strung up, just as you suggest. But all of that is mere supposition. I must base my findings on the facts. What we have before us is a man who was found hanging from a rope, with no evidence of any struggle that preceded the hanging.'

'So you will report that it is suicide?' I ask.

'What else can I do? What evidence could I present to a jury that it is anything other than what it seems to be?'

'You have no objection if I look round the warehouse?'

'I've done all I intend to do, Sir John. There will need to be an inquest, but my conclusions are already clear. If Mistress Cade has no objection to your being here, then I shall not impede you. I would wish to do nothing that would prevent your making a full and thorough report to Lord Arlington. Make it as fanciful as you wish. That is your affair entirely.'

When he has gone I make a more detailed search of the warehouse, but Truscott's killers have left nothing that will be of use to me. I walk back to the Cades' house. I knock at the door. There is no reply but the door opens when I give it a slight push. Mistress Cade is in the sitting room, staring at the empty fireplace. She looks up as I enter. Her face is as near expressionless as a face can be.

'I'm sorry,' I say. 'I have found nothing more. The coroner thinks it was suicide. I think Mr Truscott has been murdered as your husband was, but it will be difficult to prove.'

'But you think it is murder?' she says. 'Not suicide? Was there a note by the body?'

'Suicides do not always leave a note,' I say. 'Its absence is conclusive of nothing.'

'No, not something written by him, something written to him ... Something I wrote to him.'

'No,' I say. 'There was nothing at all there. And the coroner would have said if he had found something. What would you have expected him to have with him?'

She shakes her head. 'I am sorry, Mr Grey, it's the shock. Ignore me. First my husband's death, now this ... Harry Truscott wrote to me in Kent, asking me to return to London. I sent word that I would. But he must have been dead before I arrived here. And now I don't know if he even received my letter. If I'd come back earlier or never gone ... If it is murder, is his death connected to my husband's?'

'I think your husband was killed because he helped transport the goods from the Ruby and his evidence would have inconvenienced Dartford – and Pepys and Lady Castlemaine.'

'You know about the Ruby, then?'

'I know enough.'

'Well, then you'll know Harry had nothing to do with it.'

'I know he was told nothing at the time, but he'd recently found papers relating to it. Anyway, somebody may quite reasonably have thought that, as the deputy here, Truscott knew as much as your husband did. That person could also have discovered that Truscott had spoken to me.'

She looks at me blankly, then shakes her head.

'If I'd got back earlier ...' she repeats.

'Harry Truscott told me that you and he had had a disagreement,' I say.

'Then you know about us? That we'd talked of going away together to Devon?'

'Yes. Your husband must have suspected something, surely?'

'I suppose so. Cade kept talking about getting the commissioner's job at Deptford – nice house, plenty of opportunities for making money on the side. Pepys has kept the post open for a long time because it suits him to do so, but Cade reckoned he could persuade Pepys to appoint him, if they split the profits equitably. But Harry couldn't have come with us. That wasn't part of Cade's plan. So it would have been the end of Harry and me. Then Cade was killed. Harry wanted us to stay on – try to run the yard together. He'd always wanted to be master of his own shipyard. I said I'd think about it. Then there was a misunderstanding . . .'

'What was it about?'

'That doesn't matter now. Except that, if I hadn't left London, he might not have died like that. But he wouldn't have killed himself, Mr Grey . . .'

Yes, Truscott has been unlucky. I think his killer may have assumed he knew more than he did. But I also feel sorry for Thomas Cade. A man trying to save a failing yard, a man trying to save his marriage, a man trying to do right, albeit a little late, by his King. A man betrayed by his wife and his trusted deputy. A man let down by the lawyer he went to see to put things right.

'I think Dartford killed them both,' I say. 'Dartford came to see you, didn't he? The day after your husband died?'

'Who told you that?'

'Your maid,' I say.

'She's a fool – too drunk most of the time to know what was happening but very impressed by a bit of Brussels lace. Yes, Dartford came round here. That's all.'

'To ask about the Ruby?'

She shakes her head. 'I never did work out what he really wanted. He just asked what papers Cade had hidden away. It was a difficult meeting. You see Cade had tried to get Dartford to loan us some money on the back of our knowing about his involvement in the Ruby.'

'It's usually called blackmail.'

'It was a loan. A loan to a friend with whom he had shared some difficult times. It goes without saying that we didn't get our loan. Dartford's no fool. He wasn't going to let Cade push him around.'

'And, this time, Dartford really said nothing to you about the Ruby?'

'He asked about my husband's papers, but in such a vague way that I couldn't tell what he meant. It would have been very easy for him to ask outright if it was about the Ruby – that was scarcely a secret between us, was it? He was very polite, bearing in mind our past history, and he paid me many compliments. I began to think that maybe it was me he was after ... It's true that when I could provide no papers he became very unpleasant, but Pepys could be like that too – charming one moment, threatening the next. So, I still wasn't sure. But, yes, the Ruby ... what other papers could my husband possibly have had that might concern Dartford?'

'Dartford is looking for a poem – a poem he'd written that could hang him near enough, if it was found. It vanished from the King's chambers at Whitehall. At about the same time, as far as I can tell, the King sketched a ship on the back of a piece of paper and gave it to your husband.'

'And that's what he was really after? Why didn't he say? I could have told him I'd seen no such thing.'

'And give you the chance to blackmail him again, if you did happen to have it?'

'Only if I'd known what it was.'

'Of course, if he thought you did have it and were withholding it, he might have killed to get it.'

She considers this. 'True enough. Perhaps it's all as well.

As I say, when it was clear I couldn't help him, he was much less obliging than before. He told me I should burn any of Cade's papers that I came across, if I knew what was good for me. He looked at me and I looked back, and I saw the Devil, as clear as day. So, I burned everything I could. I just kept the contract – because maybe Pepys would have come good after all. But as for the rest ... well, I wouldn't want to see Dartford round here again. Not for any money. I'd do it to bring Harry Truscott back – I'd do anything to bring Harry back – but not even the Devil can work that trick.'

'You have done well,' says Arlington.

Today he wears a dark green woollen suit of clothes, the long coat and waistcoat both almost down to his knees, as ever with much lace at the neck and wrists, and a black beaver hat, broad and round. He keeps his hat on in my presence. I remove mine. Our positions in society dictate that is how it should be. Just occasionally I feel that I might like to be a duke.

'I'm running out of living witnesses,' I say, 'but I think Symonds would testify against both Buckingham and Dartford, given adequate assurances about his personal safety.'

'And the list?'

I take it out of my pocket and show it to him.

'It's very little,' I say.

'I can make it enough.'

'I assume that it is Buckingham and Dartford that you wish to bring down?' I say.

'As I have said, it is not a question of what I want, but what the King wants. It is for him to decide what to do with your report and this piece of paper. Buckingham is an ever-present danger. Having been brought up in the royal household, he believes himself to be almost royal. He looks at himself and he looks at the King and ponders the question: who is the more fit to rule? If the present King were not the son of the last King, would it occur to anyone to appoint him to the position? I merely pose a hypothetical question, you understand; I would not presume to answer it. God appoints kings and perhaps he knows something that the rest of us don't.'

'When the present King came in,' I say, 'he had much support. He has squandered a vast treasury of good will.'

Arlington nods. 'Indeed. And one day soon the country might start to think – again I speak hypothetically – we deposed one Stuart for a Cromwell, why should we not depose another for a Villiers? A maid can lose her virginity once only. The second time her conscience is easy.'

'I walked the battlefields in the 1640s,' I say, 'and saw the outcome of thinking such as that. The dead piled in heaps, as if they had neither mothers nor children to mourn them. The living cut to bloody rags. And black smoke rising from over the hill, where the nearest village lay.'

'And God forfend that we should have such a war again, Sir John. On the other hand our present King fled after the Battle of Worcester and did not return until it was safe to do so. He does not wish to fight. Buckingham may not be reckoning on a long campaign.'

'You sound almost like a supporter of the Duke,' I say.

'I am a supporter of the King. I am at all times the supporter of the rightful King, recognised by Parliament and anointed by God through the agency of his one true church.' He smiles.

Well, neither the present King nor Buckingham could find anything to object to there. The Pope would probably find it acceptable too.

'These are not matters for a simple country squire,' I say. 'I must leave Buckingham to you. But Dartford has caused two men to be killed.'

'Do you have proof?'

'Only that he had a motive for wanting both dead and that he sent men to threaten me as well.'

'We would need much more than you have told me so far to convict him in a court of Law. Of course, witnesses can be purchased quite cheaply if we have to arrange a fair trial.'

'So that was what it was all about?' I ask. 'You wanted me to produce a witness and that list, or something like it. I could have done it in half the time if you had just told me.'

'It was better like that. I have not moved against anyone – they cannot blame me in any way. You merely stumbled accidentally upon this information while undertaking another task for the King. We can both say that – we can swear it in court, without committing perjury. I mean, if perjury troubled you at all.'

'And, if things do go wrong, if anyone threatens retribution . . .'

'I can blame you. Yes, that is helpful too. I probably owe you a small favour, Sir John.'

'Good,' I say. 'I'd like to see Dartford prosecuted for murder.'

'I said a small favour.'

'Then at least I'd like to be allowed to gather the evidence.'

'Allowed to gather evidence against a murderer? Of course. Who could possibly object to that? As things stand at present, anyway.'

* * *

When I finally return to Lincoln's Inn, I am very tired and in need of dinner, but Will announces that I have a visitor.

'Send him away, Will,' I say.

'I can't, sir.'

'Will, one of your many virtues is being able to get rid of any litigant that I do not wish to see. Tell him I am busy.'

'That isn't possible, Sir John. It's not my place to say such things to him.'

'Then I'll tell him myself,' I say.

I stride into my office. The man is sitting with his back to me, with his hat on his head in my own chambers, his luxuriant black periwig flowing over the shoulders of a rich black velvet coat with white pinking. A man with money and a high opinion of himself, but I shall still explain to him that his presence is not required.

'Now, look here, my good fellow,' I say. 'Your . . .'

He turns. There is a smile on his dark-jowled face. He runs one finger along his rich sable moustache. I wrench my hat from my head and bow very low.

'Your Majesty's most humble servant,' I say to him.

Chapter 21

In the Presence of the King's Most Gracious Majesty

'Please sit, Sir John,' he says, indicating my second-best chair.
'Thank you, sir,' I say.

'I suppose you are wondering why I am here?'

'I do not receive kings in my chambers every day. Most kings need no legal advice. Or not from me.'

'Then most kings are fools – and please do not feel obliged to deny that on my account.'

'I am, of course, Your Majesty's servant to command, in that or any other respect. How can I be of service to you?'

The King leans forward in my chair. 'You have been undertaking some work for Lord Arlington?'

'Yes, Your Majesty.'

'Would you care to tell me what you were asked to do?'

Already I can see that this is a question that may need to be answered with care.

'My Lord asked me to undertake an investigation into improper payments to suppliers of goods for the Navy.'

'And what have you discovered for my Lord Arlington?'

'He will report that to you in due course, Your Majesty.'

'A very proper answer, but delivered with a caution that suggests you think Lord Arlington may not report to me precisely what you tell him and that you do not wish to allow me to compare your version with his.'

'I am sure that he would have reported to you exactly what I told him,' I say. 'No more no less, though most of it you will know already.'

'Then there can be no reason for not telling me.'

'Very well, Your Majesty. Your most senior officers habitually accept gifts from suppliers. They see it as a right. The dockyard commissioners live in considerable style, that cannot be supported on their salaries alone. There is unconscionable waste and inefficiency at Deptford, and I suspect elsewhere, but they do build ships in a scientific and workmanlike way, whatever Pepys may tell you. The men at the dockyards have amassed a collection of traditional rights and privileges that enable them to earn good money at your expense, but if you wish to stop it you will at the very least need to pay them their proper wages at the proper time. Perhaps you should do that anyway. Your workmen and your sailors. Their families would bless you if you did.'

'Yes, I know that,' he says. 'What else?'

'There is the question of the Ruby.'

'And what have you discovered about the Ruby?'

'I assume that you know most of the story already, since everyone else seems to. Lord Sandwich ordered the captain to break bulk without proper authority. Shares in the cargo were sold to a number of prominent courtiers, including the Duke of Buckingham and the Earl of Dartford. Mr Pepys had a share but sold it on, out of prudence. And I understand Lady Castlemaine may have accepted a share.'

'A large share?'

'The papers I have suggest about two-fifths. There would have been payments to various people who assisted, but she probably received a little over two thousand Pounds.'

The King smiles. 'Excellent.'

'Perhaps because of this, perhaps for some other reason, I believe that the Earl had two men killed – Thomas Cade and Harry Truscott, both of the Tower Yard. The yard was used to unload and transport the goods.'

'And again, you have proof?'

I nod. 'Less than I would like, but I have a witness, Mr Symonds, who is deputy and acting manager at the Deptford yard. Like Mr Cade, Mr Symonds has discovered honesty recently and only by chance, but he will testify, if granted immunity himself, concerning how the goods were taken and distributed.'

'And the papers you mention – what are they?'

'I have a list, found amongst Mr Cade's papers, of the intended recipients. Mistress Cade, his widow, could be questioned further to ascertain its authenticity – some of it is apparently in her handwriting. She certainly knows enough to give evidence in court. Dartford visited her recently and was pleasant to her, which was cleverly done, then threatening, which wasn't.'

'And Dartford sought to regain these papers?'

I wonder how much to tell the King. I decide that it is not for me to introduce the topic of the poem. 'I don't know, Your Majesty. But we have the evidence I have described. All in all, it could be enough, if you wish it to be enough.'

'Very good.' The King smiles again. 'You have done well in such a short time, Sir John. We can now act.'

'You will bring charges against Dartford?' I ask.

'Well, Sir John, you are the lawyer, but my understanding is that, although in any criminal proceedings I am named as a party, my judges and magistrates deal with that sort of thing. We'll need to see what they say.'

'So, the guilty parties are not to be brought to justice?'

'That is not my business.'

'Then what was the point of my investigation?'

'Didn't Arlington explain?'

'Several times,' I say, 'though never the same way twice.'

'There is only one intended target. That is Barbara Villiers, Lady Castlemaine.'

'Your mistress?' I say. 'But surely . . .'

'I could put her off with a well-chosen word? So I once thought myself. You are happily married, Sir John, as indeed I am. Do you also have a mistress?'

'No, Your Majesty. I have never found the need for one.'

'Do I detect a note of disapproval?'

'Of course not, Your Majesty.'

'I must have imagined it then. Sir John, I was, from the age of twenty-one to the age of thirty a penniless exile. When other young men were enjoying their youth in every possible way, I was in the Low Countries working night and day for the re-establishment of the monarchy. Do you not think that entitles me to a little peace and leisure now? Does the nation begrudge me a mistress or two? After all of the privations that I underwent in Flanders? Would you believe that during that time I could scarcely afford a new shirt?'

'Yes, Your Majesty. We met in Brussels during your exile.'

I also seem to recall that he had a mistress or two in Brussels, but no matter.

'We met?' asks the King. 'So we did. Remind me . . . what were you doing there?'

'I was spying for Oliver Cromwell.'

'Against me?'

'Yes, Your Majesty.'

'Of course: I remember now. Didn't I have you shot?'

'My wife – my future wife, as she then was – persuaded you otherwise.'

'If she was no more than your future wife, she showed considerable foresight.'

'She would not dispute it.'

'I had forgotten that.'

'She hasn't,' I say.

'And there's my point, Sir John. Barbara Villiers too was there during my lowest ebb. During the sad and pinched time before I was restored to the thrones of England, Scotland, Ireland and France. The time when my own country did not wish to know me. The time, too, when I might have been shot had I set foot on English soil. She feels that past service of that sort counts for something. That a bond forged in adversity is indissoluble. A marriage of sorts. Of course, the bond with Lord Chancellor Clarendon should have been that much greater, he and I being shackled together even longer, and the subservience he expected being even greater than that demanded by Barbara Villiers. I still got rid of him, thank God. Persuading Lady Castlemaine that it is time for her to graciously depart – to get her arse out of my life was how I phrased it – is proving more difficult. It is not that I am ungrateful to her, but she does not seem to understand that a man who is answerable directly to God does not wish his every action to be scrutinised and criticised by his mistresses.'

'That is normally a wife's role,' I say. 'Or so my wife tells me.'

'Precisely,' says the King. 'God has ordained it thus. It helps, of course, to have a wife, as I do, who is Portuguese and has a poor grasp of the English tongue. I would recommend that course of action to you, should you marry again.'

'I shall let my wife know that is my intention,' I say.

'If it were only what my Lady Castlemaine *says*, she might still be tolerable. She has other attractions, you understand – I don't deny that. But her need for money is insatiable. If I give her a thousand Pounds from the pittance Parliament grants me, she will have gambled it away by the morning. Or she'll give it to one of her other lovers. I don't mind her having other lovers. I just wish she'd be content with them and not bother me.'

'Can you not pay her to go?'

'I have. She's still here.'

'But if she were involved in a financial scandal . . .' I say.

'That would be providential. Clarendon was driven out of the country after people believed he'd taken bribes from the French. If she had taken money belonging to the Navy at a time when it could scarcely afford to buy rope – if she had materially contributed to our defeat on the Medway, which shamed the whole country . . .'

'The people would not stand for it,' I say.

'Not from a Catholic whore,' he says. 'Of course, personally I have no objection to Catholics or whores, but some people do.'

'And so my report to Arlington . . .'

'Oh, I think I don't need to tell you what it might say. It would be wrong for me to influence you in any way.'

'As long as it condemns Lady Castlemaine and does not mention Buckingham and Dartford?'

'I would leave Buckingham and Dartford to your discretion, but it would help if the country's ire was concentrated on a single point rather than scattered ineffectively over a wider area. Blame shared is blame watered down. Lady Castlemaine's name in your report would be quite sufficient. She seems to have taken two-fifths, which is almost half, when you think about it. The others had to content themselves with what little remained. But, of course, I haven't told you that. It would have been utterly wrong of me to have set up an enquiry into the actions of one of my mistresses. It would look a little personal and vindictive. And the mistress in question might feel that it was well within my power to suppress the facts if I wished to. But an independent enquiry by a respected magistrate on the orders of my Secretary of State – I am not the sort of tyrant who would intervene in due process of that sort. Nobody could blame me for reluctantly accepting your findings. And taking the firm and resolute action that my people would expect of me.'

'I am grateful for your clarification,' I say.

'Good,' says the King. 'Is Lady Grey still writing plays?'

'Yes,' I say. 'But there are difficulties in having them acted. Lord Dartford resents my interference in his business and has dissuaded Killigrew's actors from taking part.'

'That would be a pity. I should like to attend the next performance myself. Tell Killigrew that I shall be there when the play is performed and anyone who tries to prevent the performance will be thrown in the Tower. Tell him I'll have a troop of Lifeguards surrounding the theatre if Dartford tries anything.'

'Thank you, Your Majesty,' I say.

'Tell your wife you've persuaded me to do it in exchange for her pleas on your behalf in Brussels. Tell her that you've evened things up. She never need mention Brussels again.'

'It doesn't work like that,' I say.

'No, it doesn't, does it? Never mind. I look forward to seeing you on the opening night, Sir John.'

Chapter 22

Lincoln's Inn

'And the King guaranteed that the play would be performed without any interference from Dartford?'

'Yes,' I say.

Aminta considers this. 'Out of respect for the services that you have performed for him?'

'More likely because Dartford has fallen from favour. Perhaps the King has read the poem?'

'No, I would have heard about it from my friends at Court.'

'Then he has committed some other error,' I say.

'But to our advantage. I shall inform Killigrew this afternoon.'

'And I shall visit Arlington.'

'I think that I shall have the more enjoyable task. Thank you for speaking to the King.'

'It was my pleasure.'

'You still owe me for Brussels.'

'I never thought otherwise.'

* * *

I find Arlington at Whitehall Palace. He is not pleased.

'You should not have been speaking to the King,' he says.

'The King spoke to me. It is difficult not to reply when he asks a question. I am his subject. It is expected.'

'There was no need to tell him the truth.'

'I had not been informed that it was necessary to lie,' I say.

'I have certainly never instructed you to be honest. Nobody tells the King the truth – he does not require it. You take too much upon yourself, Sir John, indeed you do. If all my agents decided to tell only the truth, my department would achieve nothing.'

'I apologise, my Lord. Which lies did you wish me to tell? It would have helped had you explained that the purpose of my investigation was to bring down Lady Castlemaine.'

Arlington pauses in his condemnation of veracity. 'The King's present intention is certainly to bring down Lady Castlemaine. But that may not be wise.'

'Not wise? She hectors and bullies him. He is tired of her.'

'What business is that of his? The appointment of the King's mistress in chief is a matter of importance second only to that of appointing his ministers – greater perhaps, since his mistresses have greater access to him and can speak their minds in a way that his ministers cannot. Just as we attempt to place our best young men into influential roles at Court, the King's ministers vie with each other to secure places for mistresses. Nell Gwynn and Moll Davis are both Buckingham's protégées. Jane Roberts was Lord Ashley's. I have effected one or two introductions myself. A mistress cannot simply be set aside without disrupting many carefully balanced alliances within the Court. If Buckingham trades the introduction of a mistress closely related to his family for the appointment of one of my own men as a commissioner on the Tangier Committee, he wishes to be sure that the mistress's position will be as secure as the new commissioner's. Without such assurances, the trade would be meaningless.'

'When the King is with one of his mistresses, I doubt that his first thoughts are the balance of power between his ministers. But are you saying that you do not intend to do as the King wishes?'

'I shall do what I believe the King will wish me to do when he knows his own mind better. My Lady is proving more difficult to dislodge than anyone thought. Indeed, she seems to have the upper hand of His Majesty again. He is paying her four thousand Pounds a year to go and live in France, but she remains very visibly in Berkshire House. The money comes from Post Office revenues and might have paid for a ship or two to defend the capital, when the Dutch next come after us. It's not only Pepys who steals from the royal purse – the King frequently does it himself. For all that, the King believes that he is no longer under Lady Castlemaine's thumb and for the moment we all pay lip service to his belief. The French Ambassador has tactfully stopped bribing her for information, because to continue to do so would imply that she still has influence and the King would not like that. But if Lady Castlemaine really no longer controlled the King, then he would require no subterfuge of the sort we are discussing in order to be free of her. I think he will not shake her off that easily. She will continue to be a significant and somewhat vindictive power at Court. In which case . . .'

'In which case those who now seek to bring her down may be exposed to her wrath at a later date?' I ask.

'That is always a risk.'

'I am surprised that you did not let me go ahead and then blame me if the ploy failed.'

'I had obviously considered that,' says Arlington. 'It would, as you say, be a feasible plan. But you have worked for me too often in the past for me to be able to claim that I knew nothing of your activities. Or, rather, I would have claimed it, but the Lady would not have believed me. And the King too would not forgive a botched attempt, since he would be blamed by Lady Castlemaine for the action of his ministers. She would have been pacified only with jewels or property or a new title or the utter humiliation of one of his other mistresses.'

'But the King wishes me to take action. He said so. He is expecting us to help him.'

'He wishes you to take action *today*. By tomorrow, or the day after at the latest, he will almost certainly have changed his mind. Lady Castlemaine will see to that. Prudence dictates that we should keep our powder dry.'

'You could still use what I have discovered against Lord Dartford. We can bring him to justice.'

'Yes, that is true. We can, if we wish, bring down one of Buckingham's allies.'

'Is it not more to the point that he is a murderer and many other things?'

'Of course. That is what I meant to say. But we would have to be certain that we could fell him with a single shot, because there is nothing more dangerous than a wounded enemy. I am not sure that we can yet do that. You have nothing more than a list and a witness or two who may be prepared to give evidence about a misdemeanour some years ago.'

'I had hoped that would be enough, but you have given me authority to investigate further.'

'Did I?'

'Yes. I think we can prove beyond reasonable doubt that Dartford killed Cade and Truscott. I think that the men he used were the same as those who attacked me. I can track them down. We can make them talk. Kynaston thought that the more senior of the two was named Robert Makepeace. It should not be too difficult to find him.'

'I can't afford to pay you to do this,' says Arlington.

'It would be my pleasure to help you,' I say. 'No charge.'

'You should have said. You do of course have my permission to proceed. I shall arrange for arrest warrants to be drawn up – in the name of Makepeace or whatever you choose – by a magistrate who is happy to do my bidding and arguably has authority to do so in Westminster. If you need help in apprehending Mr Makepeace, then I have agents who will be of assistance. And there are places where Makepeace can be detained discreetly – I have a stinking prison on the South Bank in mind. Of course, if you fail in a conspicuous manner, then I must place it on record that I have offered you no help of any sort. In fact, I disapproved strongly of your ridiculous accusations against one of the King's closest friends and ordered you to desist.'

'I won't fail,' I say.

'Killigrew was remarkably ungrateful for all that you have done for him,' says Aminta. 'He feels that he now has no choice but to proceed with the play, but, knowing the King as he does, is less confident than you are that His Majesty will remember his promise to protect him, should things go wrong. He can afford to shut down the theatre for a while because, though he will have no receipts, he will also have few outgoings. But a massacre of theatre-goers by Dartford's men will be difficult to cover up. It will affect bookings. He is fearful, but knows that a Royal Command cannot be disobeyed.'

'With luck we can have Dartford in the Tower before the opening night. Arlington wishes me to find the evidence to convict him of murder. I am now convinced he employed the man mentioned by Kynaston: Makepeace.'

Aminta nods. 'Robert Makepeace. His usual accomplice is Peter Sleet.'

'Peter Sleet? How do you know?'

'Well, I was curious to discover who might have threatened my husband, so I asked around Court. My informant, indirectly at least, was Lady Dartford. As you know, Dartford abducted her rather than propose marriage in the conventional way. Of course he's an Earl and can get away with that sort of thing. Lady D. was distinctly unhappy with her treatment and, in complete confidence, told Lady Harvey of her ordeal. She happened to mention the names of her abductors, whom she got to know quite well. Makepeace and Sleet. Makepeace quite compact, well dressed, harder than he looks. Sleet very much the underling, tall, gangly and largely edentate. They seem to fit your description well enough. Not the most amiable of men. You were lucky to come out of your meeting with them unscarred. Not many do.'

'Did your contacts know where these gentlemen might be found? Arlington wishes me to make an arrest and question them. He will supply warrants.'

'Both come and go a great deal at Dartford House. I think you might find it difficult to make an arrest there, even with the best warrants that money can buy. A man who can abduct heiresses won't take kindly to the detention of two of his servants.'

'We'll find out where they may be more easily taken. London is a large city, but we have the advantage that they have no idea that we are coming for them.'

'I tried each of the taverns in turn,' says Will, 'starting with the one closest to Dartford House. I had to spend a Shilling or two in each on beer for myself and for landlords and customers there who might know Makepeace or Sleet.'

He speaks carefully, trying not to slur his words. But I do not begrudge Will a pint or two in the course of his duties.

'Take the money from the cashbox,' I say.

'Thank you, sir, I already have,' says Will. 'And noted it in your accounts. They seem to have avoided the hostelries nearest to their master's residence, which are respectable and charge twice the normal price for beer, preferring low houses a little way off, where the drinking is cheaper. I felt that simply asking whether the men in question drank there would be suspicious, especially since I look a little like a lawyer's clerk. I therefore concocted a plausible story that a client of my master's had left some money in a will to a Mr Robert Makepeace and that we wished to contact him. I had been told that he worked close by, with a colleague named Sleet. In the first five taverns that I tried, the landlord either did not know them or decided that anyone connected with a lawyer was not to be trusted. Then I tried a sixth establishment, in a small lane off the Strand.'

'And?'

'They both drink at the Red Bull, close to the Maypole. With regard to its clientele, it is the lowest of low establishments, but serves ale that will not necessarily give you the runs. Our two friends are usually to be found there after seven in the evening, if Lord Dartford has no other work for them. They remain for some hours. Oh, and on the night that Mr Cade was killed, they both failed to attend as usual.'

'How did you discover that last piece of information?'

'I said that I had previously looked in on that evening hoping to find them. The landlord said that he remembered they had not been there that particular night.'

'And when Truscott was killed? Were they absent then too?'

'I felt that making detailed enquiries about their movements did not sit well with the story that they were of interest merely as legatees. That they were away on the first evening still seemed helpful. I hope it is.'

'Well done, Will,' I say. 'You are right. It's all we need. We can show they killed Cade at least and they can hang only once. Take another sovereign from the cashbox. That's as a good an evening's work as you'll ever do me. Go to Arlington's office in Whitehall and ask for his deputy, Mr Williamson. He or his one of clerks will have obtained the arrest warrants by now. Then tonight we'll go with one or two of Arlington's men and make an arrest. It won't bring Cade or Truscott back to life, but I'll have done something for them after their death. This is easier than I thought.'

Chapter 23

At the Red Bull

I am sitting at a table in the Red Bull. Will has already been over to the filthy, beer-soaked counter and established that neither Makepeace nor Sleet have yet been in, the landlord being quite happy to talk to the man, with an open purse, who wishes to enrich one of his customers with a legacy from a previously unknown but happily dead uncle.

'But he says they rarely arrive later than half past seven,' says Will.

I take out my gold pocket watch. It shows me that we are five and twenty minutes past the hour. I scan the room we are in. Though it is small, you can scarcely see to the other side for pipe smoke. The ceiling is so low that almost everyone who enters the room has to duck to avoid the beams. Beer is the only drink being consumed. You'd probably get beaten up just for thinking of asking for claret or Canary. On the far side, two of Arlington's men are engaged in a long conversation, apparently unheeding of the other drinkers. They've done this before.

'But perhaps they won't come tonight,' says Will.

'We'll give them until quarter to eight,' I say. 'We're getting more suspicious looks than I would like, and lawyers don't usually put this much effort into finding lost heirs. A mug of ale before we return to our office is believable, but if we want to avoid looking like two men waiting to ambush somebody, it would be better to drink up and come back tomorrow.'

Then the door opens and two men enter.

'I think we won't need to return,' I say. 'We are about to make an arrest.'

I stand. Arlington's men, who have been more attentive than they seemed, stand too, as if ready to leave and start to stroll over towards the door. I walk across the room, no more than a dozen steps, and place myself in front of Makepeace and Sleet as they make their way to the counter.

'Robert Makepeace, Peter Sleet,' I say, 'I have a warrant for your arrest. You will accompany me now to a place nearby where I can ask you some questions about the murders of Thomas Cade and Henry Truscott.'

Sleet looks from me to Will, and then towards the door. He decides, on balance, to run for it. But he does not get far. Arlington's men have ceased to be disinterested onlookers. Each seizes an arm as Sleet tries to brush past them and he is pinioned firmly against the door frame.

I turn to Makepeace, but he is no longer there. Too late I realise that there must be another way out, at the rear of the tavern, because a door there has just slammed shut. The landlord gives me a stony glance. There is no doubt whose side he is on. He won't let scheming lawyers with lying tales of non-existent riches into his house again. I hesitate for just too long, then follow Makepeace's route. But sitting on a low stool has caused the wound in my leg to start throbbing again; I hope this won't be a long chase. The door gives directly on to a small courtyard, which in turn gives on to another narrow lane, scarcely wide enough to push a handcart down. I look in both directions. Already there is no sign of him. Has he gone south towards the Strand or north? I curse myself for my foolishness, but I am needed to question Sleet, who even now will be protesting his innocence and calling on the other clients of the tavern for sympathy and support. Once we have Sleet's confession, we can go after Makepeace. Then we can deal with their master.

Sleet was sneeringly obedient all the way down to the river and got into the small boat without protest. He remained silent when we landed him, a few minutes later, on the South Bank. Only as we saw that we were approaching the Marshalsea prison did he recall his rights as a free citizen, but we bundled him in through the gate, after which he could curse and shout all he wanted. We left him in a damp cell for an hour or so, so that he could appreciate the seriousness of his position. Now he stands before us – Will, myself and Arlington's agents – scowling and resentful.

'Can I have a seat?' he asks.

'No,' I say.

'Lord Dartford will hear of this,' he says.

'That is our intention,' I say. 'You confirm, however, that you do work for Dartford? You weren't so specific when we last met.'

'Wasn't I? I don't remember. But he'll protect me if I need it. You really think you can get me hanged for murder, don't you?'

'It will be nothing to do with me. A court will decide on your guilt. A court will get you hanged.'

'No it won't. Even Arlington will have to come up with some evidence if he wants a false conviction. I never met Cade and I've haven't even heard of the other one.'

'Henry Truscott.'

'Like I say, never heard of him until tonight.' Sleet is confidently defiant.

'Since you now admit that you work for Lord Dartford, you can hardly deny that you do that sort of job for him.'

'It's not my job to kill people – for Dartford or anyone.'

'One week ago,' I say, 'you were at Lincoln's Inn. You entered the gardens, by the gate or over the wall, then lay in wait for Thomas Cade. You watched him arrive and enter the building in which I have my chambers. You waited until he left, then, as you did with me, you called out to him that you wished to talk to him privately. When he approached you, you struck him over the head with a wooden club or some similar weapon and killed him. Then you left – probably climbing the wall.'

'You are mad,' he says. 'Completely mad. Only a lawyer could come up with a story like that.'

'Where were you seven nights ago?'

'In the Red Bull probably.'

'The landlord says not,' I say.

He frowns, then a gappy smile spreads over his face. 'No, I wasn't,' he says. 'His Lordship had a meeting with the Duke of Buckingham. Makepeace attended as the Earl's secretary. I rode on the coach with a pair of pistols – the City's still not safe at night. So, if you want a witness, I have the country's premier Duke, who will swear that my master and Makepeace and I were all at his house all that evening. Nowhere near

Lincoln's Inn. Is that good enough for you? Well, I'll enjoy reporting this back to the Earl. And he'll enjoy discussing it with Lord Arlington. I doubt he'll let Arlington forget this evening's work in a hurry.'

I turn to Arlington's men. Their expression says that this was my idea, not theirs.

'And two nights ago, when Truscott was killed?'

'Well, that evening we were in the Red Bull,' says Sleet. 'I'm sure the landlord will be happy to confirm that.'

'I'm sure he will,' I say.

'So, are you planning to let me go, then?' Sleet asks. 'Because it's past my supper time.'

'Just one more thing,' I say. 'Why is the Earl of Dartford so interested in Mistress Cade? Why did he visit her house by the Tower?'

'Is this another of your queer fancies?'

'Just answer my question.'

'You're as wrong about that as you are about my having killed Cade or Truscott. The Earl has no interest in her at all.'

'You'd know that?'

'Of course. A house by the Tower? He wouldn't venture into the City without Makepeace or me. I'd know if he'd been there. Now, are you going to summon me a boat to cross the river?'

'You can summon your own boat or you can go back via the bridge,' I say. 'I haven't forgotten our previous meeting, even if you have. I'm not paying your fare for the ferry.'

After Sleet has gone, I stand and run my fingers through my hair.

'We'll be off then, sir,' says the more senior of Arlington's men. 'Nothing more to be done here. Shall we report back to Lord Arlington or will you?'

'I'll do it,' I say. 'It was my plan.'

'Yes, sir, it was. Thank you.'

They depart. They do not invite me to join them in whichever hostelry they intend to drink in. They've been with me in one tavern already. They don't want me to order them to arrest anyone else this evening.

'It could still be Dartford, sir,' says Will. 'He could have paid anyone to murder Cade and Truscott. There are plenty of ruffians out there who'll kill for a few gold coins. The fact he was with the Duke of Buckingham means nothing.'

'It will be a lot more difficult to prove he hired some ruffians to kill Cade than it would be to show it was Dartford's men acting on Dartford's orders,' I say. 'And I've told Arlington I'd get proof.'

'Perhaps Dartford will give himself away.'

'I doubt that. It was interesting, though ... I think Sleet really had no idea Dartford had been to see Mistress Cade. Whatever Dartford wanted from her, he'd kept it quiet – even within his own household.'

'He could have all sorts of reasons for doing that.'

'I'm not sure. Dartford's one to brazen things out, not hide his deeds from anyone. Perhaps I should speak to Mistress Cade again and try to find out what I've missed. In the meantime, I have to visit Lord Arlington. Wish me luck with that, Will.'

'Good luck with that, sir.'

Strangely I feel no better for it.

'Does anyone know that Joseph Williamson got you the warrants?' demands Arlington.

'His clerk and my own,' I say. 'And the magistrate, of course. It was difficult for fewer people to know. I was unaware that it was likely to become a contentious issue.'

'Will Sleet tell anyone?'

'I should think he'll tell everyone he can. But I should also think he knows few people who really matter. If word reaches the Court, you can always blame me.'

'I most certainly shall blame you.'

'It will be no more than I deserve.'

Arlington weighs up the danger of any birds coming home to roost. 'There's nothing Dartford can do about it,' he says eventually. 'But I'd expected better from you, Grey. You seem to have allowed two guilty men to slip between your fingers.'

'I'd expected better from myself,' I say. 'But I believe Sleet. When he denied the killings he had the air of a habitual liar who is dismayed to find himself not believed on one of the rare occasions that he is telling the truth. Whoever killed Cade it wasn't Makepeace and Sleet. On the other hand, Dartford is involved in something. He has visited Mistress Cade and doesn't want anyone to know that he has. If the visit was simply a matter of pleasure, he wouldn't care who knew. It could have been in connection with the Ruby, which would link him to Cade's murder, but Mistress Cade didn't think so and nor do I. It could have been to find the missing poem, though I have no proof Cade had it – only that he visited the King at about the right time, which I think Dartford must also have found out. But the secrecy surrounding the visit makes me sure that Dartford has something to hide and that this thing is connected in some way to Cade. I should imagine that Sleet is being told, even as we speak, to keep very quiet about his arrest.'

'Excellent. The less you do from now on the better then.'

'On the contrary. I intend to discover who killed Thomas Cade.'

'I forbid that in the most absolute terms,' he says. 'I mean, really forbid it – not do it but don't tell me.'

'I had not appreciated the difference, my Lord.'

'Well, I expect you to appreciate the difference now. You may not investigate the death of Thomas Cade any further. You need make no further enquiries about corruption in the supply of goods to the Navy. Do you still have that paper about the Ruby?'

I take it out of my pocket. Arlington reaches out and closes his fingers round it. I release it to him.

'Thank you, Sir John,' he says. 'I think this would be safer with me. Just in case it is necessary to erase a name . . . or add one. In the interest of making the truth clearer than it was. I think this could be worth what I'm paying you.'

'You're not paying me,' I say.

He nods and stuffs the paper into his waistcoat pocket.

As I am leaving, I run into Williamson.

'How do?' he enquires.

This is Williamson in his bluff, no-nonsense northerner role. Of course, he can be answered in kind.

'Fair to middling,' I reply.

Williamson smiles. His accent moves a few miles southwards. 'Even after your interview with Lord Arlington?' he enquires.

'I asked for warrants for the wrong men,' I say. 'They have perfect alibis.'

'No alibi is completely watertight,' he says. 'There is always a small element of doubt that may be dangled before a jury. A good lawyer could prove that neither of us was here at this moment and that we never had this conversation about him.'

'I want to know who killed Thomas Cade.'

'You want the truth?'

'Yes.'

'Sorry, my lad, you've come to the wrong place.'

'I know,' I say. 'I know.'

Chapter 24

Lincoln's Inn and Bromley

Aminta is less sympathetic than she might be – bearing in mind that she discovered Makepeace and Sleet for me.

'Dartford could have got anyone to kill Cade. It didn't have to be one of his own men,' she says.

'That's what Will said. Of course, it will be a lot more difficult tracking down men whose names we don't know and whose faces we've never seen.'

'Still, it's interesting that Dartford doesn't want anyone to know about his visits to Mistress Cade. He is usually happy to make his conquests public knowledge.'

'I need to talk to her again,' I say. 'She might still remember something else. But she seems to have vanished again. Like her maid.'

'You're wrong about the maid. I spoke to her today. Wherever the mistress may be, the maid is certainly in London.'

'Really?'

'Yes, it seemed to me that you hadn't interrogated her quite as thoroughly as you should. So, I did it properly.'

'How?' I ask.

'There are ways of finding people. It occurred to me that, once the brandy had run out, she would need to find another job.'

'That won't be easy. I wouldn't employ her.'

'If you lived in London, my dear husband, you might have to. There's quite a shortage of maids of any sort. Too many people growing rich and needing servants, and not enough silly girls coming in from the country willing to work for almost nothing. I should think that she is sleeping off the effects of her new mistress's brandy by now.'

'Hold on. You haven't employed her yourself?'

'Of course not. I merely led her to believe that was a possibility. With so many employers and so few servants, there are agencies now that will find a maid for you – or at least will locate some respectable girls to interview. I enquired at one or two offices, saying that I was looking for somebody cheap but with experience of all types of work. They allowed me to go through their lists. I asked one or two questions about the maids' previous employers and identified one who had previously worked for a lady close to the Tower – the wife of a prominent local shipbuilder. I said that was the sort of respectable, unpretentious background we had hoped for. She proved to be called Betsy Green. I interviewed her an hour later, in a room at the agent's house, saying that I had just arrived in London and that my own home was not yet ready, but I hoped it would be in a week or so. It seemed better from all points of view not to let her set foot in Lincoln's Inn. She was anxious to impress me by telling me anything I wanted to know about her former employer. Anything at all.'

'So, had we taken her on, we might have expected her, in the fullness of time, to tell our secrets to her next employer?'

'That we might think such a thing did not seem to occur to her. She imagined that I would be grateful that she criticised every aspect of Mistress Cade's daily life. Which I was. She related many tales about Pepys, possibly embroidered slightly. I've no idea where he finds time for his Navy work.'

'Dartford?'

'I don't think there was much going on there. She was surprised that a good-looking aristocrat had any interest in her mistress, she being some years past her prime, but Betsy assured me she'd know his face if she saw it again, which could be helpful. I may have found you another witness.'

'You didn't have to pay her for any of this? She was exacting a Shilling a lover when I questioned her.'

'No, this was gossip, from one gentlewoman to another. Destroying other people's characters is usually considered an act of charity and its own reward. But that wasn't the best of it by a long way. Did you know that Truscott had a wife in Plymouth?'

'No,' I say.

'Nor it would seem did Mistress Cade. But Truscott let it slip to Betsy that that was the case.'

'How did he let it slip?'

'I think he visited Mistress Cade and left his coat somewhere that Betsy could search the pockets. Inside was a letter from his wife.'

'So Truscott, contrary to any promises he may have made to the lady, could not have returned to the West Country with Mistress Cade in tow?'

'If his wife was as accommodating as the Queen, then he might have taken the lady back as his mistress,' says Aminta. 'But I don't see how he could have married her legally. Of course, after Cade's death, he might have planned to contract a bigamous marriage to gain control of the yard.'

'It seems likely, then, that that was his intention,' I say.

'Men are deceivers ever,' says Aminta.

'Yes, you've said so before. But Mistress Cade didn't know the state of affairs in Plymouth?' I ask.

'No, I think she trusted him,' says Aminta. 'At first, anyway.'

'So, we have reached the point where Betsy knew everything and Mistress Cade did not. The question we now have to ask is how good Betsy is at keeping secrets . . .'

'She might do so for a day or two . . . or at least a few hours,' says Aminta. 'I mean, she wouldn't have gone straight to her mistress with the letter in her hand as soon as Truscott was out of the house. Unless she did, of course. That's possible too.'

'I think we can assume that Mistress Cade knew that Truscott was no better than Pepys. Hence her sudden change in attitude to him. And indeed, the slight difference of opinion that Truscott referred to.'

'Truscott's death at Dartford's hands always looked odd,' says Aminta. 'Dartford didn't know him. And, even if Truscott had knowledge of the Ruby, I'm not sure that Dartford cared. Cade's attempt to blackmail him came to nothing, didn't it? Mistress Cade, on the other hand, having been thoroughly betrayed, would have had a better motive. But would she have been able to overcome him and string him up?'

'If she had had the strength to strangle him in the first place, the rope was already in place and designed for lifting much heavier weights than Truscott,' I say. 'And he was drunk.

Yes, she could have done. On discovering that Truscott had deceived her, she attacked and killed him, then made it look like suicide. Her alibi – that she was travelling back from Kent – will, I'm sure, be supported by her brother, who will testify that she left his house at a convenient hour.'

'An extreme response to a position that many women find themselves in,' says Aminta. 'But as you say, all quite possible. And it may not only be Truscott whom she killed. There was a woman waiting outside Lincoln's Inn at the right time. Perhaps she had already murdered her husband so that she could be with Truscott. Or perhaps she got Truscott to do the killing while she waited for him. Either way, once Betsy had spilled the beans, she saw that it had been a complete waste of her time. That would be enough to annoy most people. And let's not forget that Mistress Cade found Truscott's body – so she says.'

I nod. 'I think that, for all sorts of reasons, I need to locate Mistress Cade and speak to her again,' I say.

Will has again proved invaluable. Mistress Cade is nowhere to be found, but her neighbours proved as helpful as the landlord of the Red Bull, faced with the hint of a legacy due to her, if only she could be located.

'They think she's gone back to her brother in Bromley, sir. He's called Cooper and is a blacksmith. Shouldn't be too difficult to find. The brother is a bit of a brute though, according to them. Came round and threatened Cade on one occasion when he thought his sister wasn't being treated properly. When he turned up in London again a few days ago, they kept well out of his way. You'll need to go carefully, I think.'

* * *

I should have found a place on a coach. Three have overtaken me on the way here, and my ride to Bromley over hard rutted summer roads has done nothing good for the old wound in my leg. I am not unhappy to slacken my pace as I enter the town and follow a winding street, between ancient thatched houses, to the White Hart Inn. There I dismount and leave my horse in the stables to rest, drink water and munch oats for an hour or so. The inn is crowded, a coach from London having recently arrived and one for Tunbridge Wells about to set out.

I order a pint of ale and some bread and cheese, which I need as much as my horse needs his oats, and I settle back and watch the crowds mill around the large parlour, where the waiters, coatless, run backwards and forwards with drinks and food. My meal arrives and, in due course, the bill is brought to me by the landlord himself.

'Did you get caught in the shower this morning?' the landlord asks.

'It was a refreshing change from the heat and the dust,' I say. 'It's been a hot summer.'

'So it has. Hot and dry. Are you travelling on to London or Kent, sir?'

'I'm already where I'm going. My business is in Bromley. Perhaps you could tell me where I might find a blacksmith named Cooper?'

'Which way did you come, sir?'

'From London.'

'Then you've ridden right past him – he's a bit off the London road, just as you enter the town. Has your horse lost a shoe? If so, there are other smiths I'd go to before him – I mean if you value the beast at all. Richardson on the Tunbridge Wells road is the best round here. You'll need to go a bit further, but it would be worth the extra ten minutes. Cooper can be a little heavy handed.'

'Cooper was recommended to me.'

He shrugs. 'Please yourself. Your horse, your money. It's a five-minute ride, back the way you came. But my advice is to take a look round his establishment before you decide that's where you want the work done. He doesn't get much trade from people who know him – just from strangers who arrive here late and are desperate to get their horse shod before the morning.'

'I'll take a gentle stroll back that way,' I say. 'And I'll look round as you suggest. My horse needs to rest a little longer.'

His expression tells me I'll be wasting my time. He shrugs and collects up the plate and the tankard. It's all the same to him what I do. But innkeepers rarely have a bad word to say for local tradesmen. You recommend them and they recommend you. Cooper must be pretty incompetent.

I can see how I missed the smithy. It's a few yards down a little lane, the narrowness of which must be inconvenient for whatever customers come this way. And I can see why the innkeeper suggested that I might like to take a look first. It is a low place in every sense, a single-storey building that could do with rethatching. To the right there is a workshop, open at the front, to the left the domestic premises; both halves have an equally neglected air. In the blacksmith's shop the fire is out. A heap of old iron rusts in one corner. Tools have been left scattered over the floor. The roof is leaking onto the dirt floor, where this morning's rain has left a puddle, but nobody has yet decided that it matters. Perhaps it doesn't.

A man appears out of the left-hand part, ducking as he passes through the door. He is large for such a constricted place – tall but still disproportionately wide. His beard is untidy and food adheres to it in places. He too has dined recently. He wears an old leather apron, appropriate to his trade, and carries a hammer, as if on his way to work some iron at the forge. But the fire is out, so he may have some other use in mind for the hammer.

'Yes?' he enquires.

'I'm looking for Mistress Cade,' I say. 'Is she here?'

'Who's asking?'

'John Grey,' I say. 'Mistress Cade knows me. I work for Lord Arlington.'

'Who's he?'

'The King's Secretary of State.'

Cooper spits in the dry dust. Good Republican spit.

'You must be Mistress Cade's brother,' I say.

'Well done,' he says.

There is a long pause. He's not a great conversationalist.

'I'd like to speak with her, if that's all right with you.'

'I haven't said she's here.'

This last point is however clarified by the appearance behind him of a familiar face. Mistress Cade seems much smaller, beside her brother, than she did back in London. Scarcely an adult. I try to imagine them as children together. There must have been advantages and disadvantages in having such a large older brother of so morose a character. Like the captain of one of the King's great warships, she'd have been able to bring his firepower to bear on anyone who displeased her. But how well would he have responded to the rudder? He allows his hammer to rest for a moment on his shoulder and looks me up and down. Mainly down.

'What can I do for you, Mr Grey? You've travelled a long way to Bromley,' says Mistress Cade.

'My apologies for troubling you. I'd like to speak to you again about your husband's death. And Harry Truscott's.'

'She doesn't want to talk to you,' says Cooper. 'Good riddance to both of them. She's better off here with her family. I told her not to go back to London after Truscott wrote to her here.'

Again I study the crumbling thatch and the empty smithy with its cold fireplace. It offers few comforts and the wind must blow through it in winter. You'd only come here if you really didn't like where you were before. The house by the Tower was at least large and weatherproof. The smell of tar from a dockyard isn't that unpleasant. And all of London lay at her doorstep – neighbours, friends, theatres, pleasure gardens, shops selling lace and ribbons. But I don't yet know what she is running from.

'Is there anywhere we can speak privately?' I ask her.

Cooper's grip on his hammer tightens, but she looks at him and shakes her head. 'We can walk in the garden,' she says. 'I'm sure my brother has work to do.'

The garden is larger than I expected. The grass on the paths is long and neglected, but the shade from the apple trees is pleasant and wild flowers grow between them.

'You mustn't mind what my brother says,' she tells me, as we put as much space as we can between ourselves and the house. 'He's always wanted to protect me. That's what brothers do, isn't it?'

'I never had one,' I say. 'My wife did, but he died at the Battle of Worcester, fighting for the King. I haven't had much chance to study brothers and their behaviour.'

'Well . . .' she says. The look of vagueness that I noticed in London comes over her again.

'Do you intend to stay long in the country?' I ask.

'No,' she says. 'I'll need to go back soon. Symonds has made me an offer for the yard. It's not much money, but it's not much of a yard. And I can't run it myself – not with Harry dead – a woman giving instructions to so many men.'

'Women do a lot of things these days that they did not do before the war,' I say. 'They began when the men left to join their respective armies and they've carried on ever since – especially those whose men did not return home. There are women appearing on the stage, women writing plays, women painting portraits. Women have never had so much power at Court as they have now. Times have changed.'

'I have no love of shipbuilding.'

'That is another matter entirely.'

'Why have you come here, Mr Grey? Not to enquire about the sale of the Tower shipyard, I think.'

'I'm still trying to find out who killed your husband. I thought at first that he had been murdered by Lord Dartford because he knew about the Ruby.'

She shakes her head. 'It might trouble Pepys, but not Dartford. Dartford's survived worse scandals than that – the abduction of his future wife, for example. Anyone who could get away with forcing a woman to marry him at gunpoint would shake off the misappropriation of a French ship's cargo, however valuable.'

'Exactly. I said, I *thought* it was Dartford and that his visit to you was to discover where a certain list had gone. Perhaps that was his aim – but Dartford was elsewhere when your husband was killed and so were his chief minions.'

'There it is then.' Somehow she makes it all seem reasonable and domestic.

'But somebody killed your husband,' I say. 'And somebody killed Truscott.'

'Do you really think it makes any difference to me who killed either of them? My husband courted his death. As for Harry Truscott, I loved him but it would never have worked out . . . So, here I am in Kent, back where I started and with little enough to show for what happened along the way. And now I am here, even the house by the Tower begins to look good.'

'Did you know Truscott was married?' I ask.

Mistress Cade sighs. 'Not at first. Men . . . you lie all the time, don't you? To get what you want. He told me his wife was dead. He said that he loved me and that we should run away together, back to the West Country . . . when the time was right. Not now. It was never now. Always when the time was right. So, I let him into my bed. I let him into my bed quite often. He lied and got what I suppose he wanted. So, one of us was happy.'

'*Was* that all he wanted?' I ask. 'Didn't he have designs on the yard?'

'I'm sure people might have thought that if they'd known about us . . . and people always do know, don't they, however careful you think you've been? But Harry would have realised that wasn't possible. The yard was my husband's, not mine. Of course, it was left in his will to me, and Harry could have got it after his death, if we'd stayed in London and Cade had never found out . . . What are you suggesting, Mr Grey? Harry killed my husband to marry me and get the yard? I've told you. He would have known he couldn't marry me, even if I didn't. Without a proper legal marriage, he was as far from owning the yard as he ever could be, even with my husband dead.'

'Once your husband was dead, Truscott could have found ways of gaining control of the yard, even though he knew any marriage would not have been legal. But perhaps the point is that *you* thought he was free to marry. You thought that, if your husband was dead, it finally opened the way to marrying Harry Truscott. The yard would be yours – for Harry to run or to sell and start a new life elsewhere.'

She looks at me, puzzled, as if faced with a long and complex grocery bill.

'What? Are you saying that I killed my husband?' she says eventually.

'I had discounted the possibility until now – other things seem much more likely – but the porter mentioned that a woman was standing outside the gates of Lincoln's Inn on the night your husband was murdered.'

'And that was me? Is that what you're trying to tell me?'

'You wanted to marry Truscott. The only way that you could marry him was if your husband died. He was pressing to move to Deptford and you were resisting the move. Perhaps you would have done nothing more than that, but then you found out that your husband was coming to me to denounce Pepys. If he did so, if he alienated Pepys and you lost the contract, then the yard would have been valueless. You would have Truscott but not a penny from the sale of the yard. Perhaps you suspected that, without the yard, Truscott might not even be that interested in you. So you discussed things with Truscott and agreed your husband had to die that night. You both came to Lincoln's Inn. You stayed in the Fields, keeping watch on the gate, in case your husband left before Truscott could find a way to ambush him. Truscott scaled the walls. He arrived in time to attack Mr Cade. Cade was killed with some sort of wooden club – a carpenter's mallet perhaps? Truscott would have had access to one of those, I think. Anyone at the shipyard would. The deed done, he climbed back out over the wall and you left together for the Tower.'

Mistress Cade stands there open-mouthed as I finish my account.

'Mr Grey, that is a ridiculous idea!' she gasps. 'How could you think such a thing? Harry pretty well worshipped my husband. He might have been willing to bed me behind his back, but he would never have killed him. Never.'

'The evidence suggests otherwise,' I say. 'I put it to you that something very much like what I described took place. Afterwards, you both thought all was well – your plan and Truscott's may have been slightly different, but at that point you each imagined you had achieved your ends. You thought you could marry Truscott. He thought he could get his hands on the yard. Then your maid brought you some inconvenient news. Truscott had a wife in Plymouth. He couldn't marry you. You had been cruelly deceived. He'd betrayed you. You'd plotted one murder – why not a second one? You pretended to travel to Kent, even sacking your maid to make it more convincing, but you stayed on in London. You found Truscott at work, attacked and strangled him, then, using the rope already in place, you strung him up. You carefully placed a stool so that it appeared to be a suicide that had occurred while you were away. Then you sent, not for the constable, but for me, hoping that you could pull the wool over my eyes.'

'But I wouldn't have had the strength.'

'Your brother was seen in London recently by one of your neighbours. I didn't think much about that until I met him.

He's a strong man and it would have been easy enough for him to come back with you this time.'

The vagueness has gone from Mistress Cade's expression. It has been replaced by a gorgon gaze that her brother would be proud of.

'So, I've killed both my husband *and* my lover? And my brother helped kill Harry? That's what you think? It's very early in the day for you to be drunk, Mr Grey. The ale that they serve at the White Hart must be stronger than I remember.'

'It's true though, isn't it?' I ask.

'You're right about Betsy,' she says. 'She told me that she'd seen a letter from Truscott's wife. Lord, I didn't even know that idiot girl could read. But she comes to me and says that she's taken a paper from his pocket while he was in the bedchamber with me. She laughed that I'd been such a fool. I did go straight over to the yard and confront Harry. He denied it, of course – said he told me the truth, his wife was dead, but I could tell he was lying.'

'How?'

'He was a man and his lips were moving. So, I told him that he could leave the yard at the end of the week and never come back. I went straight down to Kent. Yes, I was furious with him and I told everyone how I felt. It was difficult stopping my brother coming back to London to kill him. Harry wrote to me, asking me to come back so that he could explain. Sent the message by hand. Stupidly, I relented. I replied the same way, saying I'd come as soon as I could, but when I arrived in London I was too late. He was already dead. Perhaps it was as well – he'd have only told me another pack of lies and I might have believed him. I don't know who killed Harry Truscott, but it wasn't me. And my brother was here in Kent.'

'Then tell me who else it might have been.'

'One of his other women, perhaps. Maybe that wife of his in Devon. She'd have had cause, don't you think?'

'Perhaps we should stick to what is likely,' I say. 'Nobody has reported seeing Mrs Truscott or any other strange woman about the yard. You, on the other hand, could come and go as you chose, almost unnoticed.'

'Listen, Mr Grey . . . listen carefully. Harry Truscott didn't kill my husband. He respected him too much. I didn't kill Harry – I was still travelling back when he died. If Harry didn't commit suicide then I don't know who killed him. But I do know this: all I have to do is to call out and my brother, who will be standing by the door trying to overhear our conversation, will be out in the garden before you know what's hit you. And what will have hit you is the hammer that he carries around with him, even though he's annoyed half the town and has almost no proper work to do with it. Two violent deaths in one month is enough for me, else I'd summon him now.

'Return to London, Mr Grey. Go back to your master Lord Arlington. Tell him you have no idea who killed my husband. None at all. I'm going back to the house now and when I get there I'm going to explain to my brother, in simple words that he will understand, exactly what you just said to me, including the bit about his being my accomplice. If you begin walking to the inn now, you'll be five minutes ahead of him when he comes for you. That should be enough time to mount your horse and start riding. Ride fast, Mr Grey, and don't even think of coming back to Bromley.'

Chapter 25

Lincoln's Inn

The journey back is even harder on the old wound in my leg than was the journey out, and I am not displeased when I finally enter Southwark and make my way slowly through the crowds towards London Bridge. There is a horse ferry at Lambeth, in the west, but riders entering London from the south-east must be content to plod slowly over the gently rising cobbles, following the wagons and the people on foot, stopping and starting again as the long queue moves forward at a snail's pace. We pass under the great stone gate, still decorated with the heads of past traitors, tarred and stuck on poles. Though the King has undertaken to add no new ones, they are a sufficient reminder of the misfortunes of those who plot against the State. And it's easier for the King to leave them there than take them down. Then we are out in the late afternoon sunshine again, on one of the open stretches of the bridge, with a fine view across the river to the City, three-quarters blackened ruins and a quarter bright new red brick, with small boats dodging backwards and forwards on the water, propelled by sail or oars. But the bridge is a home as much as a road, and a gloomy tunnel of houses soon swallows us up again, the sound of horseshoes on the stones and human voices all echoing off the walls. Eventually the road starts the gradual descent to the far side of the river. There are more shops and houses, more shuffling and cursing, another gateway, and finally we can step into the City of London. The whole crowd breathes a sigh of relief and dissipates gratefully amongst the streets and lanes on the north side, and I can ride through the ruins and back to Lincoln's Inn.

'That Mistress Cade denies everything does not mean that she didn't kill her husband,' says Aminta. 'Like so many wives, she had a motive.'

'I hope you're not suggesting that all women have a motive for killing their husbands. The facts suggest otherwise. It is more common for men to kill their wives.'

'That merely shows that women are capable of greater restraint than men.'

'I still wonder about Truscott. He was very troubled about Cade's death. He spoke to me of his guilt. Could that be because he was in fact the killer?'

'Perhaps. I have however found some interesting information myself while you were in Bromley, and without getting the dust of the road on my clothes. I spoke to Lady Sandwich today.'

'And?'

'And Pepys did not have supper with her and Lord Sandwich the night Cade died.'

'He lied to me?'

'You sound surprised.'

'So, where was he then?'

'It may be worth asking. But it will wait until tomorrow.'

I know that Pepys is an early riser and that he will be at his desk when men like Arlington and Dartford are still asleep. Or usually so. Leaving Lincoln's Inn, I pass a richly gilded coach with four horses; a voice calls me to a halt.

'Sir John! A word with you, if I may.'

I turn. Lord Dartford is not in his bed after all. He is leaning through the open window of the carriage, a silk-covered elbow resting lightly on the sill.

'How can I be of service to you, my Lord?' I ask.

'Why don't you join me in my coach? We'll be more comfortable here and it will be more private than anywhere else.'

'Is that what you said to your wife?' I ask.

Dartford's face clouds over, then he bursts out laughing. 'I'm not planning to abduct you,' he says. 'Anyway, if I'd wanted to do that, I could have done it on the road. I know that you left for Kent yesterday. Where did you go?'

'Bromley,' I say.

'For what purpose?'

'I don't remember.'

'Let's talk. Then maybe you will. Don't worry – I want to be your friend.'

I climb up into the coach, waving away his proffered assistance. I want to get out again owing him as little as I possibly can. I lower myself onto the leather seat opposite him.

'Mistress Cade is in Bromley,' I say. 'She confirms that you visited her at the Tower, but she doesn't know why. Nor do I. Do you want to tell me?'

'I am happy to be completely frank with you. I thought she had some papers that I needed.'

'The Ruby?'

'That's old history.'

'Your poem?'

Dartford narrows his eyes.

'What do you know about that?'

'I know what most of the Court knows – that you wrote it and accidentally sent it to the King. I also know, as you seem to have done, that Cade visited the King at about the same time. The King drew a sketch of a ship on the back of something and gave it to him. I think if we ever found the sketch it would have your poem on the other side.'

'You're well informed.'

'So is the King. He'll find out sooner or later.'

'I agree the King's no fool. But he'll have heard already. Of course, he never takes action on anything unless he has to. Until he's actually confronted with it, he'll ignore it, because it's easier to ignore it. But, if it became known that he knew, then his dignity as God's anointed would mean that he had no choice but to take action. He'd send me to the Tower because he'd be too idle to think of anywhere else to send me. And as long as the poem is out there, that remains a possibility. So, yes, you're right. I need the poem back, or I need to know that it's been destroyed. Maybe you can help me there.'

'Probably not. I've seen some of Cade's papers. But on your instructions, Mistress Cade has burned a lot of them. If Cade had it, then I think it's gone. But I can't even be sure he did take it.'

'You haven't taken it yourself?'

'No.'

'You'd tell me if you had.'

'Not necessarily. But I haven't.'

'I'd pay you well for it.'

'So would Arlington, and he'd have first refusal. I still don't have it.'

Dartford looks at me. Men who lie as habitually as Dartford always assume others lie too, but I think he believes me.

'So you think she burned it?'

'There was a pile of ashes in the fireplace. A burned poem and a burned invoice for timber look much the same, just as one day we'll all look the same in our graves.'

'That's dangerous Puritan nonsense. On Resurrection day, the God of the Established Church will be able to tell an earl's dust from a commoner's.'

'He is omniscient,' I concede.

'And therefore also knows that I had nothing to do with Thomas Cade's death,' says Dartford.

'Cade knew about the Ruby, of course,' I say.

'I've said: that's long in the past. If it became public it might have brought about the downfall of Pepys, but I've never claimed to be an honest servant of the Crown. Why should I worry about what Cade knew or didn't know? If you want to find Cade's killer, you should look closer to home.'

'Who had you in mind?'

'Your master might have wanted him dead.'

'Arlington's not my master.'

'He has you running around for him though, doesn't he? And he seems to have set you off on your current quest just after Cade died. Do you really think that was a coincidence? You may say that Cade was only a simple shipbuilder, but in so many ways he was only one step away from so many of

Arlington's friends – and his enemies. How anxious is Arlington that Cade's murderer is found?'

'He has other priorities,' I say.

Dartford smiles. 'Just consider this: when did Arlington ever tell you the whole truth about anything?'

'That's between me and Lord Arlington.'

'Well, consider it in private then. And bear in mind that Arlington would love to see me executed for the murder, if he could do it without getting his hands dirty. So why not arrange the murder of somebody he'd heard had tried to blackmail me, then see if he could pin it all on me? Have you thought of that?'

'I agree he might enjoy watching you hang.'

'I must correct you there – you might hang for murder, squirming your way to Hell on the end of a rope, but, as a peer, I'd expect to have my head cut off in the time-honoured way.'

'I'm sure Lord Arlington would wish everything to be done fairly.'

Dartford laughs. 'You're determined to be Arlington's lapdog to the very end.'

'I'd rather be his lapdog than yours.'

'You are certainly loyal to your master. I like that in a lapdog. How well is he paying you?'

'He is not paying me at all. What I do, I do out of loyalty to the King, not Arlington.'

'Which you have to prove constantly, to make up for your past service to the Republic?'

'It is as you say. Too many of us served Cromwell in the past for the King to be able to sweep us all away, but he watches us to see if a trace of old homespun wool still shows beneath the new velvet and lace.'

'But you still have some sympathy with the Good Old Cause?' he asks.

'Only hardened Republicans speak of the former regime in that way. It's not an expression I would use.'

'That is very wise,' says Dartford. 'But the Good Old Cause is being talked up again in certain circles – some say that England was merrier as a Republic.'

'That is not what men said then.'

'But they say so now. They also say that my Lord Buckingham is more fit to rule than the King. They say that his hand would be lighter than Oliver's, but that things would be run as they were then, when we could beat the Dutch every time. England would be respected again throughout Europe – not laughed at. I merely repeat what they say.'

'And what do you say, my Lord?'

'A wise man says no more than he has to. But he listens to what others tell him. You look like a wise man, Grey.'

'Appearances can be deceptive,' I say.

I descend from the carriage. I hear Dartford's driver crack his whip and the great wheels of the carriage grinding on the hot, sun-baked ground, but I do not look back.

Pepys keeps me waiting for half an hour before he condescends to see me. He scowls at me from behind his desk when I am finally ushered into his presence.

'I have told you that I have nothing further to say to you about naval contracts,' he says. 'You are wasting my time and your own. I do not believe that Arlington really has the authority of the King to act as he has. I would suggest that, for your own sake, you desist immediately. I shall, should the King ask me, assure him that you had no choice but to obey your master and that no blame should attach to you. I would do that, of course, on account of our long friendship and that we are both alumni of the same most worthy college.'

'I have already spoken to the King,' I say. 'He found my brief report to him quite useful.'

Pepys looks at me open-mouthed.

'What did you tell him?'

'You will understand entirely if I inform you that anything I said was in the strictest confidence.'

'I demand that you tell me, Grey.'

'Sadly you are in no position to demand anything. Especially since you were not dining with Lord and Lady Sandwich when Cade was killed.'

'Who dares say so?'

'Lady Sandwich. Yes, I know, you probably told Lord Sandwich that he should confirm your story, but Lady Sandwich slipped your memory. Perhaps you didn't think she was important enough – that we would not question a mere woman if we could ask her husband. Or are you saying that she is wrong?'

'Wrong? No . . . it is simply that I must have misremembered what I was doing that evening. I think you are right. Yes, I recall things more clearly now. I was elsewhere. Well, if that is all, I shall let you go and continue your very valuable enquiries. You must have a great deal to do.'

'So, where were you?' I ask.

'You surely do not need to know that?'

'If you tell me, I can judge for myself.'

Pepys goes over to the door, which is partly open, and closes it. He returns to his desk and sits down.

'Why don't you take a seat, Sir John? You must be

uncomfortable standing there. You received a leg wound, I believe, in the King's service.'

'Most of the time it troubles me no more than Arlington's nose wound. I'll stand, if that's acceptable to you. So, where were you?'

Pepys glances at the door. Then in a much lower voice he says: 'With Mistress Knipp.'

'The leading actress in Aminta's play?'

'Yes. Just so. A most talented lady. I had met her after her performance in *Macbeth* and we went to a nearby tavern. We engaged in conversation and were there some time. The meeting was wholly innocent. You should not think otherwise.'

'Good. Then there can be no harm in people knowing that.'

'I would rather my wife didn't know. She suspects . . . you see, Mistress Knipp writes me letters sometimes – under the name of Barbary Allen – from the song she often sings on stage, you know. My wife discovered one of the letters but cannot be sure it is to me because Mrs Knipp addresses me by an assumed name.'

'What name?' I say.

Pepys glances at the door again. 'Dapper Dicky.'

'Well,' I say, 'I'm happy that should be our little secret anyway.'

'There is no need to tell anyone, surely? About where I was. I mean, you do believe me, don't you?'

'Of course. I would never doubt anything another Magdalene man told me.'

Pepys grinds his teeth but says nothing.

'Well, I must go,' I say. 'I am due at the theatre later today. Mrs Knipp will be there. Shall I send her your best wishes?'

'I am sure,' says Pepys, 'that you will do as you damned-well please.'

Chapter 26

At the Play

Outside it is mid-afternoon, but here inside the theatre daylight is replaced with dozens of candles. They flicker constantly, so that the shadows they cast are always in agitated movement. It is as if nothing in this artificial space has the patience to remain still for a second.

The pit is filling up. That is the place to be, even though the benches have no backs and are covered with nothing more than green cloth. This is where the Men of Quality and the wits wish to be seen. They chatter to the ladies around them. That is why they are there. Nobody expects them to fall silent when the play begins. The galleries behind the pit rise up steeply. The better lit, lower ones are occupied by respectable tradesmen and their wives; the more obscure ones, higher up, are the domain of those who are, even now, stowing away their orange peel to throw at the most appropriate point in the drama. Above the stage are the side boxes, still empty, in which the King or Lady Castlemaine or some other dignitary may appear in due course. The noise is already growing. Many of those there are already drunk and looking for trouble. Orange girls pass amongst them selling ammunition. They will continue to do so even after the play starts. They need to sell oranges and people want to buy them. Only the most optimistic of playwrights expects every word of the drama to be heard.

This, I reflect, is Aminta's world, as remote from my drowsy, paper-filled office in Lincoln's Inn as Lincoln's Inn is from my estate in Essex.

Killigrew is at least more or less sober. 'Things have changed since Shakespeare's day,' he says, 'and changed for the better. Now there are wax candles and many of them; then not above three pounds of tallow. Now all things are civil, no rudeness anywhere; then it was as a bear garden. Then two or three fiddlers; now nine or ten of the best. Then all was open to the sky; now . . . well, you see, Grey, the fine building that we have constructed. We can make the Devil appear from the bowels of the earth. We can make men fly across the stage on ropes that are almost invisible. It is a shame that your wife has not permitted me to do so tonight.'

'There is nothing in the plot to require it,' says Aminta. 'The play is set in London in the present day. Nobody in London flies twenty feet or so attached by the waist to a very obvious piece of rope.'

'You might as well say that nobody flies in *Macbeth*,' says Killigrew reasonably. 'But many of the audience came just to see the flying forest.'

'No flying,' says Aminta.

'You may find that the takings on the third night are less than you hoped for.'

'Nevertheless, no flying – people or trees.'

Killigrew is not happy. He would doubtless prefer the actors to sing Aminta's lines while swinging from a trapeze, but realises that authors can be difficult about these things.

I scan the audience. Could any of them be Dartford's men? Several in the pit carry swords. I look up again at the boxes. There is no sign of the King, nor did I encounter a troop of dragoons outside the theatre. Killigrew was right not to trust the King's memory of a promise given in an idle moment.

We stand there and watch the remaining seats fill.

'Do we wait for the King?' I ask.

'Only if we want a riot on our hands. The play will begin at the hour indicated, or they will storm the stage. If you will excuse me, I shall go to the tiring room and tell the actors to commence.'

Aminta's play begins, as is conventional, with two world-weary rakes discussing life in general and the arrival in London of an old acquaintance of theirs and his beautiful new wife. The combination of Aminta's script and the presence of Hart and Mohun is sufficient to quieten even the upper tiers of seats. The only sound is appreciative laughter. Then there is a commotion from behind the stage. Hart and Mohun, to give them due credit, do no more than glance at each other, then continue with the play, but a moment later two men enter, swords drawn, through one of the entrance doors. The audience gasps at this bold twist in the plot, which I (having read the script many times) know does not exist.

'Well, gentlemen,' says one of the intruders. 'I think we can put an end to your games.'

There is a murmur amongst the audience as the gentlemen in the pit confidently explain this development to the ladies.

The ladies are somewhat doubtful but defer for the moment to their men's greater knowledge. Of course, if I were there with them I could explain the missing parts of the story – the rivalry between Arlington and Buckingham, my investigations, Dartford's threats, the King's forgotten promise . . . But without this background the next few minutes will be inexplicable and quite exciting.

From where I am, I could reach the stage only by clambering through the pit. I am not sure I would be able to manage to climb up onto it, especially after my ride to Bromley, unless Mohun or Hart has the leisure to help me up. At the moment both are fully occupied.

'Are there just the two of you?' asks Mohun.

'Two will be more than enough,' says the second intruder.

'I think you should both leave,' says Mohun. 'While you can.'

I have to say, he's good. He hasn't departed from his stage role at all. I hope he doesn't have to die in character.

The man laughs. 'Us?' he says. 'Get you gone and take your stupid words and blunt swords with you.'

It is perhaps the reference to blunt swords that finally stirs Hart and Mohun into action. They look at each other and both draw their weapons at the same moment. The blades flash in the light of ten dozen wax candles. Then I realise, as do the intruders, that these are no blunted props. Hart and Mohun have brought, as many actors do, their own swords as part of their costumes. They are not required to use them in earnest during the play, so their razor sharpness is no disadvantage. But it could be useful in this particular scene being written before my eyes. Do the intruders know that they are facing two veterans of the late wars? I think they do now.

They start to back away, holding their swords before them but with less confidence than before. One makes a lunge at Hart that is easily parried. If they had any doubts that actors can really handle swords before, they know the truth now. With Hart and Mohun closing in, they turn and run. Mohun succeeds in prodding a retreating rump with the point of his weapon. There is laughter and applause. This buffoonery is not Lady Grey's usual style of writing, but it is entertaining nevertheless. They feel that the look of panic on the intruders' faces was very well done – a little exaggerated perhaps, but comical enough.

Killigrew's face appears round a door on the other side of the stage. 'Have they gone?' he asks.

More laughter from the audience. They know Killigrew and are pleased to see that he will be playing the part of a scatter-brained old man with his periwig awry.

'These out of town ruffians are no match for a true London fop,' says Hart to the audience. 'They lack our cut and thrust, they do indeed.'

'It is a pity that they did not remain to be skewered on our city wit,' says Mohun. 'I had a phrase or two that would have run them through the guts and left them shitting epigrams for a sennight.'

'Even more a pity that we were not able to introduce them to our friend Sprightly and his new wife,' says Hart. 'He always loved to use his sword at every opportunity. He could make a woman swoon just by drawing it.'

'Since his marriage his blade is almost never in its scabbard,' says Mohun. 'I am told his wife loves to take it out and polish it.'

'My own sword is a little rusty,' says Hart. 'Do you think she might be persuaded to make it clean and bright?'

'No, I am told she has sworn to clean one sword and one sword only.'

'Well, I intend to ask her anyway,' says Hart. 'A shiny sword gives me more pleasure than I can describe.'

The gentlemen in the pit do not have to explain any of this dialogue to the ladies. One or two hold up fans to their faces, since they wish it to be known they are blushing. There is much laughter and applause from the shadowy heights.

'Do you think Sprightly will be here soon?' Mohun asks Killigrew pointedly. 'I think it would be best if he was. I do believe that, without him, we are running out of things to say to each other.'

'What?' says Killigrew. 'Oh, yes. I see. I'll go and find him.'

There is a brief pause and Kynaston appears with Mistress Knipp on his arm and the dialogue resumes where it had left off before the interruption.

But the play still cannot continue undisturbed. A few minutes later there is a flurry of activity and attention is briefly diverted to one of the boxes above the stage. The actors pause for a moment, look up and bow. The actresses curtsey. Then the action recommences as the King and his party settle into their seats. I receive a gracious nod of the head from Lady Castlemaine. The King too sees me standing by the stage and also gives me a smile. He has kept his word. He has come to protect us.

'I couldn't stop them,' says Kynaston. 'They came in through the side door over there and pushed straight past me. I went to fetch Killigrew, but by the time we could reach the stage, you'd already dealt with them. I'm not complaining. I'm just saying that we did all we could.'

We are seated in the tiring room. The performance is over. Everyone has agreed that it has all been a great success, and the sword-polishing business in particular. Dialogue like that would not have been possible in Cromwell's time. Aminta has received many compliments on her daring style. But the audience, even the wits who insist in visiting the actresses backstage, have now departed to discuss the new play in the coffee houses and inns around Drury Lane, and we are left alone. In the meantime, Hart and I have carried out a thorough search of the theatre before joining the others. The intruders might have left surprises for us almost anywhere, but it seems they have not. Killigrew has opened several bottles of wine in celebration of our deliverance.

'The war cost me a great deal of my acting career,' says Hart, 'but I learned something of the soldier's art in return.'

'You couldn't have actually run them through, you know,' says Mohun. 'Not on stage. The audience wouldn't have stood for it.'

'I agree. Not during a comedy. It would have been different if we'd been acting *The Duchess of Malfi*. A couple of bodies more or less wouldn't have been noticed. We could have told the audience afterwards that it was just pig's blood that was spilled.'

'Why did you have to prance in through the door like that?' Mohun asks Killigrew. 'It was difficult enough trying to squeeze two intruders plausibly into the plot, without having to explain your presence as well.'

'I was making sure you weren't dead,' says Killigrew.

'And what would you have done if we were? Soliloquised over our bodies for an hour and a half?'

'Well, you weren't dead. And you carried it off very well.'

'So we did,' says Hart. 'The Duke's Company would have

fled, leaving the stage bare. We of the King's Company are made of sterner stuff.'

'They'll expect that sword-polishing business tomorrow as well,' says Killigrew. 'They liked that.'

'I've noted it,' says Aminta. 'I'll need to polish it up a bit, if I can still use that expression to mean merely making something shine, but it wasn't so bad for an impromptu exchange of wit. And I can refer to it later on, when Sir Know-all Halfwit is in the garden with Mistress Sprightly. I can have him reach for his sword and give it a tug but be unable to draw it. They'll know what that means. Oh, and the orange girl in scene five can say that, in addition to selling fruit, she also polishes swords for gentlemen. She does, actually, when not engaged at the theatre. Did you see Pepys go off with her, by the way?'

'No, I must have missed him while I was carrying out the search.'

'I think he didn't want you to see him – in the auditorium earlier or going off with an actress. He looked worried but hopefully he managed to forget his troubles. His needs are not complicated.'

'Well, I don't think he had anything to do with the intrusion,' I say.

'No, they were Dartford's men, I assume,' says Killigrew.

'I think so. But again, it was just intended as a warning – to show what he might do. They weren't the most competent of ruffians, but they did manage to get in. If they'd chosen to start a fire rather than interrupt the performance then it might have been much nastier.'

'They'll return,' says Killigrew. 'The King won't be at every performance.'

'Perhaps,' I say. 'So far we've got the better of them, though.'

*

But on our return to Lincoln's Inn I discover that they have got the better of me.

The first thing I discover on entering my chambers is a heap of papers on the floor, books pulled from the shelves and disorder everywhere. The second thing is Will, lying face down, with dark blood matting his hair. I kneel by his side. He is at least still breathing. With Aminta's help I lift him up and we carry him to his bed. This would have been a job for Mother, who was adept at fixing broken bones and bandaging wounds, but Aminta and I do well enough with a basin of water to clean away the blood and one of my old shirts to be torn up for bandages. We are completing our work when Sparks arrives.

'Who did this?' he asks.

It is at this point that Will stirs on his bed and opens his eyes. 'I tried to stop them, sir,' he says.

'Who, Will? Who?'

'Dartford's men. Sleet and the other one. They wanted to go through your papers. I'm sorry, sir. I tried, but one came up behind me as I was trying to throw the other out . . .'

'Don't worry, Will, it's not your fault.'

'Did they take anything?' asks Sparks.

I survey the mess before me.

'It may take days, even weeks, to answer that question,' I say.

'Then there's nothing to be done but to tidy this away,' says Sparks.

'Yes, there is. I'm going to see Dartford.'

'I'll come with you,' says Will, raising himself on one elbow.

'No, even if you were fit and able to come with me, I'd need to do this on my own,' I say.

All three look at me. They are silent but their meaning is very clear.

'I can look after myself,' I say.

'I'll have more bandages and ointment ready for your return, in that case,' says Aminta.

I shake my head. 'I don't think you'll need them,' I say.

'And if you don't come back at all?' she asks.

'Tell the King I died his loyal subject,' I say.

Chapter 27

Dartford House

This time I am not kept waiting very long. I think Dartford was expecting me. I am shown quite quickly into his study. The heavy door closes behind me.

'Ah, Sir John! This is a pleasant surprise.'

'You have arranged a number of surprises for me today.'

He raises his eyebrows. 'You speak in riddles, sir. I have arranged nothing for you.'

'Your men tried to disrupt my wife's play. Fortunately Hart and Mohun saw them off very easily. Had you forgotten they were formerly soldiers?'

'I have no idea what you are talking about.'

'I think you do. Then you raided my chambers and left my clerk bleeding on the floor.'

'I have been here all day.'

'Your men have been elsewhere, going through my papers.'

'If you say so.'

'You seem to have issued me with three warnings,' I say.

'But there must be easier ways of making yourself clear than disrupting my wife's plays and striking my clerk over the head. Is your wish merely that I should return to Essex? If so, then perhaps you should simply explain why.'

He considers this. 'That is certainly what I would have advised you to do, had you asked me my opinion in the matter a week ago. Arlington clearly intended to inconvenience the Duke of Buckingham in some way, and my duty was to ensure that nobody made the mistake of helping him. But now . . . I really think it would be helpful if you remained in London. Our party is in need of good men – men, like you, who are not easily frightened off. Men who, whatever their loyalties to the present King, still remember the days of the Republic. Oliver was no tyrant, whatever men say now. But it is not a question of King or Parliament, as it was in 1642 – it is a question of Parliament working harmoniously with a good ruler or Parliament shackled to a bad one. Do you not agree, Sir John?'

'Nobody would disagree that a good ruler is better than a bad one.'

'Precisely. So, if you have a bad one – one who is disinclined to rule in a way that is for the good of his people – then it is simply a matter of how you set such a ruler aside and put in a better one.'

'Even an anointed king?'

'Anointing is merely a ritual. The anointed man is still flesh and blood.'

'But he is descended from kings for all that.'

'Is he? You know that for certain? There are those who say that the present King does not resemble the last one in any way. The last King was short, our present one tall, the last King quite fair, our present one very dark, our last King chaste . . .'

'I don't listen to Court gossip.'

'It's not gossip, so listen. The late King's wife, Queen Henrietta Maria, was and still is much attached to Henry Jermyn, Earl of St Albans. He was her Master of Horse. And a hard drinker. And a gambler. The King much resembles him.'

'I'd call that gossip.'

'Ask Arlington if you don't believe me. There's evidence in his papers. His most secret papers. He's got a report dated the thirteenth of August 1660 from Captain Francis Robinson, who overheard Nathaniel Angelo, a Windsor clergyman, asserting that all the royal children were Jermyn's bastards. Ask Arlington if you can see the report. Robinson's report. From what you say, he'd trust you with it.'

'You have remarkable faith in Captain Francis Robinson and in his hearing.'

Dartford nods. 'That's right, I do.'

'You really believe that the King is Jermyn's son?' I ask.

'It doesn't matter what I believe. It could be true, or people could be led to believe it was true, which is much the same thing. But the real point is that the King cannot claim he is the undoubted heir to the throne any more than you and I can. There is always doubt. And if such a claim is unprovable, then what value is it? Of all the claims to the right to rule us, descent in the male line is the most tenuous. Why should we not be free to choose our own leader?'

'Why are you telling me any of this?'

'Because such a thing can happen only if enough good men combine to bring about that change. They need a leader around whom they can coalesce – somebody with the skills required to rule the country. Richard Cromwell was a good man, but he lacked the experience needed to manage the factions that emerged after his father's death. General Lambert might have done the job, but he never courted popularity. The people never warmed to him. Even his own troops deserted when he tried to march on London.'

'But Buckingham has both the skills to manage the State and the ability to be loved?'

'Your words, Sir John, but I do not disagree with them.'

'What would you want me to do?'

'What are you offering to do?' he asks.

'I asked my question first.'

'You still have Arlington's trust?'

'Nobody has Arlington's trust, except perhaps Joseph Williamson.'

'I think you underestimate yourself.'

I shrug.

'I need to know what Arlington is thinking,' he says.

'Ask Arlington.'

'I'm asking you. Why has he set up this enquiry now?'

'You're not the target,' I say.

'Who is?'

'I can't tell you that.'

'Good. I like loyalty. At least in principle. Is Arlington loyal to the King?'

'So long as he sees the King's interests and his own as the same thing.'

'Can he be detached from the King?'

'I think not. He has thrown in his lot with the King and his brother, the Duke.'

'And Lady Castlemaine? Perhaps she is Arlington's target? I know you have spoken to her. What are her views?'

'She too is loyal to the King in her way.'

'But you have the information that would bring her down? I think you must have.'

'Not enough – not yet – if she retains the King's support as Arlington thinks she will.'

'But you could find out more?'

'You want me to work for you and against Arlington?'

'If that wouldn't inconvenience you.'

'And you would then cease to attack me and my family and my servants?'

'You could be confident that I would protect you in a way in which Arlington clearly cannot.'

I nod.

'So, you are with us?'

'Arlington's star is on the decline,' I say. 'Buckingham's is on the ascendant.'

'Just so.'

'A wise man does not allow himself to be dragged down by a falling patron,' I say.

'But rather to be pulled upwards by a rising one,' says Dartford. 'You have a way with words, Sir John.'

'I'll report back when I have any news,' I say.

'Thank you,' says Dartford. 'Of course, it would be helpful if you had news sooner rather than later. I mean, that I had solid proof of your support. Proof that you required no further inducement to come over to us. I always hate having to offer more inducement than is necessary.'

'I understand completely,' I say.

'The missing poem, for example,' he says. 'I'd like you to find it, if you haven't already, and give it to me rather than Arlington.'

'I don't know where it is.'

'I think you can find it. I don't know why, but I think you have a better chance of finding it than anyone else.'

'I'll try,' I say.

'Good,' he says. 'You have a small son, I believe?'

'Yes,' I say.

'And he is in excellent health, at present?'

'Yes.'

'Let us hope he remains so. I have only one question for you before you go: you didn't need to agree to work for me. You could have just run back to Essex.'

'Perhaps I still remember my old loyalties. Perhaps there is unfinished business from the days of the Republic.'

Dartford nods. 'I look forward to your reports,' he says. 'And the poem.'

'How is Will?' I ask, on returning to Lincoln's Inn.

'Sleeping,' says Aminta. 'But he complained of the pain in his head and could not stand the light from the window. He is in his bed with the curtains drawn.'

'He'll sleep it off,' I say. 'I've had worse.'

'Maybe there is less inside your head than his. But with luck he'll recover, as you say.'

'You sound doubtful.'

'When I went in to see him half an hour ago, he thought I was your mother.'

'I'm surprised. Will usually thinks he's my mother.'

'Don't joke, John. I'm worried about him.'

'He's had a blow to the head. That's all.'

'How did your meeting with Dartford go?'

I pause. 'He's not a threat any more.'

'Are you sure?'

'Yes, I'm sure. You're safe. Will's safe. Killigrew's safe. Little Charles is safe.'

Aminta looks at me uncertainly.

'Don't worry,' I say. 'Everything is fine.'

Chapter 28

From a Diary

Paying off ships crews all morning, with many complaints that the men were to receive tickets promising settlement at a future date and not hard cash as they had reason to expect. Some went off and sold their tickets at a great discount as soon they received them, but the King is slow to pay and indeed may never pay his many debts, so they may have been wise to do so at any price. One woman, collecting for her dead husband, lately killed at sea, asked how she might feed her children with a ticket and was so irate that I had to get two of my clerks to throw her out into the street, where she lay in the dust crying and cursing the King and the Navy Board, but at length went away since there was nothing she could do. It is wrong that the men who fought bravely for us through the Dutch wars and their widows should be treated so, but unless the Treasury can get us more money there is no alternative. The King's coffers are bare.

I was then told that Sir J. Grey was present and wished to see me. I told my clerk I was busy, and, knowing Grey has a wound to his leg, instructed that he should be left standing in the antechamber, in the hope that he would get tired and go away, but after half an hour he was still there and I had no choice but to see him. We spoke again of Cade's death and I was obliged to say that I had been with Mistress Knipp when the deed occurred, which I would not have done for all the world, but that I had to.

Since Mrs Knipp was appearing in Lady Grey's new play, I went to the theatre to see if I could speak to her, but she was already backstage and so I bought a ticket for one of the more obscure parts of the theatre, lest Grey should see me and wonder why I had come. I pushed my way to a seat, my Lady's reputation being high with the town and the theatre being full, and was squeezed against the very pretty daughter of a grocer who was there with his wife, my thigh pressed hard against hers, which I did not dislike, though I dared not place my hand on her knee, her father being so close. I had heard that the King was to attend with my Lady Castlemaine, but he was not come when the play began.

Hart and Mohun played two gallants who intended to cuckold their friend, newly wed to a girl from the country, and there was much merry talk between them. Then they were interrupted by two men with drawn swords and drove them off with ease, but afterwards their friend arrived and they each attempted to divert him while the other tried to seduce his wife, turn and turn about, which was very droll. There was much expectation that the comical swordsmen would return, but they did not and I could not see why they had made an entrance at all, then a man near me said that they were not players but hectors and the creatures of my Lord Dartford and there only to spoil the play, but Hart and Mohun had so much the better of them and carried it off so well that in truth I know not whether they were actors or no. But if they were Dartford's men he will be much displeased with them, for they put up no fight and were most amusingly trounced by Hart and Mohun, who prodded one in the rump with his sword as he fled.

After the play, when Grey was occupied elsewhere, I visited the tiring room behind the stage, but, Lord, what a poor show the men make once they have quit the scene, in their threadbare coats and cheap lace and false gems, though they look brave enough when they are performing and speaking their fine words. Knowing Grey would be back soon, I was unable to speak to Mrs Knipp for long, but enough to assure myself that Grey has not questioned her, which was a great comfort to me. She promised, if asked, to say I was with her the night Cade was killed, which I hope she will. I took the actress who played an orange seller in the play to a tavern nearby and had a merry time with her there in a private room and *nulla puella negat*, to my great satisfaction.

Then home to my wife who had burned supper waiting for me and would pick a quarrel on account of it, but I went to my study and made up the accounts for the paying off of the seamen today, and there will be more tomorrow and still no money withal.

Chapter 29

Whitehall

'I'm sorry, Sir John, Lord Arlington has been called away,' says Williamson.

'The matter will keep for another day,' I say.

'You know your business better than I do,' he says, 'but my advice would be not to trouble him with further reports on the naval contracts. He now has all of the information that he needs. If you wish to pursue the matter of Mr Cade's death, then you should do so discreetly and ensure that no ripples trouble the surface of his Lordship's pond.'

'He wanted me to investigate. He must expect a few ripples. Is Lady Castlemaine now his ally?'

'Who can say? We know these things only with hindsight. But for the moment there is no need to bring her down, nor should you do anything to trouble her.'

'And Dartford?' I ask.

'Why do you ask?'

'I am merely curious.'

'He serves Buckingham,' says Williamson. 'Arlington and Buckingham are two giant stags who cannot live in the same forest in peace with each other. Arlington will win, of course.'

'Your loyalty to him is noted.'

'No, I mean it. And if you've any sense, you'll listen to me. Merely view the thing as if you were the King. Arlington is fighting to be the King's chief advisor. Buckingham is fighting to be the King. His Majesty cannot allow Buckingham to rule these woods. So, Buckingham will have to go. It's the largest and noblest beasts that are the easiest to hunt down. They are used to chasing, not to being chased. All of their experience suggests to them that if they stand and fight, they will win. The lesser beasts know to run the moment they hear a twig snap behind them.'

'Well, I'm certainly one of the lesser beasts,' I say.

'We're all lesser beasts, John, at least when measured beside the King. We accept his rule and are allowed to graze contentedly in his sight. We are permitted to test our antlers against each other, but not against the King. Only the most foolish of beasts would risk attacking the leader of the herd. Unless they were certain they could win.'

'You've lost me,' I say. 'Is this an allegory of life at Court, or are we actually talking about hunting?'

'Oh, hunting, of course. I miss it greatly, down here in London, don't you?'

'I never hunt.'

'Allegorically or in reality?'

'Both,' I say.

'Good. Then stay away from Dartford.'

'Why do you say that?'

'Because you've been seen at his house.'

'I had business there. Lord Arlington knows that.'

'He has forbidden you to investigate Cade's death any further. You would have no other reason to talk to Buckingham's closest ally.'

'He can forbid me only if he's paying me. Otherwise, I'll investigate any death I choose. I'm a magistrate after all.'

'You are a magistrate in Essex, where there are presumably crimes committed as well. And I should warn you that whatever you say to Dartford, whatever he says to you, will be reported back to Lord Arlington.'

'You have spies in his house?'

'You know I can't tell you that.'

I yawn. It's a hot day and Williamson is boring me.

'I know what game Dartford is playing,' he says. 'And, if you don't, you're a fool. You are getting into water that is far too deep for you.'

'If there's one thing Arlington did,' I say, 'it's to teach me to swim.'

Chapter 30

The Tower

'We've started to lay the men off,' says Morgan. He's the third master of the Tower Yard in as many weeks. That might make some men pause for thought before they took the job on. But not Morgan. He's built like an ox in all respects. He still has a slight Welsh accent, but he's been in London for some time. Like so many who have sought work in this City, he will soon be as much a Londoner as any who were born here. He wears a leather apron over his grey linen shirt and brown woollen breeches. It wouldn't occur to him to give himself airs and graces now that he manages things here and the men call him 'sir'. He may be the last man in London to buy himself a periwig.

'I can see that's difficult for you,' I say.

'Yes, sir. I'd often dreamed of running a yard such as this. I little imagined that I'd come to it through the deaths of two colleagues, within days of each other. Nor did I imagine that, when I did take charge, my first task would be to sack my fellow shipbuilders, one by one. But there's nothing for them to do now.'

'You've been unlucky,' I say.

'Mr Cade's death was very unfortunate, but Mr Truscott's was downright strange.'

'What do you mean?'

'Well, here's what it is: I don't understand why he would hang himself like that.'

'I agree there doesn't seem to be a reason.'

'More than that, sir. I wouldn't tell you any of this if Mr Cade or Mr Truscott were still alive, but Mr Truscott had finally achieved what he wanted, if you see what I mean.'

'That he was finally in charge of things?' I say.

'No, I meant him and Mistress Cade ... Well, it was no secret in the yard that he and Mrs Cade were friendly, as you might say. And, fair play, she seemed as keen as he was. It wasn't just him trying to get possession of the yard, as some said. It was difficult for Truscott, though. Mr Cade gave him the job of deputy when he was down on his luck – he'd come up from the west somewhere looking for work. He owed Mr Cade everything, so he always said to me. But he didn't feel that Mr Cade treated his wife with respect ... he expected her to butter up men like Pepys who could give them contracts. That was wrong.'

'I see,' I say.

'And yet, Mr Cade was his master and a good one, as far as the work in this yard went. Then Mr Cade died and we were all very sorry for it, but it did seem to leave the way open for Harry. Strange that that was when he decided to hang himself.'

'Yes,' I say. 'He had some falling out with Mistress Cade.'

'I noticed he was low, sir, but no more than that.'

'He had family in Devon?'

'Yes, sir. He told me he had a wife there, but she died some years ago.'

'Not still alive and capable of writing letters?'

'No, sir.'

'Not capable of coming up to London and murdering him?'

'Not in the normal way of things.'

I consider this.

'So, how can I help you, Sir John?' he says. 'Or did you just come to ask about Harry Truscott?'

'I'm looking for a paper,' I say. 'It may be amongst Mr Cade's documents.'

'Oh, that!' he says.

'You know what and where it is?'

'I wish I did. But I know there was some important paper missing. The morning after Mr Cade died, some very grand person showed up at the yard asking for Mr Truscott. He was out, as it happened, so I spoke to the visitor myself. He said it was some paper he was after. He said that he'd spoken to Mistress Cade and that she'd given her consent to search the plans we keep here. So, we went through everything together. I kept an eye on him, I can tell you, in case that wasn't what he was really after, but we found nothing. Nothing at all. He gave me a sovereign, which may have helped me forget to check with Mistress Cade that she really had given permission. Still, there was nothing there and nothing taken away, so no harm done.'

'Does the yard often get visitors like that?'

'Like that? A visit from the nobility? Never! Mr Pepys comes to the yard quite often, of course. And Symonds from down river poked his nose in every now and then, when he could think of an excuse to talk to Mr Cade. We treat him with caution whenever he comes. He knows we're the better yard and I have no doubt he spies on us to find out how we do things. But even if he knew our secrets, well, they don't have the skill there that we do here. It would do him little good.'

'Thank you,' I say.

'Is there anything else I can do for you, Sir John?'

'No,' I say.

'I hope you find out who killed Mr Cade, sir. Mr Truscott said you were trying to discover him. He mentioned it quite often – before he died himself. Always talking about it. I think it worried him – that we didn't know who the killer was.'

'Yes,' I say. 'Whatever I do, I intend to find that out.'

The rear wall is quite low and the lane narrow and deserted. The Tower stares down at me disapprovingly. Lawyers are not supposed to break into houses.

I try the back gate first, but it is firmly locked. I could try picking the lock, a skill that I have acquired along with lying and skulking in the shadows, but that will take time and somebody could come round the corner at any moment. So, I look again at the wall. I think I can just about do it. I stretch out my hands and grasp the rough bricks at the top. Then I pull myself up, using my one good leg and a convenient hole left by a missing brick. I sit astride the wall for a moment surveying the lane in both directions, then the yard below me. The drop is only about six feet and there are no obstacles that will trip me up as I land. Then I hear footsteps. My plan to lower myself slowly and gently has to be abandoned. I swing my leg over and drop to the ground. I know in advance that this will be painful, and it is. The jolt as I hit the baked earth is almost as bad as when I received the wound, many months ago. But I am safe and out of sight of the people whose footsteps I hear on the far side of the wall. The back door is also locked, but I am fortunate to find a window with a badly fitting catch. A little pressure from my shoulder and it springs open. This time the climb is easier, the sill being little above waist height. I am back in the Cades' kitchen.

I think that Mistress Cade was genuinely in ignorance of the location of the poem, if it is here at all. I think that Cade may have known where it was, but never appreciated its value. The kitchen, Mistress Cade's domain, is the wrong place to look then. So is the great chest in the bedchamber.

I search the parlour. At least I now know what I'm looking for. There is a cabinet with drawers in it, but it contains letters from Mistress Cade's brother in Bromley and a kitchen accounts book. Anything else of interest has been taken by Mistress Cade. Then I see the books of poetry and the bookmark sticking out of *Paradise Lost*. Yes, of course. I stride across the room and lift it from the dresser. I unfold the bookmark. On one side there is a drawing of a ship. On the other there is a poem. I can see why Dartford might have liked this back.

We are gathered round Will's bed. He is sitting up now. He claims to be well enough to wait on us all, but Aminta assures him that he is not. He will stay there until he has been waited on a little more. He has just read through the poem. It has cheered him up a great deal, even though it was the cause of the attack on him. He is now admiring the drawing, which is boldly done. Sparks has just joined us.

'The sketch is signed by the King,' says Sparks, looking over Will's shoulder. 'Or somebody with the same initials. C. R.'

Will turns the paper over for him and Sparks raises his eyebrows.

'Yes,' I say. 'I thought so too.'

'This is the poem for which Mr Atkins was attacked?' asks Sparks.

'Just so,' I say.

'But it is about the King,' says Sparks. 'It accuses him of neglecting his duties in favour of whoring and gambling. As for what it says about his . . . his . . .'

Aminta nods. 'Dick?' she suggests. 'I think that is what the poet intends when he refers to the King's glistening sceptre. It would certainly be odd – possibly sacrilegious – if he really used the coronation regalia in that fashion.'

'But this would hang the author as soon as the King read it,' says Sparks.

'It was not intended for His Majesty's eyes. It was delivered to the King wholly by mistake. But I doubt that, having received it, His Majesty even glanced at it. He reads very little that is put before him unless somebody obliges him to. He probably turned it over, unread, and then sketched the ship,' I say. 'Cade took up the sketch and carried it off. His wife said he had his own ideas about what the ship should look like. He wasn't planning to actually use the sketch. Later he needed a bookmark. It ended up marking page four of *Paradise Lost*.'

'But would Dartford dare write such a thing?' asks Sparks. 'To circulate obscene poetry – yes, of course. That is common amongst courtiers, as I understand it. The King would find that amusing. A vicious barb against Lord Clarendon – what possible harm could there be? But to hand him this – it is *lèse-majesté.* It is out and out treason. It would, if unpunished, be to declare to the world that Charles Stuart lacked the power to defend his own name and reputation. It would say that he was no longer King.'

'In that sense it would strengthen Buckingham's hand greatly,' I say. 'I have no doubt this is Dartford's work. This is the poem Dartford wished to recover.'

Aminta considers. 'I agree. Few others would dare. And he is a competent poet; you will observe that this is no mere doggerel. Shakespeare would not have owned it, but it is written competently in pentameters. "The Ladies swarm as Bees do to their Hive / Around his Sceptre that's so apt to swive / And get them baby Dukes of new Creation / Indeed he is the Father of his Nation." And further down the page: "No whore's too low for our King to disdain / He'll stoop e'en to my Lady Castlemaine." And here: "One at a time, the ladies seek his Door / And then his Bed, while Lord A pimps for more." The author is not frightened of making enemies. And he strikes at Buckingham's rivals.'

'I am no judge of verse,' says Sparks. 'It seems to me somewhat crudely done, compared with Milton or Marvell. But it is not entirely unflattering. And it is true that the King has spawned more bastard dukes than any other monarch since the Conquest. Who can deny it? Still, the greater the truth, the greater the libel, as the Law would have it. I fear for Dartford if this became known to the King, I do indeed.'

'If it became known,' I say.

'But you will give this to my Lord Arlington?' says Sparks.

'He's asked for it,' I say.

'Then that's the end of Dartford,' says Sparks. 'And quite right too.'

* * *

Later I am sitting beside Will's bed. He is slumbering but suddenly he awakes and sees me there.

'You will give the poem to Arlington?' he says.

'I need to decide,' I say.

'You wouldn't return it to Dartford?'

'Don't worry about it, Will. Just try to sleep.'

'You're planning to go over to Dartford, aren't you?'

'What I'm planning to do is safer, Will. Safer for all of us.'

'Don't, sir. Arlington is arrogant, penny-pinching and ungrateful, but he's on the right side. He believes in peace and good order. Dartford is evil.'

'I'm sorry, Will. I realise that Dartford caused you to be here, bandaged and in bed.'

'It's not that, sir. I rather he came and hit me over the head every day for a week than that you supported such a man. Please, whatever you do, just give the poem to Arlington. Then go back to Essex and leave him to deal with Dartford.'

'I have to do it my way, Will. I know what I'm doing.'

'Very well, sir. I'm sure you know best. I just wish you wouldn't.'

'Don't tell my wife or Mr Sparks.'

'No, sir. Of course not. If there's anything I can do, let me know.'

'Just sleep, Will,' I say. 'Sleep and get better. I'm so sorry.'

Chapter 31

From a Diary

Left the house on ill terms with my wife, her parrot having again fouled the clean linen cloth on the dining table and eaten some strawberries from the kitchen, where it also shat on the cooking pans, though they being still dirty from last night it is but a little more cleaning for the maid. The parrot also said some words that, if my wife taught him, shock me greatly.

To White-hall where I have business with Mr Williamson. He tells me that Sir J. Grey is now reputed the creature of Lord Dartford, which I find it hard to credit, their characters being so wholly alien, each to the other. I asked if that meant that Grey no longer intended to report on the matter of naval supplies, but he did not know. Mr Williamson said that the King still wishes to rid himself of my Lady Castlemaine but that he knows not how, and is like to let her remain at Court because it is easier than chasing her away. But he is still enamoured of Frances Stewart and will have her, whatever my Lady C. says, and has decided to send her husband, the Duke, to Scotland that he may be more free in his addresses to la Stewart, which I am sorry for, the lady being one of the few at Court who is truly virtuous. The Duke of Bucks has said that he will put the Queen out of the way, if the King desires it, by kidnapping her and sending her to one or other of the plantations in the Americas, but I do not believe this. It would become known and be a great discredit to His Majesty, so why should the Duke consider this? Mr Williamson claims the King has in any case refused the offer, pretending to regard it as a jest, though he knows it was not.

Stopped at the apothecary on my way home and enquired whether he has a poison that would kill large birds. He said that he could acquire a powder that might do this, but he seemed so suspicious of my intent, the powder also being fatal to people, that I said I should think on the matter and come by at some other time. Which I shall.

Chapter 32

Drury Lane

We are standing in a box, looking down at the stage. The theatre is again filling up. We shall have a full house for the third performance.

'There was no need to bring your clerk,' says Killigrew. 'My own man can add up.'

'Will has suffered at the hands of Dartford's men,' I say. 'I thought that a little diversion would be good for him.'

'He could simply take his place on one of the benches below. Or I could have made a box available to you and your people, Sir John. It would have been my honour and pleasure.'

'Will likes to make himself useful,' I say. 'It's how he amuses himself. We trust you completely.'

'No, we don't,' says Aminta. 'Will is going to remain where he is until the last of the money is in and accounted for – that means until the first act at least is done. The second act of my play is where I have placed my best lines – all too often the opening scenes are lost as the audience drifts in and one half criticises the other's clothes or morals. By the second act, everyone is seated, the important judgments have been made and they can concentrate on what is happening on the stage. Then we count the entrance money and not before.'

'You've left Hart's extempore lines in there, I hope?' says Killigrew.

'They're my extempore lines now. Never say anything in front of a writer that you don't want them to steal.'

'I'm told that nobody in London can mention polishing a sword without the risk of being misunderstood,' says Killigrew.

'Take heed of him,' says Aminta. 'He stabbed me in mine own house, and that most beastly. He cares not what mischief he doth, if his weapon be out. He will foin like any Devil. He will spare neither man, woman nor child.'

'Did you write that too?' asks Killigrew.

'Shakespeare,' says Aminta. 'Henry IV Part II. I think you'll find the whole sword thing is an old joke, though mine is better – or at least dirtier – than the Stratford man's version.'

'Anyone who wishes to make money must write for the times they live in,' says Killigrew.

'And have a good agent to ensure they are not swindled,' says Aminta.

'You are most untrusting,' says Killigrew.

'It is the spirit of the age,' says Aminta. 'Don't blame me. I didn't invent mistrust. I just found it lying around and used it.'

'Then who should we blame?' asks a tall, dark man, entering the box behind us.

'Not you, Your Majesty,' says Killigrew.

Killigrew bows as little as he can get away with. I bow awkwardly – I'll never quite get used to it. Aminta curtseys very prettily. The King nods his approval.

'Who then?' he asks. 'Cromwell? Things were very prim and proper in my father's time. The theatre was quite genteel. Then Cromwell banned everything. Now the citizens of London are still catching up on the good times they might have had.' He looks at me pointedly.

'Your Majesty is as right as you always are,' I say. 'No more, no less.'

He laughs. 'Well said, Sir John. For a Puritan you make a very plausible Royalist.'

'I must protest—' I say.

'Your Majesty is correct,' says Aminta. 'My husband is an unreformed Puritan in red velvet. It is the clothes that lie and the hair that tells the truth.'

'Your wife must bespeak you a periwig, Sir John,' says the King, 'or I shall begin to suspect you are a traitor. Tomorrow you go to a periwig maker or to the Tower. Cover your head or lose it.'

'Don't give him a choice,' says Aminta. 'You've no idea which he'll settle on. I'll just take him to be measured for a periwig.'

'Once again, your wife has saved your head,' says the King. 'In both senses.'

'I am the most fortunate of husbands,' I say.

'Your Majesty does us too much honour in visiting my theatre again,' says Killigrew, returning the conversation to his preferred subject of himself.

'One performance of Lady Grey's work is never enough,' says the King. 'I hope that Lord Dartford has not troubled you further?'

'No, Your Majesty,' I say.

'You have reached an understanding with him?'

'I think so.'

'I had heard something of the sort.'

'You have heard correctly.'

'Well,' he says. 'If that is really what you want . . . And now I must return to the Queen. It is good that she and I are seen together from time to time, or people might form the wrong opinion of us. It's not advisable for people to hold the wrong opinion of you, Sir John. All sorts of things can happen if they do. I don't often give advice, but I'm giving it to you now.'

Afterwards Aminta says to me: 'What did the King mean, "an understanding" with Dartford?'

'Nothing,' I say. 'Just that he will not bother us again.'

'And in exchange?'

'Nothing of importance.'

'People like Dartford always want something in exchange.'

'We'll go back to Essex soon,' I say. 'He won't trouble us there.'

The following day I am sitting at my desk, sorting the last of my papers, when I hear a knock at the door. After a short pause, Will brings me a letter. I open it.

'I'm going to have to go out,' I say.

'Is there anything you need, sir?'

'No, Will. Nothing. I'll be back as soon as I can.'

Chapter 33

Whitehall

'You summoned me, my Lord?'

Dartford looks at me and smiles. 'Yes, Sir John, I have a small errand that I would like you to run for me.'

'I am yours to command,' I say.

'I am pleased to hear it,' he says. 'You won't regret coming over to us. Nor will Lady Castlemaine.'

'She is of your party?'

'Not yet. That is your task for today.'

'I think you ask the impossible.'

'No, she very much respects you. She sees you as being honest and incorruptible. Once she knows that you are on our side, half the work is done.'

'And the other half?' I enquire.

'We will offer her what she really desires.'

'Gold?'

Dartford laughs. 'No, not that. Give her gold and she gambles it away. No, what she really wants is the King.'

'And you can deliver that?'

'Yes, I think so.'

'But when Buckingham comes to power, there will be no more King.'

He shakes his head. 'That was the mistake that Parliament made in 1649. They believed that it was a question of King or Parliament. And that came back to bite them on their arses. My Lord's thinking is somewhat different. Buckingham will revive the office of Lord Protector and govern the kingdom. But the King will not be sent to the block or even into exile. He will remain here, at the Palace of Westminster, or on the racecourse at Newmarket or at the tennis court, entirely as he prefers. He may even sit on the throne from time to time in ermine robes and wear a gold crown. In short, he will continue to do the things that he enjoys and Buckingham will do the things that the King does not enjoy – that is to say, managing Parliament and levying taxes and negotiating treaties. We shall be a Republic again, but there will be no need for the Royalists to rise against it, because the King will still be there, large as life.'

'Not everyone will agree that is a good plan.'

'We are picking them off one by one. We arranged things so that the loyal Coventry was sent to the Tower. Arlington and the Duke of York are our next targets. We need merely to stir up the mob against Catholics. Soon the King will be completely alone.'

'And the King will then just stand aside?'

'He will be persuaded. He is very aware of how it ended for his father. He does not wish to be the last of the Stuart line. And he won't be. He will have the leisure to extend his line almost indefinitely.'

'And you want Lady Castlemaine to persuade him? What's in it for her?'

'I said: the King. She will marry him, and will become Queen. And all those who have called her a Catholic whore will have to lick the dust from her shoes.'

'I can see that would be an attractive offer.'

'And you will convey it to her. If it came from Buckingham, if it came from me, she would see it as a trick. But if you say that we will keep our word . . .'

'I cannot guarantee success,' I say.

'That is not what I am asking for. I am asking that you put the offer to her.'

'What happens to the present Queen? Am I allowed to ask that?'

'She will be returned to Portugal. In a sense she never really left it – not in her heart. She is still more comfortable talking to her Portuguese ladies or listening to Jesuitical sermons in her gloomy chapel. If she refuses to go . . . Well, there are other ways of ensuring that the King is no longer encumbered.'

'Very well,' I say.

'You ask for nothing for yourself, if this succeeds?'

'No,' I say. 'I ask for nothing for myself.'

The Palace at Whitehall is a great disappointment to many who do not know it. They imagine a vast edifice with much glass and stone and many elegant pillars. It is a rabbit warren of old buildings of many styles, some lofty and regal, some low and tumbledown, living in comfortable proximity to the dirty Thames. It would take a lifetime to study all of its two thousand rooms, its winding cobbled passages, its river walks, its gardens and its rush-matted corridors. Too many people inhabit it for it to smell sweet, even when the rooms are sprinkled with rose-water. It is true that lords and ladies may be seen strutting in silk and velvet through the lily-bordered gardens; but there are also serving men, pages, clerks, cooks, scullery maids and those like me, who have no desire for people to discover what we do.

Lady Castlemaine's quarters at the Palace are not far from the King's and look out over the bowling green. They are panelled in a pale wood and furnished with tables and cabinets of polished walnut and chairs upholstered in new rose silk. For some time now she has been standing by the tall sash window, observing the fashionable world drifting by, considering what I have said to her. Finally she turns to me.

'I am disappointed in you, John,' she says. 'To serve Lord Arlington must be trying at times, but it is honourable work for all that. To be the creature of that snake, Dartford, on the other hand ... How could you stoop so low?'

'I support the cause, not the man,' I say.

'Republicanism?' She spits the word at me.

'Peace,' I say. 'If the King continues as he is doing, there will soon be a rebellion again. He is losing the support of the people. They will rise against him, Buckingham or no Buckingham. Just as the later stages of the last civil war were bloodier and more brutal than the opening campaigns, so a renewed conflict would be more horrible still, as each side attempted to revenge whatever defeats were inflicted on it by the other. In Ireland, Cromwell burned cities, laid waste the countryside. I don't want to see this here too. I don't want to see the flames rising over Cambridge as they did over Drogheda. The settlement that Buckingham proposes – a powerless King who reigns but does not rule, a Republic in everything but name – would bring us peace for a hundred years.'

'And I would be a powerless Queen?' she asks.

'Not with your cousin Buckingham as Lord Protector. I think that you might play one man off against the other very nicely. You could be more powerful than either of them. You'd enjoy that.'

'Your Republican sentiments would permit it?'

'It would not be my concern,' I say.

'So, what are you in this new regime?'

'I am a country magistrate in Essex, if you permit it my Lady, remembered in history mainly as the husband of a noted playwright and poet.'

'Has Dartford offered you nothing?'

'I have not encouraged him to.'

'You could be so much more than Dartford's lackey, John. You are so much better than he is.'

'I think you can see what I am very clearly. What answer shall I take him?'

'Tell him that you made his case as well as it could be made. Better than he deserves it to be made. If he disposes of Arlington and the Duke of York as he says . . . but I must be Queen, properly crowned. Crowned at Westminster Abbey, with trumpets and sackbuts and boy choristers in white surplices all madly in love with me. An anointed Queen – not merely a mistress in chief, with the next mistress waiting in an anteroom for the King to desire something younger.'

'I shall make that clear, my Lady.'

She half holds out her hand towards me, then changes her mind. She turns on her heel and marches towards the door, her lapdogs scrambling after her. I find my own way out into the gardens and from there back to Lincoln's Inn.

* * *

'The letter came for you while you were out,' says Will, handing me the folded and sealed sheet of paper. I do not need to open it to know who is writing to me so often.

'Thank you, Will,' I say.

'Did you have a useful morning?' he asks.

'I think so,' I say.

I break the seal and quickly read what Dartford has to say. It is brief and assumes that I have nothing to do this afternoon other than wait upon him.

'I'll need to go out again,' I say.

'Lord Dartford?' he asks.

I can see his point. I am dancing attendance on the man who caused him to be struck over the head.

'Yes,' I say. 'Is there anything to eat here before I go? Some bread and cheese or something?'

'I don't think so,' he says.

'Could you fetch me something? From the tavern?'

'Mr Sparks has asked me to draft a will for him,' says Will. 'I said that I would do it immediately.'

'Of course,' I say. 'I understand completely.'

I take my hat and head for Westminster again. This time to Dartford House.

'You should have come straight here,' says Dartford. 'I expect my men to report back to me at once.'

'I apologise, my Lord,' I say. 'But I am happy to tell you that it went well. The Lady is inclined to accept your proposal. You'll need to find some sackbuts and cherubic choirboys, but otherwise she's content. I think her doubt is that you can dispose of Lord Arlington and the Duke of York. But that's not my affair.'

'I got rid of Coventry. His weakness was his vanity. Once he'd been lampooned in that play, his pride was hurt and getting him to challenge the Duke to a duel was very simple. What's Arlington's weakness?'

I consider this carefully. 'His daughter,' I say.

'What, kidnap her?'

I shake my head. 'Nothing that difficult. He wants her made a duchess. That's the bait to lure him with.'

'Go on.'

'Send him the offer of the hand of one of the King's bastard sons in marriage. He'll snap it up.'

'Why would the King do that?'

'He won't do that. You will, implying that it is on the King's behalf. Once you have Arlington's reply – which will be an emphatic "yes" – then all you need do is to make it public that he is plotting to link his own undistinguished family to the Stuarts. When Clarendon married his daughter to the King's brother it was one of the most unpopular things that he did. People don't like ambition of that sort. The King will like it even less.'

Dartford nods. 'Well done, Sir John,' he says. 'Yes, I like the way you think. We'll do that.'

'One other thing,' I say. 'It would be good to get Joseph Williamson on board as well. He's a good man of sound views. If you approve, I'd like to go and see him this afternoon.'

'Be careful what you say. He is Arlington's loyal servant.'

'So was I, once.'

'Well, if he can serve me as well as you, he will be a valuable asset indeed. You have my permission to speak to him.'

'Thank you,' I say. 'Now, if you'll excuse me, I'll go and get some dinner.'

'Go down to the kitchens. You'll find some of my other men there. The cook will serve you with some ale and bread and cheese.'

'Thank you, my Lord,' I say. 'I am grateful for your hospitality.'

I find the kitchens eventually. Dartford House is elegant and symmetrical above ground, a maze of tunnels beneath.

I am served by a reluctant cook, who informs me that the other servants finished eating an hour ago. I do however recognise a couple of them, still lolling on their benches, battered tankards in their hands.

'I was told you changed sides,' says Makepeace. 'Glad to have you with us, Grey.'

I nod and cut into the hunk of cheese on my plate.

'We're sorry that we had to warn you off the other day,' he adds. 'You'll not bear us any grudge for that?'

'I hope I gave as good as I received,' I say. 'In any case, I must apologise for having Mr Sleet arrested.'

Sleet laughs. 'You were well wide of the mark there, as his Lordship could have told you.'

'So, his Lordship knows who it was?' I ask. I pick up my tankard and drain it.

Makepeace glares at Sleet.

'That's not what Sleet meant,' says Makepeace. 'And it's not our place or yours to enquire any further.'

'Of course,' I say. 'I understand completely. What's it to us if his Lordship does know?'

'Exactly,' says Sleet. 'Just what I was saying the other day. What's it to us what we all know?'

I pretend not to notice Makepeace kick Sleet for the fool

that he is. These are after all now my friends. I wish to leave here on good terms with everyone.

'Well,' I say, 'I had a more pleasant task this morning than enquiring into a murder.'

'I know,' says Makepeace with a grin. 'I made sure you were followed, just in case. His Lordship doesn't entirely trust you yet, Grey. So don't do anything that he might find suspicious, or you could end up dead in an alleyway. I'm just warning you, as a friend.'

'I know I was followed,' I say. 'I saw your man, clear as day. I could have given him the slip at any time. I hope you have better than him, or you'll never know where anyone is. Anyway, Lord Dartford knows exactly where I am going next. I made sure I told him. Follow me there if you want to. I won't stop you.'

'Very wise,' says Makepeace. 'Dartford's not a man to cross. Not in any way.'

My meeting with Williamson, which takes place in a tavern rather than his office, is satisfactory in all respects. He takes little convincing. In another age, and we both remember such an age, he might have hesitated longer, might have been less willing to stoop as low as I proposed. But he agrees. I shall be able to report, when I need to, that he gave me every assistance. I am making progress.

Will has gone out on Mr Sparks's business. That is to be expected. Sparks is Will's future. I am merely his past, and a disreputable one, as he has now discovered. His absence gives Aminta the chance to speak her mind.

'Are you mad? How can you work for Dartford?'

'Who says I am?'

'The whole Court says you are! Everyone knows that you have switched sides and that he treats you like one of his lowest servants. Please forget the fact that I am mortified and humiliated. That doesn't matter in the slightest. Arlington never had the slightest care for your safety, but he did value you. Dartford does not even do that. You mean less to him than two halfpennies in his breeches pocket. You will not be alive at the end of the month.'

'Then you will not be troubled further by what the ladies at Court say about me.'

'But why are you doing it? If you are afraid of him, then let us just go back to Essex. He will not follow us there. But you remain, just so that he can drag you lower and lower.'

'I have a debt to pay,' I say. 'One that goes back a very long way.'

'How far?'

'Brussels,' I say.

'When the King threatened to have you shot?'

'Yes,' I say. 'Exactly that.'

'And you haven't forgotten?'

'How could I?'

'You've harboured that all this time?'

I say nothing.

'Not long ago,' says Aminta, 'you told me that, as Arlington's spy, you had to live the part you were playing. You had to believe that was who you really were. Is that what you've been doing all these years? Pretending to be a loyal subject of the King? Pretending to be a loving husband and father? But just waiting for your chance to be revenged on Charles Stuart?'

I say nothing. There is nothing to say.

'You're right,' she continues. 'He is the most disappointing king in living memory. I can understand why people look back on Cromwell with regret. But even so – the risk of siding with Buckingham is enormous and you haven't even asked him for any reward. You're mad.'

I nod.

'I'm going back to Essex,' says Aminta. 'First thing tomorrow. You may follow me or not as you wish.'

'I still have things to do in London,' I say.

'Then do them,' she says. 'Do them and go to your new master for a pat on the head. Just remember he has more important dogs than you.'

Of course, she is right. I've have fallen very low. But I have a little further to go before I can stop.

Chapter 34

At a Tavern

'How did you find me?' asks Betsy.

'I was aware that you were looking for work. I was aware that you could be contacted through an agency that deals with such matters. I made a guess that you had not found work yet and would respond to an invitation to an interview.'

'They all want references,' she says. 'That bitch didn't give me one.'

'They also probably want a maid who is sober, at least when meeting her new employer for the first time.'

'Well, I don't think you're about to employ me, so it matters little what I've drunk. The weather is hot and I'm thirsty.'

I call for more ale for my dishevelled friend and allow her to quench her thirst a little.

'You're right. I wouldn't employ you if you were the last maidservant in London,' I say.

'Charming.'

'But I'll pay you for information.'

'Like you paid last time?'

'You left before I could settle up,' I say. I count out five Shillings and push them across the table. She stuffs them into a pocket under her skirt without thanks or comment.

'What do you want to know?'

'First, tell me about you and Harry Truscott,' I say.

'I loved him,' she says.

'And did he love you?'

'He might have done. If she hadn't let him into her bed.'

'She being your mistress?'

'He's not going to look at a maid when he can have the mistress, is he?'

'But you didn't give up on him?'

'I gave him time to come to his senses ... How much you paying me for this?'

I take a half sovereign out of my purse and hand it to her. 'There's more,' I say. 'But I need the truth. And if you try to lie to me, then I shall ensure that your life is not worth living. Because I can do that.'

'I'm not afraid of you,' she says.

'Whether you are afraid of me will make very little difference to what happens to you,' I say. 'It will still happen. I know people whose job it is to make the lives of others unbearable. And they enjoy doing it. So, tell me, why did you inform Mistress Cade that he had a family in the south-west?'

'Because he did,' she says.

'How did you know?'

'I read it in a letter.'

I take *Paradise Lost* out of my pocket and open it on the table. 'Read what you see in front of you,' I say.

She opens her mouth, then closes it again. 'Can't,' she says.

'No, you can't, can you? So you read nothing in a letter.'

'All right. I made it up. It might have been true.'

'But it wasn't. It was a lie. He had no more wife living in Devon than you did.'

'It worked though. She believed me. She told him to sling his hook.'

'He came to you for help, didn't he?' I say.

'How do you know?'

'He told me he wrote to Mistress Cade at her brother's. He had to get that information from somewhere. Cade was dead by then. You were the only servant. You were one of the few people who might have known where she'd gone.'

'I loved him,' she repeats. 'Do anything for him. Yes, he was really miserable after she'd gone. So I said I'd take the letter to her. In Bromley. If that's what he wanted. Been there, hadn't I, when she visited her brother? Knew just where it was. Not the name of it, or anything, but where it was. He said bring back her reply. If I wasn't back in two days, he'd know there was no hope. Well, I reckoned I knew what the answer was likely to be. Once she'd said "no" that would be everything sorted out nicely. Then I could cheer him up a bit.'

'Did you get back in two days?'

'Sort of. Got back to London, but when I went to the yard, Symonds was there. He said to come for a drink. So I did. We went to a tavern and he asked me a lot of questions. I can't much remember what happened after that. I didn't know where I was and didn't much care as long as the drink was flowing. Next morning, or maybe the morning after that, I woke up in a bed somewhere in Southwark with a splitting headache. The innkeeper said somebody had paid all my bills for me and I could sling my hook. I went to find Harry and give him the letter, but he was dead.'

'Are you saying he hanged himself because no reply had come to him?'

'Maybe. But why? Even if he didn't have her, he had me.'

I consider this doubly unfortunate outcome. But Truscott does not seem the sort of man to kill himself simply because he had been disappointed in love. There has to be something else that I've missed.

'Where was Truscott when Mr Cade was killed?' I ask.

'At the yard,' she says. 'I saw him there.'

'So, he couldn't have been at Lincoln's Inn that evening?'

'No. Unlike Mistress Cade. I saw her going off shortly after the master left the house. He left. She followed him.'

'To Lincoln's Inn?'

'I don't know where else she'd have gone.'

I hand her a gold sovereign.

'Thank you,' I say.

'Do you want me to testify against her in court? If so, that's another five Shillings.'

'Maybe. I'll let you know when I've been to Bromley.'

This time I travel by coach. I may need both legs in good working order.

I descend from the coach, dusty and shaken by travel over the hard summer roads, and fortify myself with a much-needed tankard of ale, for the price of which I am able to confirm that Mistress Cade is still resident at her brother's house. My journey has not been wasted.

I set out for the smithy, winding my way through the narrow streets. The overhanging upper floors of the houses provide much-needed shade, but I am sweating by the time I arrive at the lane that leads to Cooper's modest residence.

Any hopes that Cooper might have gone into town on some errand are dispelled by his very obvious presence as I enter the front yard.

'I thought I'd told you to get out of my house and never return,' is his greeting.

'If you did say anything of the sort, it wasn't within my hearing.'

'No, it wasn't, was it? You made yourself scarce as soon as you'd finished threatening my sister. A man might have stayed to face her brother, but you didn't.'

'That's very true,' I say.

'Well, you can go now. She doesn't want to see you.'

'I don't deny the truth of that either, but I need to see her. Perhaps you'd let her know I'm here.'

'Make me.' He picks up, from the heap of scrap iron by the forge, a rusty sabre. A soldier would get himself flogged for having a sword in that condition, but I do not doubt that it could still do damage.

I draw my own sword. For once, I think I may win in a fair fight. Hopefully I'll need do no more than run my blade through his arm.

'Let's discuss this like adults,' I say. But before I even finish the sentence his blade flashes through the air in front of my face. Like so many who have rarely used a sword, he believes that it is necessary to draw the blade right back before taking a swing, exposing his whole body to a leisurely thrust into his guts.

'I have no argument with you,' I say. 'I'd prefer your sister was able to concentrate on talking to me, rather than have her waste her time binding up your wounds.'

His response is another swing of his sabre at chest height, which I parry easily with a half hanger. His blade is deflected to one side, leaving him looking surprised. He really has no idea how to fight with a sword.

'I'll give you one last chance,' I say. 'Drop the sword.'

He repeats his previous move. This time I simply step back to show how easy it is to avoid the blow. My foot, however, strikes one of the many pieces of scrap on the floor of the smithy. I stagger backwards, into something even larger. Then I am lying on the ground, more than a little stunned, with my sword spinning away across the floor. I remind myself never again to opt to fight fairly, even against an idiot who has never had a fencing lesson in his life.

Cooper advances on me slowly, an evil grin on his face. The rusty blade, I decide, won't be very effective for cutting, but whatever he does next is still likely to hurt. Then I hear a woman's voice.

'Stop that at once! Both of you boys, stop it! Fighting like that never solved anything. Tarquin, put that sword down now!'

'*Tarquin?*' I say.

'I can't help what my parents named me,' he growls.

'Even so,' I say.

Tarquin drops his sword to his side.

Mistress Cade looks down at me. 'What do you want now?' she says. 'It had better be good. His middle name's Satan.'

'Really?'

'It's only a nickname he was given by the people who really know him. The priest told my parents he couldn't actually baptise him that. Why are you here, Mr Grey?'

'Betsy can't read,' I say. 'There was no letter from Devon. Harry Truscott had no wife – at least no living wife.'

'The lying cow,' she observes.

'But she didn't need to read in order to see you heading off to Lincoln's Inn the night your husband was killed.'

'Is she going to testify to that effect?'

'Only if I can find the five Shillings she plans to charge for her testimony.'

She looks at me lying on the ground at her feet.

'Let's talk,' she says.

We are strolling through the garden again.

'For once that silly trollop is telling the truth,' she says. 'I did follow Cade. Harry came round that evening – came to the back door where Cade wouldn't hear us. He told me that he and Cade had had a conversation. My stupid husband had told him he had been trying to see you and was going back for one last attempt. He was going to tell you everything – Pepys, the Ruby, the lot. It would have been the end of the yard. We'd have never built another ship for the government. Harry said there was nothing to be done, short of killing the fool before he left the house. I said, fine, let's kill him then, but Harry was on about how Cade was a good master and had given him a job when he needed it. I knew if anyone was going to stop Cade it was going to have to be me. That was the point when I heard the front door slam shut.

'I hurried after Cade, hoping to catch him before he reached Lincoln's Inn. It was getting dark, but I followed him across the City, through the ruins and out of the gate on the far side. Maybe if he'd been going slowly I could have kept up with him in my skirts and petticoats, but I couldn't. The gatekeeper at Lincoln's Inn held him up, no doubt questioning him about who he wanted to see at that hour. But he was entering the

Inn as I caught up with him again. I had no idea where he had gone – I didn't even know your name to ask directions – Harry had just said a lawyer at Lincoln's Inn. So, I decided the best thing was to wait under the trees until he came out again. I'd find out what he'd done and strangle him on the way home through the ruins if I had to. But he never did appear. In the end, I got a link boy to see me back through the City. Next thing I heard about Cade was that he'd been killed.'

'Why didn't you say this before?'

'I said I'd have killed him myself that night. Why should I turn in the person who did kill him?'

'So, who did kill him? Truscott? You left him at your house but he could have followed both of you and climbed into the garden without your seeing him.'

She shakes her head. 'It wasn't Harry.'

'You might like to believe that—'

'No, it really wasn't. When Harry came to me that evening, one of the things he told me was that Cade had already blabbed to too many people about his plans. One of them had come to him an hour or so before to ask what Cade meant to do. Harry told him that Cade was going to see you. Later, when Harry heard what had happened to Cade, he blamed himself. Said that first he'd betrayed his master by bedding me. Then he'd caused him to be murdered by telling the killer exactly where to go.'

'So who was it who came to see Harry Truscott that evening?'

'Symonds,' says Mistress Cade.

'He may have told him, but that doesn't mean he went to Lincoln's Inn—'

'I saw him there,' says Mistress Cade. 'He didn't see me, but

I saw him in the Fields. He was working his way round the wall, looking for a place to climb in.'

'I know he was involved in the Ruby business,' I say. 'But, even if he was there that evening, would he really have killed your husband?'

'Oh yes. He had plenty of reasons for wanting Cade dead. For a start, Symonds had been acting manager at Deptford for a long time. He wanted to be commissioner there, but didn't have the influence or the money to buy the post. My husband did. Symonds also knew how much more efficient our yard was than his. He was always round trying to find out how we did things. There was every chance he'd lose even what he had without a powerful patron to protect him. I'd heard Symonds was trying to get in with Dartford – he hoped if he did him a few favours Dartford would buy him the commissioner's job. Dartford hated my husband, of course, for trying to blackmail him. That Dartford didn't fear exposure was irrelevant – it was the insult of being threatened by a mere tradesman that he'd never forgive. I suspect he and Symonds did some sort of deal. I'm sure Symonds thinks he's safe. Of course, Dartford's influence won't be worth much if the King sees that poem you talked about.'

'No,' I say. 'It won't.'

'Lord Dartford's man left this for you,' says Will as I come through the door. He hands me a folded and sealed sheet of paper as if it were a cold dog turd that he had no choice but to pick up in his bare hands. And he's had a lot of turd to handle lately.

I open the letter. It is, as expected, another summons to wait upon Dartford.

'Could you take a message to Mr Williamson for me, Will? If you've nothing more pressing to do for Mr Sparks, of course.'

'Is Mr Williamson now of your party?' he asks stiffly.

'Yes,' I say. 'Very much so.'

'I'm sorry to hear it. I always thought he was an honest man.'

'Nevertheless, I'd be obliged if you'd take him my message. After that, if you no longer wish to serve me, you may quit and I shall not blame you.'

Will takes a deep breath. 'Very well, Sir John. I'll take your message. For the sake of our old friendship. Then I'd be grateful if you'd accept my resignation from your service. Do you wish me to fetch a pen and paper?'

'No, there are some things better not committed to a written document. You'll be able to remember the message.'

'And what is it, sir?'

'Just find Mr Williamson and tell him: "Now." That's all.'

'Only that?'

'Only that.'

He turns and heads for the door. I hear his footstep on the stairs, just as I once heard Thomas Cade's. As my old Republican friend Probert would have once said: *alea iacta est*. The die is cast.

Chapter 35

Whitehall

'You were to tell me where you were going,' says Dartford. 'Forgive me, my Lord. My understanding was that your man was to follow me, skulking in the shadows where I should not see him.'

'Don't be impertinent, Grey.'

'But it's true, nevertheless. You have had me followed.'

'That's my business.'

'Well, tell him not to follow people quite so obviously. It's too easy to give him the slip.'

'Is it? So, where have you been then?'

'Bromley.'

'I did not tell you to go there.'

'I was unaware that I could only go where you instructed me to go. I have provided you with information on Arlington. If you don't trust me after that, then there is little I can do to convince you. My name is mud in Arlington's camp. You must know that?'

Dartford seems a little mollified. 'I'm sorry, Sir John. Yes, of course. It is common knowledge that you and Arlington have parted company. He reviles your name. My wife knows Lady Arlington. Lady Arlington has no doubts on the matter. She spoke of you in the most disparaging way possible. My wife also knows your wife a little and was able to observe her very genuine unhappiness.'

'Then there is nothing more to be said about that,' I say.

'So, what business had you in Bromley?' he asks. 'You visited Mistress Cade?'

'She is an attractive widow, my Lord.'

I look him in the eye. Does he know anything that I have done in the past few hours? The real test will be whether I am attacked and beaten up as I leave the house, but I think I shall not be. Not this time.

He laughs. 'She's not to my taste, but very obliging, I'm sure. Did you speak to Williamson?'

'Yes, my Lord.'

'And was he helpful?'

'He could not have been more so,' I say.

'Good,' he says. 'We make progress then.'

'We do indeed,' I say.

It is now late, so I do not call on Williamson until the following day. He nods at me as I enter his office.

'Did you get my message?' I ask.

'Yes. And acted on it last night. Could it not have waited until today?'

'I had to go and see Dartford. Whenever I do that, I have to allow for the fact that I may not get out alive. I wanted to make sure that things went as planned.'

'Well, that is how it is when you play dangerous games, John. But I suppose old habits die hard.'

'Will Lord Arlington see me this morning?'

'I think so. I've told him what you are doing. Most of it.'

'Good,' I say.

'You might have explained your intentions better,' says Arlington.

'It could only be done this way,' I say. 'I had to get inside Dartford's circle. I couldn't tell you or anyone else the truth. Your wife's conviction that I was a traitor to you was possibly the only thing that saved me from being summarily dispatched by Dartford's men last night. Lady Arlington is not alone in believing me to be a dangerous Republican. My own wife is similarly convinced. It really couldn't be helped. I have a lot of explaining to do to a number of people.'

'So, what have you discovered?'

'First, Buckingham really does intend to make himself ruler of the country – and sooner than you may have thought. Dartford is actively working for him. Lady Castlemaine is ready to switch sides – it is only a matter of how much cash and which title she receives. Queen would be her preferred one. But it is to be done not by casting the King aside. The plan is that Buckingham will first dispose of you and the Duke of York and then reduce His Majesty to a mere puppet, tied firmly to his kinswoman, Lady Castlemaine. He will begin by trying to discredit you – I hope, by the way, that you did not respond to a letter from him offering your daughter the hand of a royal duke?'

'Not yet,' says Arlington. He is not pleased to hear that the offer was insincere. He had hoped otherwise.

'Good,' I say. 'Well, don't.'

'Did you discover anything else?'

'Thomas Cade was murdered by the Acting Commissioner, partly on his own account but partly for Dartford. Dartford's involvement is of course arm's length. But you have the papers relating to the Ruby. With that and with any evidence Symonds will give while trying to save his own skin, we can bring Dartford down.'

'Indeed, we might.'

'Surely you mean we will do so?'

'Let us not be too hasty. I think that we might persuade Dartford to come over to our side. He is a man of many parts.'

'Indeed. He is a murderer,' I say. 'Or at least an accessory. He is also a debauched drunkard whose influence upon the King is wholly evil. He abducted an heiress who refused to marry him. God alone knows what else he has sunk to. Our cause is better for the absence of all of his talents.'

'We should still not act in haste,' says Arlington. 'It would be wrong to make him an enemy before we have to. I suppose that you didn't discover that poem of his?'

'I do not have it, my Lord.'

'Well, that's a pity. If I had it to return to him, it would have been an inducement for him to come over to us.'

'So, he will not be brought to justice?'

'You can, of course, arrest Symonds. I can assist you there. I have men who can help.'

'Thank you. I have in fact already discussed with Mr Williamson how that might best be done. But Dartford is the greater evil. Symonds is just a fool whom Dartford has used.'

'Just be satisfied with Symonds,' says Arlington. 'Dartford is much too important and well born to hang.'

'He explained that he would accept nothing less than the axe.'

'He won't face that either. Trust me, Sir John. There's nothing you can possibly do. Take Symonds as my gift. Leave Dartford to me. I think we can work with him.'

I am sailing down the Thames again. In the boat with me is Will, with whom I have had a difficult but ultimately satisfactory conversation, and the same men that Arlington loaned me to arrest Makepeace and Sleet. They are understandably sceptical about this expedition. So, I fear, is Will. We must extract the manager of the dockyard from the midst of the men he employs and whose many privileges he has protected and nurtured. But Williamson has already prepared the ground for us.

The absence of noise from the yard is obvious even as the boat makes contact with the jetty and the boatman leaps ashore to tie up. I see Symonds marching towards us. He is not happy.

'What's going on?' he demands, as I get out of the boat. 'My deputy – idiot that he is – has given the whole yard the afternoon off, to celebrate St Tarquin's Day. I've never even heard of St Tarquin! I don't believe he even exists. The first I heard of it was when I got back to the yard and found it empty, except for one cripple who couldn't get to the inn without help. They'd left him behind in their pious wish to start drinking St Tarquin's good health as soon as they could. The cripple told me what had happened and asked me to help him get to the inn, since he was thirsty himself. He's still in the storehouse if you want to speak to him. All of that was very odd indeed, but then you show up again like a lead sixpence you thought you'd got rid of at the grocers, but you get back in change for a good Shilling the next day. Don't tell me it's just a coincidence you're here. So, I repeat – what's going on, Grey?'

'You are quite right,' I say. 'Both about St Tarquin's place in the church calendar and about my arrival here. Lord Arlington has agents everywhere. One happens to be your deputy at the yard. He was given instructions to dismiss the workforce for the rest of the day in case any of them should decide to intervene when we came here to arrest you for the murder of Thomas Cade.'

Symonds laughs. 'There was no need for that. I'd have come with you quietly enough.'

'You admit to it?' I say.

'I'm not signing any confession,' he sneers. 'But I wanted him dead. Of course I did. He was about to buy the post of commissioner. Which of us deserved that? He or I? I've spent my life here, trying to coax what effort I could out of a work-force with more rights and ancient customs than anyone could hope to remember. But Cade had the ear of the King. And he constantly dripped poison into it about the inefficiency of this yard. I went to Dartford. He said he wasn't troubled one way or the other. Said it was up to me what I did. But I could tell he hadn't forgotten the insult of Cade's trying to blackmail him. I knew I had his support. So, I went to the yard and his deputy kindly told me where Cade was going that evening. I followed him to Lincoln's Inn and waited for him in the gardens.'

'And killed him,' I say. 'You were seen there, of course. Mistress Cade saw you. The case against you is a lot more watertight than one of your hulls.'

'Mistress Cade saw somebody like me. Who knows who it actually was? Juries can be persuaded to have doubts. Dartford can afford to employ the best lawyers for me.'

'Possibly. They'll need to be very good, because later you were somehow involved in Truscott's death. You intercepted Betsy, the Cades' maidservant, on her return from Bromley, and ensured that Mistress Cade's message did not reach him. You got her drunk and kidnapped her.'

'Yes, I met her at the yard and she said she had a message from Mistress Cade to Truscott. I thought maybe it was about Cade's death and what one or other of them had seen. I knew Betsy's weakness, so I took her to an inn to get her drunk and find out exactly what people were saying about me. She started to tell me all sorts for things about the Cade household. She said she had to get her message to Truscott or she thought he might kill himself. Well, I thought, that was worth trying. I arranged for the inn to keep her locked in a room for a couple of days with enough brandy that she'd have no idea where she was. Then I went home.'

'She didn't get back to the Tower for a day or two. But you couldn't have been sure he would hang himself.'

'Of course not. More likely he'd just clear off to Devon, but that was fine too. Then you came here still asking questions. I realised you'd put two and two together eventually, even if Truscott hadn't worked it out for himself, so I knew Truscott would have to go. I might have Dartford's protection today, but if there's one thing I've learned it's that you can't trust an aristocrat to look after a working man. Sooner or later they'll forget you. So, I left you eating and took your boat back to the Tower. I wasn't expecting to find Truscott hanging from a rope, and he wasn't, but when I arrived at the yard he'd already drunk about half a bottle of brandy to console himself that Mistress Cade had not replied. As you know, there was little work to do in the yard. He'd already sent the men home.

'I told him I'd seen Betsy and that she'd told me how things had gone – he wasn't going to see Mistress Cade ever again. I also told him how he'd betrayed his master to me. He'd deliberately directed me to Lincoln's Inn in the hope I'd kill him. I told him we were in it together, and that there was no point in going to the authorities because he'd hang too. He'd just have to live with it for the rest of his life.

'I got him even drunker in order to console him. He agreed he was to blame, because brandy does that to you. He said he should kill himself anyway – he wasn't fit to live. I said it wasn't as easy as he thought – maybe he should try tying the knot and getting up on a stool with the rope round his neck – he'd soon see he didn't want to die. Well, he was drunk enough to go along with it. When he was standing there, saying I was right and he preferred to live, I kicked the stool away. Kicked it good and hard. When he tried to grab the rope and save himself I whacked him on the hands and arms a couple of times with a stick. He was too drunk to do much, though.

'I waited until I was sure he was dead, then I took the boat back to Deptford and finally let Betsy go and deliver her message to a dead man. So, that's two murders, if you like, and not one, as you thought. Well done, Grey. Arrest me. Try me.'

'I intend to. These gentlemen will escort you to the boat, and then to the Tower, where you will be held pending your trial.'

He laughs again. 'Do what you like. I don't have to worry. Dartford may not protect me for ever, but he'll see me through this. So long as he is the King's drinking companion, neither he nor I will hang. My men at the yard will thank you for their half day's holiday, but otherwise my arrest will do you no good at all.'

Arlington's men look at me doubtfully. They've been made to look fools before.

'Get him in the boat,' I say. 'I want him back in London before nightfall.'

As Symonds is bundled into the bows of the boat, where we can watch him, Will whispers to me: 'They're right, sir. Dartford will protect him, and Lord Arlington seems determined to protect Lord Dartford. We're going to look like dupes again.'

'Only if Arlington can protect Dartford,' I say. 'He'd like to. It's in his interests to do so. But I think it may already be too late for even him to perform that trick. Williamson's seen to that.'

'I have come to take my leave of you, my Lord,' I say. 'It is my intention to return to Essex and resume my former life.'

Dartford's face bears a frown of absolute disapproval. 'I thought that we had an understanding? Do not be too hasty, Sir John. In a year – perhaps a little more – our party will be in power. You can only benefit by remaining with us. And you know a little too much about our plans for us to allow you to simply walk away.'

'I find myself reluctant to work for a man who abducts heiresses and connives to murder honest shipbuilders.'

Dartford laughs. 'I have only ever abducted one heiress. It is not something that I make a habit of doing. The shipbuilder's death had nothing to do with me. Anyway, I do not believe that your old master, Lord Arlington, would hesitate for a moment to order a death if he believed that it was necessary for the good of the State.'

'For the good of the State,' I say. 'Not to revenge himself for a personal slight long past. Arlington has principles of a sort.'

'You really intend to go back to Essex?'

'Yes,' I say.

The friendly smile fades. 'You will regret this,' he says.

'I think not. I have just come from Deptford, where we have arrested Symonds for murder. He will of course implicate you over the Ruby and perhaps other matters as soon as he needs to give evidence to try to save himself. He's not a man to go quietly to the gallows out of loyalty to another. Your reputation might survive the revelation of your gains from the Ruby, but maybe not the associated murder. Taken together, the whole enterprise starts to look a little grubby.'

'Where is he? Newgate?'

'The Tower. It seems more secure.'

'Then he will be out of the Tower by this time tomorrow. I shall speak to the King and arrange his release.'

'Your influence with the King tomorrow will not be great,' I say.

'You presume a great deal,' he says.

I take a sheet of paper from my pocket and pass it to him. He reads it, then stares at me open-mouthed.

'This is my poem,' he says. 'Who has dared to have it printed? I shall have the printer's throat cut.'

'I think not. As I say, your powers to do anything will be much reduced, once every Londoner has a copy of this in his pocket. I think you will be joining Symonds in the Tower.'

'That won't stop me squeezing the name of the printer out of you before I go.'

'You can try. It won't help you much. The poem is already on the streets of London as we speak.'

'How many copies of this exist?'

'How should I know that? You assume that I am in contact

with the printer. I can promise you that I have no idea who it is. However you plan to make me talk, that is one piece of information that I have no way of giving you. Anyway, you don't have time to deal with me. If I were you, I would be packing my bags ready to flee the country. The King's dragoons could be here to arrest you at any moment.'

'It wouldn't take long to kill you, Grey.'

'But you wouldn't risk that. Cade was of no account. The death of a shipbuilder who had tried to blackmail you is something you could arrange with little risk. It wouldn't surprise me if you get away with it in the end. But the Law takes a dim view of the murder of a magistrate – even one from an obscure part of Essex. You'd lose your head for that. I'll leave you to pack, my Lord. You wouldn't want to miss the tide.'

Chapter 36

Lincoln's Inn

'Why is it that I have to rely on Will for information about what my husband is doing?' asks Aminta.

'I would have written as soon as I had time,' I say. 'To tell you and ask you to return.'

'Begged me to return,' says Aminta.

'I should have begged you in the most eloquent way,' I say.

'Will was quite eloquent himself. And he explained things more clearly than you probably would. Anyway, if I'd seen your writing, I would have probably thrown the letter into the kitchen fire unread. It was only because I saw that it was from Will that I opened it at all.'

'Then it is as well that Will dealt with it,' I say.

'I almost didn't come,' she says. 'Even with Will's very biased and plausible account of your actions. I may be back in London but that doesn't mean I have forgiven you for not telling me what you were planning.'

'I couldn't tell you,' I say. 'I've said before: as a spy you have to live the part you are playing. You can't stop being the person you claim to be, even for a moment.'

'You thought I couldn't keep your secret?'

'Nobody knows if they can keep a secret,' I say. 'It wouldn't have been fair to you that, had Dartford killed me, you were left wondering whether it was something you said that had given me away. You wouldn't have forgiven yourself.'

'I probably would. I am a very charitable and forgiving person in some respects.'

'The same applied to Will. And to Arlington.'

'Very well, I forgive you, but you can add it to Brussels in the general accounts.'

'Thank you,' I say.

'So Dartford is finished?' asks Sparks.

'Yes. I had to let Williamson in on the secret. I gave him the poem and told him to find a printer to produce five thousand copies. For the printer's sake, I was not to know who it was – just in case Dartford tortured me to find out – only that the man was in London and could act quickly. When the time was right to distribute the poem round London I would send Williamson a message. Just the word "now".'

'The poem has proved very popular,' says Sparks. 'The town talks of little else. But why not just show the original manuscript to the King?'

'Because he would have put it away, pondered on the best course of action and ultimately done nothing. But now it has been published, and everyone in London knows that it is Dartford's, he has no choice but to act. Private disrespect can be ignored, even laughed at, but a public humiliation of this sort has to be acted on. A warrant for Dartford's arrest, on a charge of treason, is already out.'

'And Symonds is in the Tower?' asks Sparks. 'You have ensured that Mr Cade's murderer was caught, as you set out to do.'

'Yes. Of course, Symonds was not solely responsible for Cade's death. I think Truscott really did know what he was doing when he told Symonds where Cade was going, and Mistress Cade could frankly have tried harder to find her husband and warn him. And then there is Dartford. He didn't order Cade's death. He merely made it known that it was something he'd rather like to see, then sat back, a bit like Arlington, ready to deny responsibility when it occurred. A lot of people killed Thomas Cade.'

'And where is Dartford now?'

'Nobody knows. He has fled, leaving Lady Dartford in sole possession of Dartford House and what remains of her fortune. Arlington was not pleased with me, of course. He wanted Dartford for himself. But he has been able to tell the King that one of his agents – unnamed, I suspect – has uncovered a plot by Buckingham, Dartford and Lady Castlemaine to make Buckingham Lord Protector. The King will have to reward him in some way.'

'But why subject any of us to the dangers you have?' asks Aminta. 'I can see that you felt responsible for Cade's death, but you didn't need to bring down Dartford. That was a disproportionate risk. True, if nobody had done anything about Dartford, the King might have been deposed, but, as a Republican, would you have objected so strongly to that? You've said before: he doesn't deserve to rule.'

'I told you. It's about Brussels,' I say.

'Because the King threatened to have you shot there?'

'No, because he didn't have me shot. He could have done. It would have been very reasonable that he should have shot me as one of Cromwell's agents. Especially since my job was to lure him back to England and his probable death. But he didn't.'

'And you believe that, by saving the King now from the fate Buckingham had in store, the King will somehow think that the debt has been repaid?'

'Perhaps,' I say.

'It doesn't work like that,' says Aminta.

'No,' I say.

'Anyway,' says Sparks, 'constitutionally, what Buckingham proposed would be ridiculous. A monarch who reigned but did not rule, allowing their first minister to do as he pleased, running roughshod over the wishes of an elected Parliament. That could never happen.'

'True,' I say. 'The people would never allow that. However unlikely some parts of this story have been, that would be the most unbelievable of all.'

Postscript

From a Diary

To St Giles, where I paid Deb a visit, which I have not been able to do for many days, for fear that my wife might discover it. I told Deb that I had had to lie to many people over my last seeing her, telling Sir J. Grey first that I had dined with Lord Sandwich and then, my falsehood being revealed by Lady Sandwich, that I had visited Mistress Knipp, which I would rather my wife believed than that I had discovered again where Deb was living, which God forbid. This tale made Deb very merry and I dallied a while with her. *Et j'ai fait tous que je voudrais avec elle, avec grand plaisir.*

Then away to White-hall, where all of the talk is of the Earl of Dartford, who has fled the country and is said to be in Paris. The King is wrath against the Earl for writing the poem and would hang the printer, but nobody can tell who the printer may be. Some say that an enemy of the Earl's caused the poem to be issued, but Mr Williamson tells me that the printer lives some way out of London, and that the man received the instructions to print from the Earl himself, at which I marvel greatly. But I expect truth out of Lord Arlington's department as much as I expect snow in July.

My Lord Buckingham is also in ill favour with the King, though none knows why. The King will neither receive him at court nor drink with him. My Lord Arlington, however, is much esteemed. It is said that he will soon be made an Earl and that the King intends to bestow the hand of his eldest son by Lady Castlemaine on Arlington's daughter and will make the son a Duke and Arlington's daughter a Duchess, which is a fine thing.

I also hear that Symonds, who managed the Deptford Yard for us, is arrested for the murder of Thomas Cade and his deputy at the Tower Yard. He claims loudly that the Earl of Dartford caused him to do it, but unless the Earl chooses to return, Symonds will hang alone. His departure does mean however that I shall be able to make much-needed changes at Deptford, with the advice of Sir Anthony Deane, the only truly scientific shipbuilder in the country. In the meantime, the order for the new frigate can go to the Tower Yard, if other matters there are satisfactory. Mistress Cade has written to me to say that, though she is much affected by grief at her husband's death, she is already tired of life in Kent, and plans to carry on work at the Tower with the support of one Morgan, who has run the yard since Truscott's death. I intend to go over to the yard tomorrow and offer the poor woman what comfort I may. It would be an act of charity to do so, whatever inconvenience it may cause me personally.

Notes and Acknowledgements

I am occasionally asked which points in my various books are true and which invented. I invariably reply that the more unlikely the assertion, the greater the chance that it is true. Lord Arlington really did marry his daughter, then aged five, to Henry Fitzroy, son of Charles II and Lady Castlemaine, later Duke of Grafton. Shipbuilders really were allowed to carry off as much wood as they wished, provided each 'chip' was under three feet long. This may or may not be the origin of the phrase 'cheap as chips'. The practice continued until 1753, when a mean-spirited government ordered that the bundle should be limited to what a man could carry under his arm instead of on his shoulder. Riots followed. Buckingham really did see himself as man of the people, though the people didn't quite see it the same way. He eventually died alone and in squalor, 'in the worst inn's worst room, with mat half-hung, / The floors of plaster, and the walls of dung' – but that is another story. Peter Pett really did claim that it would be better for the Dutch to capture the actual English fleet, rather than his collection of model ships. Lady Castlemaine really did accept a bribe of four thousand Pounds a year to go and live in France, and then decided to stay in London after all. And at the same time the families of sailors starved because their pay was so much in arrears and the King had no money left to pay them. Her hold over the King was progressively eroded until, in 1676, she finally left for Paris, but not before she had been made Duchess of Cleveland, allowing her to rename Berkshire House as Cleveland House. Lord Arlington's residence, Goring House, was renamed Arlington House in 1677. It was later bought by (a different) Duke of Buckingham, who of course named it Buckingham House, and later by George III, who created Buckingham Palace on the site. Lord Dartford is an invention – a composite of various Restoration rakes – but those who know the period will see a lot of the Earl of Rochester in him, including the abduction of an heiress and accidentally sending the King a satire on his sexual prowess. I have toned Samuel Pepys down a little to make him halfway believable. Yes, he did most of that. Yes, really. Joseph Williamson was also a real person – a hard-working and unfairly neglected public servant, who was later knighted and founded a mathematical school in Rochester (against which my school used to play cricket). Will Atkins, Mr Sparks and Aminta – oh, and John Grey, of course – are all fictitious, though in many ways more real to me than many of the historic figures.

As usual I consulted a number of sources when researching this book. These include: J. D. Davies, *Pepys's Navy, Ships, Man and Warfare 1649–89*; J. R. Jones, *The Anglo-Dutch Wars of the Seventeenth Century*; Elizabeth Hamilton, *The Illustrious Lady* (a life of Lady Castlemaine); Philip W. Sergeant,

My Lady Castlemaine; *The Cambridge Companion to the Restoration Theatre*; Montague Summers, *The Restoration Theatre*; John H. Wilson, *A Rake and His Times* (a life of the Duke of Buckingham); Ian Mortimer, *The Time Traveller's Guide to Restoration Britain*; Liza Picard, *Restoration London* – and of course, *Pepys's Diaries*. They are all worth reading, especially the diaries.

My thanks are as ever due to Krystyna, Amanda and the whole team at Constable, and to Charlotte for her careful copy-editing (without which you would already be emailing me to point out a number of chronological and historical inaccuracies). I am grateful for the continuing support of my agent, David Headley, the good advice and all the chats over coffee. And finally, my thanks to my wife, Ann (who has the unenviable task of witnessing the actual production of my books), and to the rest of the family, including the newest arrival Ieuan, to whom this book is dedicated, though it may be a few years until he is actually able to read it.

New in 2021!

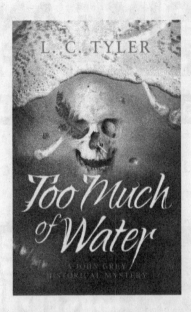

Eastwold, 1670, and local legend tells how on a still night, if you stand on the beach there, you can still hear the bells of the drowned church of St James tolling mournfully beneath the waves . . .

Eastwold, once one of the greatest ports in England, has been fighting a losing battle with the sea ever since it was granted its charter by King John. Bit by bit, the waves have eaten the soft cliffs on which it stands, until only a handful of houses remain. But rich men from London are still prepared to pay well for the votes of the dozen or so remaining burgesses of the town.

The voters are looking forward to a profitable by-election, only for the Admiralty's candidate, the unpopular Admiral Digges, to end up in a fishing net, every bit as drowned as his prospective constituency. Is it an accident, as the coroner has ruled, or has Digges been murdered, as the Admiralty fears?

John Grey, Justice of the Peace and former spy, receives a request from the authorities to uncover the truth.

Newport Community
Learning & Libraries